Daphne, Woman of Law

J.C. Fairbanks

Published by J.C. Fairbanks, 2019.

DAPHNE, WOMAN OF LAW

First edition. July 28, 2019.

Copyright © 2019 J.C. Fairbanks.

ISBN: 978-1393958772

Written by J.C. Fairbanks.

Also by J.C. Fairbanks

Love and Desire
Two Days In Florida
A Kiss in Carolina
Love and Desire in Paradise

Standalone
Daphne, Woman of Law

Watch for more at https://www.facebook.com/jcfairbanksromance.

1

Chad

"**F**uck you, Chad! Get the hell out of here! Get the hell out of my life!" I threw my coffee mug at his god-damned head. Prick. It shattered against the wall two inches from him.

"Jesus Christ, Daphne! I thought we were both adults here. You've known it hasn't been good between us for some time now. There's no need to resort to violence!"

"Oh yes there god-damned is! You think you can do this to me? To ME? No one scorns Daphne Williams! Don't you know who I am? I'll bury you!"

"Don't you know who *I* am? Go ahead and try."

"Oh, yes, the great Chadwick VonHenley. Get the fuck out!" I threw a fountain pen at him and ink spattered down his shirt.

"Fine. I'll be sending you the cleaning bill for this." He turned on his heel and slammed the door behind him.

I sank to my knees and my breath came in ragged gasps. I'd never lost it like that. Never. Damn it, Daphne, get ahold of yourself!

Sure, we'd been together a year and a half. So, he'd kissed Elena Holmes on the way to a corporate retreat. In front of everyone in the limo. Then fucked her in his hotel room that night. Asshole! I was going to kill him!

No, I would do worse than that. I would kill his reputation. Murder his financial portfolio. Tell everyone his dick was limp. Shit.

I wasn't going to do any of that. I never loved Chad. Why should I waste my time on him now? He was a momma's boy. A hot, fucking animal in the sack, hard-bodied, complete wuss. But he looked damn fine in a suit. I could take him anywhere and be the envy of everyone.

But that's all he was to me. Arm candy. And a hot lay, as far as that went. When he wanted it, he was on fire. But he never wanted it as much as I did. And that had become a problem for me. Now how was I going to keep my bed warm? And my arm decorated?

I walked into my office and flipped through the planner on my desk. Damn. The Lantana event was this weekend. Great timing. I began flipping through my mental rolodex. Who did I know that could fill out a suit like that, but wouldn't have me chewing fire by the end of the night?

It hit me like a hammer to my head. David. Of course, David. I'd never really thought about him like that before. Not since the first time I'd set eyes on him when I came to interview at the firm. I'd lost my voice for a second when I met him. Those green eyes that burned like fire and looked right through me.

But I'd put him out of my head immediately. He was already a partner at the time. My boss. And I was not one to mix business with pleasure. David, however, had been out with his fair share of paralegals, lawyers, and even a judge one time. I didn't think he'd scoff at the idea, anyway.

My phone rang, jolting me back to my senses. I looked at the screen. David. Well I s'wannee, didn't that beat all. Fate must be looking out for me after all.

"David, I was just thinking about you," I answered.

"Oh? Something going on?"

I never realized how darn sexy his voice was before. "Actually, yes. I find myself in need of an escort Friday night to the Lantana gala, and I was hoping you would lend me your services," I said in my most 'damsel in distress' voice.

"Ah, of course, Daphne. But really, seems like overkill for both of us to be there, don't you think? They're not one of our top priorities right now."

"Yes, but Nathaniel Eldritch is expecting me to be there, and you know I can't see him alone, the lecherous old coot. And Chad won't be available. I need someone who can protect my back."

"You mean your backside," David laughed. "Sure, Daphne, I'll be there. Anything for you. Listen, I called about..."

David went on a few minutes more about a case we were deep into at the moment. I paid attention, but my mind longed to wander back to the thoughts I'd been enjoying before. I started to form a plan.

2

David

Once upon a time there was a little girl. She never had it hard. She was never poor or downtrodden. No one ever told her she was plain, or dumb, or worthless. The exact opposite, in fact.

She'd grown up knowing she was the most beautiful girl in all of Kenton County, Kentucky. And the smartest. She rode ponies, then horses as she grew. She was prom queen, then Debate Team Captain in undergrad, as well as valedictorian. Law school brought multiple offers from prestigious universities and firms. Daphne Williams had it all.

And she was grateful and happy with all of it. Everything had gone her way her entire life. Dating had been no different. Men worshipped at her feet. They fell madly in love with her. Except no matter how many men she went through, none of them could seem to satisfy her for very long.

Chad had been the longest. And he only lasted as long as he did because she'd begun to think about settling down. Chadwick VonHenley was a natural choice. Sole heir to a vast fortune, though his family had dropped out of all the prominent social circles in the last decade. Still, thirty was fast approaching and wasn't a girl supposed to be married and have a baby by then?

I played the story in my head. I was always the heroine in my stories. Strong, independent, and awe-inspiring. I tried to live my life like the heroine I wanted to be. That was how I'd ended up partnered with David Monroe.

I knew I was hands down the best female lawyer in South Carolina. Probably the best lawyer at all, but I would never tell the men that. A girl's gotta keep their egos inflated, after all. Makes them much easier to deal with.

After undergrad I'd wanted to get away from my family, set out on my own. I had a bit of a Scarlett O'Hara complex, truth be told. I'd read the book at least fifty times in my tween years. And every time I desperately hoped I'd turn the page and Rhett would come back and sweep Scarlett off her feet. I'd picked Charleston for that reason.

David had caught my attention. Not the man per se, but the success he'd achieved over his very short career. He was beyond even me in his accomplishments. The youngest partner at the most prestigious firm in the city. And I wanted to learn from him.

So, I'd interviewed. I was already more nervous than I'd ever been in my life when I sat down in that room. When David came in and turned that smile on me, lord I thought I'd faint right there. And then none of my usual tactics seemed to work. I flirted and got a blank stare. David made me work for it, but in the end, I got the offer I wanted. And a healthy respect for the man.

From the start we'd shared the same passions. One thing and one thing only drove both of us. Winning. We were both driven to be the best, and we were. David loved to take the hard cases and I welcomed the challenge. Clients turned away by other firms came to us and we won them handsome settlements.

Now, David's reasons for winning were not quite the same as mine. I had no righteous cause for which I was fighting. David truly wanted the world to be a better place, to be fair. A strange sentiment in a lawyer, but there it was. He fought for the little guy. I never told him, but my family's money came from tobacco. Thankfully I'd never had to choose where my loyalties lay as we'd never been asked to fight big tobacco.

Almost three years after hiring me David had decided to leave the firm and strike out on his own. He'd offered me a partner position and I saw my chance to move up. It was risky, sure, but with David and I at the wheel I was sure we'd succeed. And we had.

Today I felt like celebrating. I almost forgot about Chad. I was going to buy a new dress for tonight. Something sexy as all get out. Nathaniel Eldritch be damned!

I got into my car and turned the key. Nothing happened. I tried again. Nothing. Arrrgh! Why were the fates doing this to me? First Chad, now my car? I pulled my phone out and called a tow-truck, then a Town Car.

My shopping trip was quite successful. I'd found a deep green satin gown that I was sure matched David's eyes. The front and the back plunged dramatically, and I had the perfect pair of stilettos to go with it. I marched into the auto repair shop that afternoon looking forward to the evening ahead and anxious to get my car back so I could go home and begin working on my hair. My long, golden locks took forever to tame.

I walked into the shop's waiting room and tapped the bell on the counter. No one came. It was like a ghost town. I rang the bell again impatiently and waited another minute. No one. I decided to go find my car.

I walked into the garage and spotted it. I strode over and saw a pair of legs sticking out from under some small economy thing. No one else seemed to be around.

"Excuse me," I said impatiently.

"Yes?" came the reply from under the vehicle.

"I would like to get my car now, please. I'm in a bit of a hurry. Can you help me?"

The legs moved and began to slide out from under the car. "Now, ma'am, I'm going to have to ask you to step out of the work area..." he began, but cut off abruptly when he saw me standing there above him.

I had a very short skirt on that day, and very high heels. His eyes ran up my long legs, over my body and finally stopped on my face. I felt a surge of power over him and I liked it. I crossed my arms and stared into his eyes.

"My car?" I said, raising one eyebrow at him, a la Vivien Leigh.

"Um, yes, ma'am. Right away." He jumped up and brushed his hands on his pants. He was wearing a dark t-shirt, and it strained against his wide chest. I found my eyes coursing over him as he turned to set something on a table. His back was broad, and his arms were huge. I wondered if he even needed a jack for the cars, or if he just lifted them himself.

"I'm going to guess you belong to the Mercedes, ma'am?" he asked. His smile revealed two deep dimples and his hazel eyes sparkled at me. I lost my train of thought for a moment.

"Yes, well, *it* belongs to me, actually, Mr.?"

"Trevor Bond. Pleased to meet you. I'd shake your hand, but..." he held up a gloved hand with oil on it.

"Daphne Williams. Nice to meet you."

"So, Miss Williams, you had a short in your electrical system. And your battery was pretty old. I fixed the problem and installed a new battery for you. I checked over all your other systems and everything looks good. You shouldn't have any more trouble."

My, he was thorough. "Thank you," I said and smiled back at him.

"If you'll step this way, please. Just sign here."

"So, everything was alright? You're not going to tell me I need a new oil pan or a seal or a plug of some kind?"

"No ma'am. That's not how I operate. I know the last owner of this place ran things a bit differently."

He was right. I'd learned a fair amount about auto repair so I wouldn't be swindled, and the previous owner tried every time to sell me something I didn't need. Not to mention took forever to fix the tiniest things. I was becoming very impressed with Mr. Bond.

"This is the total? Is this correct?"

"Yes ma'am. It was a rush job, so it's a little higher..."

"No, no," I cut him off. "It's much less than I expected. Huh. An honest mechanic. Rare find."

"Not really. I know quite a few. May I ask what your line of work is that makes you so cynical?"

I was surprised. Not many people voiced their opinions so honestly and non-aggressively. I wasn't used to it. I smiled at him in anticipation of his response.

"I'm a lawyer."

He laughed as I expected he would. I found myself laughing, too.

"Well, talk about the pot and kettle," he laughed again.

"I suppose you're not entirely wrong, Mr. Bond."

"Trevor, please. Listen, if you have any problems, with your car, or..." he smiled his dimpled smile at me as he handed me a business card. "This is my cell number. Feel free to use it. Anytime."

I took the card and placed it in my purse, smiling back at him. I was used to men flirting with me, but I didn't usually enjoy it this much. There was something about him. Maybe I was ovulating. That could account for the intense flush of heat I felt deep in my pelvis when he handed me my key and his hand brushed mine.

I drove home even more distracted than I had been before. My sexual frustration was reaching a dangerous peak. If I didn't find release soon, I would burst. And self-gratification was only going to get me so far. I cursed Chad again for his sluggish libido. If he'd been keeping me happy, I probably wouldn't be ready to explode right now.

That night I walked out of the house feeling like the belle of the ball. I felt as pretty as a peach, and as juicy as one, too. I hoped David really meant it when he said he'd do anything for me.

David picked me up looking like he stepped out of some European magazine. He was tall enough that even in my stilettos, and my natural 5'9" height, he still had a few inches on me. As he drove, I stole glances at his broad chest and flat abs, his tight body visible through his fitted dress shirt. Maybe we could make it an early evening.

When we arrived, the party was in full swing and everyone was there. This wasn't the dinner jazz and passed hors devours I was expecting. A live band had set up in one corner of the great hall in the old plantation house. Nathaniel Eldritch was a horny old libertine, and he certainly knew how to throw a party. Everywhere I looked people laughed, or danced, or drank. I began to enjoy myself.

I spotted Mr. Eldritch holding court in a circle of armchairs off the side of the main hall. I signaled David that it was time to go in. We made our way over.

"Good evening, Mr. Eldritch," I began as I approached the group.

"Daphne! Why so formal? You know I like you to call me Nathaniel. Come over here and say hello," he bellowed over the music.

"Mr. Eldritch, it's great to see you," David stepped in, directing me to a chair while he reached out to shake Nathaniel's hand. Nathaniel looked momentarily disappointed at having lost his chance to grope me and slobber on my cheek.

"David Monroe! How the hell have you been? So good to see you at my little gathering. Thank you for bringing my favorite girl," he said, winking at me.

"Wouldn't miss it," David smiled. The woman next to me sighed. Her eyes were locked on David. David took a seat in between me and the woman and I thought I heard her squeak.

"Now, Daphne, tell me all about what you've been up to since the last time I saw you. Any more parasailing adventures?" He chuckled and stared at my breasts.

At a party a few months ago, Chad had told an amusing little story about my bikini top flying off over the water in Mallorca, and Nathaniel reveled in bringing it up every chance he got. I decided to play with him a little tonight. I crossed my legs and let my dress slide half-way up my thigh. I let him ravage me with his eyes before I got down to business.

It all went very well. We secured him as a client for another year. His account alone was enough to keep us in business. Everything else was just gravy. And, thanks to David's skill as an escort and a diplomat, Nathaniel didn't even get to touch me once.

I couldn't have been happier as we made our way around the rest of the party. I figured we could leave after rubbing a few more elbows, and was about to suggest as much to David, when someone caught my eye.

There were two men standing by the bar laughing heartily at something a third man was saying. They formed a tight little circle and seemed to be having a private conversation. The laughter had turned my head, but the dimples had caught my eye. It couldn't be!

But it was. Trevor Bond stood there in a tuxedo, looking more like James Bond. His coal-black curls were neatly styled except one curl that fell defiantly across his forehead. It gave him the look of a devilish playboy out for a night of debauchery.

I stared for a moment, and then one of the men standing with him burst out laughing so hard my eyes moved to him. He was even taller than Trevor, tousled golden-brown hair, with a perfect light stubble beard. He was in a suit, but his manor made me think country boy through and through. Or maybe it was the beer in his hand.

I let my eyes drift over to the third man. While the other two were tall, this man was probably only a few inches taller than me *without* my stilettos. But what he lacked in height he made up for in width. His broad chest strained against his dress uniform. Navy, I thought. His blonde hair was cut short in back, and I thought momentarily about running my hand over it to feel the soft, short bristles.

"Oh, Daphne, you need to get laid," I whispered to myself. And I started to turn away.

As if he'd heard me, Trevor looked up and our eyes met. He smiled and motioned for me to come over. I almost ran away. But something drew me over and my feet moved of their own will.

"Daphne Williams," Trevor said as I approached them. "It's so nice to see you again." He turned his dimples on me and my breath hitched.

"Hello Trevor," I smiled.

"Let me introduce you to my friends. This is Hunter Falco and Ace Butler. Gentlemen, Daphne Williams. She's a client."

I reached a hand out to the man in uniform first and he took my hand, shaking it firmly, but gently. "Ace?" I asked.

"It's a nickname. My name's Reed, ma'am. Pleasure."

I reached out my hand to Hunter, the country boy, and he grasped my fingers, lightly kissing the back of my hand. "Pleasure to meet you, ma'am," he said, staring at me with deep chocolate-brown eyes. Damn.

"Please don't take this the wrong way, Trevor, but I didn't expect to see you here," I said, and immediately regretted it. Why was it I always seemed to say the wrong thing around him?

"Not sure there's a right way to take that," he said, but he smiled. "I'll forgive you, accounting for your profession and all."

The other two looked at me, their eyes running over me. I suddenly felt self-conscious.

"She's a fancy lawyer, boys," Trevor laughed, seeing they had jumped to a very wrong conclusion.

Country blushed. Navy looked a little disappointed. I supposed my dress could lead them to think I was a VERY high-priced escort. I laughed a little, too.

"Daphne," David said, appearing at my side. "If you don't mind, I'd like to call it a night. I've got a phone call to make."

"Sure," I said. "David Monroe, meet Trevor, Reed, and Hunter."

"Pleased," David said, shaking hands all around.

"Well, it was very nice to see you, Trevor. And to meet you both," I said.

"Good evening, Miss Williams," Trevor said.

I glanced back over my shoulder as we walked out the door. The three of them were watching me go. I smiled to myself.

3

Trevor

"**C**ome in for a drink?" I asked as David pulled down my street.

"I've got to make that phone call," he started. But I wasn't going to let him get away that easily.

"David, I could really use a friend right now. I didn't tell you everything when I asked you to come with me tonight. Chad and I split up."

"I'm so sorry, Daph."

"Oh, don't be. He's an asshole."

"Wow, guess you're over it already, then," he chuckled. I hardly ever used profanity. It wasn't ladylike. But Chad deserved it.

"Yes, and no. I think I've been over Chad for a while now. But it still hurts getting dumped."

David parked the car and looked at me. "I have a hard time believing *he* dumped *you.*"

I laughed. "Stranger things have happened."

"Not often," David said, climbing out and coming around to open my door. "Let's get that drink."

David leaned his shoulder against the wall as I unlocked my door. Good heavenly days, he looked fine!

"Come on in. Wine or liquor?" I asked.

"Wine, please. Still have to drive."

Not if I could help it. I grabbed a bottle and popped it open, pouring out two glasses.

"So, what is this important phone call you keep talking about tonight? Anything I should be worried about?"

"No, it's not work. Nothing you need to be concerned about." But his eyes sparkled in a way I'd never seen before. I started to worry.

"Well," I said sitting down on the sofa next to him, "I won't worry then. Cheers." I touched my glass to his, then took a long drink. David sipped at his.

"Nice work on Eldritch tonight, by the way. You do have a way, Daph," he said.

"Let's not talk about work," I said, setting my glass on the coffee table. I leaned closer to David and looked into his eyes. "Let's not talk at all."

David cleared his throat and reached up to loosen his tie. "I really need to go, Daphne," he said, standing.

I leaned back and adjusted my skirt innocently, revealing more of my legs. "Are you sure?" I whispered.

"Yes, um, really need to make that phone call. But text me if you need anything, really."

I knew when I was beat. This clearly wasn't going to happen tonight. I stood and walked him to the door.

"Goodnight Daphne," he said, opening the door.

"What?" I said, stepping next to the open door. "No goodnight kiss?"

David leaned in and kissed my cheek. A fire spread through me. But then he all but ran out the door. "Goodnight," I whispered and closed the door behind him.

I walked back and fell onto the sofa, grabbing my phone as I went. I lay on my back and stared at the screen. My body was on fire and I thought I might go mad. Maybe I was already there, I thought, as I began typing the text.

-Hello again, this is Daphne. Enjoyed seeing you tonight. Wondering if you'd like to come over for a nightcap?-

I sent it. Dear lord, I sent it! What in the world was I thinking? Well, no matter now. It was done. Oh, please let him respond. And please don't let me be rejected again. I didn't think I could stand it three times in a row.

My phone buzzed.

-A nightcap? Do people really still say that? Guess you're an old-fashioned girl. What's your address?-

I breathed hard. He was coming. I typed again.

-No, not a lot about me is old-fashioned. 23 Gadsdenboro Street.-

He responded immediately.

-Very happy to hear that. I'll be there soon.-

My heart pounded. I threw back the rest of my wine and David's, washing and drying his glass. There was a tap on my door. He was certainly fast. I opened the door.

Trevor stood there, leaning on the doorframe, a pink and white daffodil in his hand. He smiled at me and I fought the urge to run my fingers over his dimples.

"Come on in," I said, holding the door open for him.

"Thank you. I brought this for you. Not too old-fashioned, I hope." He held the single flower out to me.

"Gee, no. I've never heard of a single daffodil before. I don't think you're in danger of living up to some fairytale stereotype."

Trevor eyed me appraisingly. "You're not easy to please, are you?"

I supposed I was being a little harsh. I didn't care. "No, I'm not."

"Good. I like a challenge."

"You want a drink?" I asked, holding the wine glass out.

"Not really. Open bar at the party and all. So, Daphne Williams, what happened to your date? I was pretty surprised to get your message. Unless you're only inviting me over here in a professional capacity. Something else go wrong with your car?" he laughed.

I set down the wine and walked around the kitchen island to stand right in front of him. In my heels I was almost at eye level with him, but not quite.

"David is my partner at the firm. Tonight was more work than play for me. But I'm finding it frustrating. I called you because I feel like playing." I reached my arms around his neck and stared into his blue-brown eyes. They burned for me and I felt my blood rushing in my veins.

Trevor lowered his lips to mine. His kiss was soft at first, his arms slipping gently around my waist. But then he pulled me into his body and his mouth pressed mine, forcing my lips apart. He ran his tongue over my bottom lip, and I quivered. My breath rushed in.

"Daphne," he whispered against my lips.

"Yes?"

"What's your middle name?"

"What?"

"Your middle name. What is it?"

I pulled back. "You have a very strange way of talking dirty."

"I just thought, before we do this, I'd like to know something about you. Besides that you're a lawyer and you live on the swankiest street in Charleston."

"Olivia. Now, will you kiss me?"

"Yes, Miss Daphne Olivia Williams. I *will* kiss you."

Trevor's hand came up into my hair and he crushed me to him. I ran a hand down his arm and felt the muscle bulge through his jacket. I pushed his jacket off and untied his bow tie.

"Not a clip-on?" I teased him.

"You really are determined to fit me into your little box, aren't you?" He sounded a bit annoyed.

"I'm sorry, it's just, most people don't surprise me, and you keep doing it." I started to unbutton his shirt.

"Daphne, you'll find that people have a lot more going on than you give them credit for."

I had his shirt off and the sight of his sculpted chest sent a flood to my panties. I bit his neck and whispered in his ear, "Why don't you show me."

Trevor moaned and ran his hand down my back, sliding the zipper down. His eyes ran over my shoulders as he slowly slipped the straps of my dress down until it fell to the floor.

"Mmm, another layer. I knew you had more than one, Daphne. Even if it was skillfully hidden," he said eyeing my plunging corset.

I grabbed his belt as I looked into his eyes and unbuckled it. I unzipped his pants and he kicked them off.

"Where's your bedroom?" he asked, running his hand down my neck, his fingers caressing me over the top of my corset. I shivered again.

"This way," I said, taking his hand and leading him in. Once I had him inside, I took my time running my eyes over his body.

The impressive arms I'd seen before, but now I could see the large star, in dark and light shades counterchanged, tattooed on his left shoulder. On the right was a set of wings, two hammers crossed over them. I'd never been with a man who had tattoos before. It had me even more bothered.

His dark skin accentuated the ridges of his abdomen. Fine, dark hairs were sprinkled over his massive chest. I looked back up to his face and he smiled.

"Like what you see?" he asked, turning those dimples on me again.

I did. Oh lord, I did. But I wasn't going to tell him that. I ran my hand over his cheek, caressing the little divot, and up to the curls on his head. They were soft as I ran my fingers through them.

Trevor reached around me, burying his face in my neck. I felt his tongue caress me as he deftly unhooked my bra. Shockwaves ran down my neck and my corset fell.

Trevor's mouth moved down and he pulled my waist to him as his tongue found my nipple and skillfully circled it. I thought I was going to cum right then. A low moan rose from my chest. My arousal spurred him on. His massive arms held me even tighter and his teeth came down on my nipple.

"Oh, god, Trevor! Fuck me, please!" I begged him.

"Yes, ma'am," he said, a wicked smile on his lips.

Trevor lifted my whole body in his arms and laid me down on the bed. I was losing my mind. He grabbed my thong and slid it off, tossing it aside. "Let's get these off. I don't feel like being accidentally impaled tonight," he said, slipping my shoes off.

He stood before me and dropped his boxers to the floor. Oh lord, I wanted that cock inside me! He was massive; long and thick and beautiful.

He stood over me, his eyes running over every inch of my body. Normally I liked to be the one in control, but Trevor had a quiet command over me that was unlike anything I'd experienced before. And then his head was between my legs.

His tongue was hot fire as he spread my lips apart. He ran it up and down the length of my sex and circled my clit. I cried out. He circled faster and slipped two fingers inside me. He slammed his fingers into me, and my orgasm exploded.

I screamed and writhed as my muscles spasmed in wave after intense wave. Every part of my body tensed and released. Lights flashed behind my closed eyelids and my chest heaved, unable to get in enough air. Finally, I began to come down and remember where I was. I opened my eyes.

Trevor stood, running his huge hands down my thighs. "Jesus, Daphne, you weren't kidding about being a little frustrated, were you?" he said, wiping his mouth.

I couldn't speak. My body refused to obey me. All I could do was feel the sweet anticipation for what was about to come next. Already I felt the fire burning in me again.

Trevor kissed up my body, sucking a nipple as he went and sending a pulse through me. Then I felt him there, ready, hot and hard.

"Do you want me inside of you, Daphne?" he asked, looking into my eyes.

"Yes, Trevor, please," I begged again. I'd never been this submissive, never begged. But I'd never wanted a man as much as I wanted Trevor right now.

He looked into my eyes and I felt him penetrate me. Slowly he slid the head of his cock into me, and then the shaft. Then he sank the whole thing in, deep and hard. I cried out again. Trevor moaned my name.

"Daphne Olivia, you're so fucking wet. Uuunnnghhh!" he moaned, thrusting into me again.

I'd never had a man use my middle name during sex before. It was incredibly hot, like I was a naughty child and he was calling me out for it. I felt my pussy throb on him.

"Holy shit," he murmured, biting the side of my neck.

He thrust into me hard and deep and I thought I might split in two. The pressure was exquisite. I could feel another orgasm building fast. Trevor's hand slid down my thigh and he grabbed onto my ass, shoving himself even deeper into me. One more thrust and I was cumming again. The feeling of cumming on his huge cock was more intense than anything I'd ever felt. I clawed at his hard back, bucking my hips and crying his name.

"Oh, holy hell," he cried as my body clenched around him. I grabbed his hard ass and pulled him deep, and his cock throbbed and burst into me. I could feel him pulsing, cumming in me and my pussy throbbed in response.

Trevor's head fell to my shoulder and his breath came fast. My own heart was pounding a mile a minute. His arm came around my waist and he pulled my body into him, kissing me deeply. I ran my hand through his now wild curls. He looked into my eyes and smiled.

"Now you've surprised me," he said.

"Mmm, how's that now?" I asked, my voice raspy from screaming.

"I pegged you for the don't wrinkle the sheets, fake an orgasm type. Glad to be proved wrong." His fingers played down my side, leaving a trail of fire in their wake.

"Well, if that's what you thought of me, why did you even come over?"

"*I* like to give people the benefit of the doubt. Plus, I don't think there's a straight man alive who would pass up the chance to be with a goddess like you."

"Mmm, well, thank you. You're not so bad yourself," I teased him. But he seemed to take it to heart.

"Not so bad? Well, I'm going to have to fix that," and he kissed me passionately.

4

Hunter

My eyes refused to open. My lids felt heavy and my head was foggy. What time was it? I forced my eyes open and grabbed my phone off the nightstand. I bolted upright. Eight a.m.? Phooey! Then my eyes caught something else and a wave surged through me.

Beside me Trevor lay on his stomach, sound asleep. His arms were raised and the muscles in his shoulders were round and taught. The thin sheet only covered him to his waist, and I admired the smooth curves of his back.

Last night had been... well there just weren't words for it. I'd never known such pleasure. Had almost never seen such stamina. I did have this boyfriend in college once who could go all night, but he wasn't good enough to want to bother going all night with. Trevor, on the other hand...

We'd worn each other out. I thought I'd be surprised that he was still here, after what was clearly a late-night booty call, but I wasn't. If he felt anything like I did he probably couldn't drag himself out of the bed, much less dress and drive home.

I almost never slept this late. I woke before the light most mornings. We had some clients overseas and it was necessary at times. And there was always work to do. Like today. David and I had brunch with clients in two hours and I had loads to prepare. How could I have slept this late? And now I was going to have to get rid of Trevor, too.

My eyes fell back on his slumbering frame. I really didn't want to kick him out. I wanted to stay here with him all day, in fact; a feeling that was altogether new to me. I felt a pull toward him, deep in my chest. I reached a finger out and lightly traced the wings on his upper arm, just below the shoulder. He stirred.

"Mmm," he mumbled into the pillow. Then he seemed to think of something. "Oh, hey there. Wow, morning already, huh?"

"Yes. Listen, it's not that I want you to go, I really don't, it's just that I've got a meeting in a few hours and I have a lot to prepare."

Trevor sat up. "Say no more. Busy life of a litigator." Then he reached his hand up to my cheek, caressing it. His hand came up into my hair and he pulled me in for a kiss. I started to breathe hard.

"How did you know I was a litigator?" I asked breathlessly.

"Don't you think I googled you first thing after you left the shop?"

"Oh," I breathed.

"You're ready to go again, aren't you?" he whispered, smiling.

"Honey, I'm always ready to go again. Even when I've been thoroughly slaked until four in the morning."

"You're incredible," Trevor whispered, kissing me again.

"I know. But I really have to hit the shower now, and no, that is not an invite," I said when his eyes lit up. His face fell and I felt a little bad. "Later, tiger, I promise. I'm free tonight."

"Can't tonight, angel eyes. I'm heading out of town this afternoon. Be back tomorrow. I would love to see you again, though. Maybe I can find out more than your middle name next time." He flashed his dimples at me and kissed me again.

"Uuuhhh," I moaned. "You really have to get out of my bed now before I lose all control and miss my very important meeting!" I pushed him playfully and he grabbed me to him, throwing me down on the bed underneath him.

"Yes, ma'am," he said kissing me, then he hopped out of the bed. I watched as he slipped his boxers on over that tight ass and walked into the living room to find the rest of his clothing. He had a way of saying 'yes ma'am' that really meant 'I'll do what I want with you and you'll like it'. And I did like it.

The rest of the morning was a blur. I managed to make myself presentable enough to be seen in public. I managed to get everything together we needed for the meeting. I wasn't managing keeping my mind off of Trevor so well, though. Why did he have me so distracted? I couldn't concentrate on anything else.

Until I got to the restaurant and saw David sitting at the table. I watched him for a moment. He was reading and taking notes as he always did. He took a sip of water and I wished I were the glass.

I realized something then. I was in love with David. I must have been in love with him for a long time now. But I'd never admitted it to myself. For one thing he was my boss until recently, and I had my rules. But also, because he'd never shown that kind of interest in me. But that had to be because I'd never encouraged him. And because he would never take advantage of someone directly below him. He wasn't that kind of man.

David valued people. He valued their thoughts and feelings and hopes and dreams. It was admirable, sure, but not my area of expertise. I preferred people who could keep their own acts together. People who had drive and ambition. Like David.

I walked to the table and David looked up as I got there. His green eyes met mine and I gazed into them for a split second before he was up and pulling out my chair. His dazzling smile was on high beam today.

"You're awfully chipper. Guess you got more sleep last night than I did," I said, taking my seat.

"No, not really. Didn't sleep much at all, actually. It's just such a lovely day, don't you think?"

"I suppose it is. And what kept you up all night? The mysterious phone call?" I asked, hoping he would say no.

"Yes, actually. To tell the truth, Daph, I haven't been sleeping all week. I'm sorry, I'm just..." he sighed and fidgeted in his seat.

"Distracted?" I asked.

"Yes. I've got a date tonight and I can't stop thinking about her. I'll try to focus, I promise."

I didn't doubt David's focus. He'd never let personal matters get in the way of work before. I turned my head in the direction of the door and pressed my lips together tightly. I felt a twinge. Why now, did he have to meet someone? Why, when I finally realized my feelings for him, did he have to go and find some new relationship?

I took a deep breath. It wouldn't matter. This one would be over soon like all the rest of them. And I would be there when it ended, a soothing shoulder for him to put those full, sweet lips on. I imagined his hot kisses trailing up my neck. I shook my head and realized the clients were headed in our direction.

"...and so, the short answer to your question is yes," I finished and turned to David for his input. He was almost bouncing out of his seat. I placed my hand on his knee and squeezed. Mostly to get his attention, but I certainly enjoyed it.

"Oh, yes, of course." David said, snapping back into it. "Ms. Williams is correct, but allow me to bring up the other issue we're likely to face..."

It had been successful. We were both worried about this case, though. Our star witness had received multiple death threats and they were increasing in frequency and credibility. David was rabid to win this one, and when he spoke about it the flash in his gorgeous green eyes was dazzling.

The clients left and I leaned back and sipped my Arnold Palmer. "Are you in this when we have to put him into hiding?" I asked.

"Do you even need to ask me that? We're going to crush them. With Ibi's testimony it's a lock. He's a natural and everyone will believe him as soon as they hear him." David waved his arm to our server. "Check please."

"Alright then, because *I'm* not sharing a motel room with him for a week," I said.

"Huh? Oh, yes, of course, it would be me," David said, quickly tossing several bills in the black folder the waitress handed him. "Daphne, you were brilliant as usual. I don't know what I'd do without you."

David leaned down and kissed my cheek. It wasn't unusual, but this time I savored it.

"Gotta go! I will see *you* tomorrow." And he ran off, a huge smile on his face and a spring in his step. I slumped down in my chair.

One more sip of my drink and I walked out. As I left the patio through the little arch covered with flowering vines, I almost ran head-on into someone coming down the sidewalk. "So sorry," I mumbled, not even glancing up.

"Daphne?" a deep voice said.

I looked up and my eyes locked with the soft, brown, puppy dog eyes of Hunter Falco. I was caught off-guard yet again.

"Hunter," I said. "How lovely to see you."

He was so tall I had to look up into his face. He was quite handsome, I realized. His fawn-colored hair was tousled on his head, and he pushed it back from his forehead with a large, strong hand. There was something boyish and wild about him. Indiana Jones, I thought. He reminded me of Indiana Jones.

"It's mighty nice to see you again, ma'am." He bowed his head to me and blushed in a very endearing way.

"Well, have a lovely afternoon," I said, and started to turn down the sidewalk.

"Wait, Miss Daphne," he paused. "I don't mean to be too forward ma'am, but would you allow me to take you out for lunch? Seeing as how we're both here, 'n' all."

He was so shy and adorable as he said it, I almost couldn't bear to say no.

"Thank you, Hunter, I'm mighty flattered, but I'm just coming from lunch, as you can see."

He glanced over at the restaurant I was exiting and hung his head a little.

"Well, shucks, guess it'll just have to be dinner, then," he said, raising his head and winking at me, suddenly bold. He extended an elbow out to me and when I didn't move, he picked up my hand and placed it in the crook of his arm.

"Let's take a walk through the park. It's really a beautiful day."

And then we were walking. Or, rather, he was walking, and I was being walked. I didn't know why, but I went along with him. I didn't have anything better to do, really. And besides, it would take my mind off of David's date. The less I dwelt on that the better.

We walked for a few minutes in silence and then Hunter guided me over to a bench under the shade of a massive Magnolia tree. He held my hand while I sat down and then sat next to me.

"Don't you just love the summer?" he said, sighing and leaning back, his hands behind his head.

"Um, sure. It's great," I said.

"Me, I love the summer. It's warm, people move slower. I love the beach. Do you like the beach?"

"I guess so."

"Next month I'll be heading home to visit my family for a few weeks. Help with things around the farm. Nothing quite like going home, is there?"

So, I was right. A country boy after all. "No, I suppose not. Where is home?" I asked, curious now.

"Bourbon County, Kentucky."

"Really?" I asked, surprised. "I'm from Kenton County. What kind of a farm do they have?"

"Well don't that beat all, a Kentucky girl! I knew I liked you as soon as I met you, Daphne." He looked into my eyes as he said it and his soft stare made me shift in my seat a little. "Got an orchard. Apples, pears, peaches, some berries. I help a few times a year. It's about to be peach season."

"And what do you do when you're not down on the farm?"

"Well, didn't Trevor tell you? No, I guess you don't know him that well. I work at the garage with him."

I smiled to myself. No, Trevor hadn't told me, but I wouldn't exactly say I didn't know him that well.

I found myself at ease with Hunter. We talked for a very long time, telling lots of stories about high school. His were more interesting than mine. There was something about Hunter. He felt familiar and calming. And he was oh-so-sweet.

"You like to swing?" he asked me suddenly.

My eyebrow shot up. What exactly was he asking me? Before I could find out, he was up and going.

"Come on, my legs need to move." He grabbed my hand and pulled me up from the bench.

We walked down the sidewalk through the park, hand in hand, like a couple of teenagers, or senior citizens. I wasn't sure which one I felt like around Hunter. He was probably at least five years younger than me.

Soon we reached his goal, the playground. Hunter pulled me over to the swing set.

"Are you serious right now?" I asked, pulling my hand back and stopping ten feet from the thing. At least there were no kids here, so I didn't have to feel like a complete fool.

"Come on over here, it's not gonna bite," Hunter said, smiling at me.

"No, thank you, I outgrew the swing set when I hit puberty," I said, crossing my arms.

"Aw, don't be shy now, Daphne. I'll even push you. Come on, now." He took a few steps toward me and I started to back away.

"I'm not shy, I'm just confused as to why two grown adults are standing alone in a playground."

"You don't remember how fun these things are, do you?" Hunter took another step toward me. I stared him down.

Then he lunged. Suddenly his hands were all over me and I yelped. I couldn't speak because he was tickling me devilishly. "Stop, stop," I managed to get out in between laughs. He stopped right away.

"Are you going to get on the swings with me now?" he asked, challenging me.

I had an idea of what might happen if I said no, and I realized I kind of liked it. Definitely a teenager, I decided. I gave him my best Scarlett O'Hara eyebrow, daring him with my eyes. "No."

He grabbed me around the waist and tickled me again. This time I didn't tell him to stop. I hadn't been tickled in decades, probably, and it was a lot of fun.

Hunter wrestled me over to the swing set and let me go in front of one of the rubber and chain contraptions. I looked at it skeptically. He jumped onto the swing next to mine and began pumping his legs.

"Come on," he said. "You know you want to." Then he smiled at me with those warm eyes and I realized I did want to.

"What the heck," I whispered and climbed on. Hunter was pleased as punch. I pushed the ground with my feet and swung back and forth gently. Hunter was already soaring high above my head.

"Oh, don't tell me you forgot how to swing? How old *are you*, anyway?"

I think he meant it as a rhetorical question, but I answered him anyway. "Twenty-nine. About to be thirty."

"Oooh, getting up there. I knew you reminded me of my Meemaw." He jumped off his swing and flew through the air, landing a few feet in front of the swing set. "You have to pump your legs. Here, I'm gonna push you."

He ran behind me and grabbed the chains just below my hands. He pulled me back and I squeaked when he got too high. Then he let go and I went sailing. The wind felt wonderful. When I came back, I felt his hands on my back give me a gentle push and I flew higher.

"So how old are *you* then," I called over my shoulder. "Ten, eleven?"

"Please, I'm at least thirteen," he laughed. He pushed me again.

"Ok, high enough!" I said.

"What's that? Higher? Ok, but you're wild!" He pushed me again and I flew into the sky.

"No! Enough!" I shrieked.

"Not enough? Well, if you say so." Hunter pushed me again, but not so high this time. My pulse was rushing with adrenaline.

"Let me land now, Hunter. I think I can remember how to swing now."

Hunter hopped back on his swing and began swinging in perfect sync with me. I wondered how often he did this. After a few minutes I slowed down and he matched my pace.

I stopped my swing and sighed. "That was crazy, you know," I said.

"Not really. Next time I'll take you down the twisty slide," Hunter said, straddling his swing and inching closer to me.

I laughed.

"Will you let me take you to dinner now, Daphne? I'd sure like to."

The sun was getting low and the sky was starting to turn shades of pink. I hadn't realized it was getting so late. And I was hungry after all the walking and swinging.

"A girl's gotta eat, I suppose," I said, smiling at him.

Hunter moved closer to me, until his swing was pulled right up to mine. He looked at me with those puppy dog eyes, and my heart fluttered. I didn't think about it, it just happened. Maybe it was the sunset, or how sweet he was, or how he made me feel carefree, but I leaned toward him, still clutching the chains of my swing, and I kissed him.

It was a soft kiss, innocent and honest. He almost didn't move as I placed my lips against his. But then his lips were moving on mine, slowly, gently, taking their time. His soft beard tickled my face.

Hunter pulled back an inch, his eyes a little wider, and he looked back at me in wonder. Then he suddenly swung back in his swing and jumped up.

"Whoo-wee!" he yelled. "Ain't I the luckiest." He stood in front of me and held out his hand, helping me up.

I laughed at his reaction. It wasn't one I was used to. He didn't try to kiss me again or put his hands on my body. He just held my hand, gently caressing it with his thumb as we walked.

"Where are we going?" I asked after a few minutes. I realized I'd been following him without even giving it a second thought. Not my usual practice. I liked to be the leader. But with Hunter, there really was no leader. I felt more equal with him than with any man I'd ever been around. I didn't feel like I had to be better than him because he didn't seem to be in a race. He didn't even seem to be aware of the race. He just was. And I could just be. It was an incredibly freeing feeling.

"I'm following my nose," he said. "Smells like pizza this way. Chinese over there. Waffle house down this block. You like waffles?"

"No!" I said. I wasn't really a teenager, after all. If I ate that many carbs, I'd gain five pounds.

"What do you like, beautiful?" he asked me softly. I looked up and he was blushing a little. I giggled.

"Sushi?" I asked.

"Raw fish?" he said and made a face. Now I outright laughed, covering my mouth with my hand.

"You're right, I forgot. You're thirteen. No sushi. I bet I know a place we might both like. Come on, race you!"

I don't know what came over me. I was wearing heels, for goodness sake! But Hunter had awakened something in me that wouldn't be put back to bed now. I ran in the direction of a steakhouse I knew. They had a decent vegetarian selection and the best cocktails in town.

Hunter was hot on my heels, but I got there first. Maybe he let me win, or maybe because he didn't know where the finish line was supposed to be. But he was a gracious loser regardless.

"You can really run when you want to!" he said as he came to a stop next to me. He wasn't even winded, I noticed.

"Shall we?" I asked, pointing to the front door.

"This looks absolutely wonderful. I'm hungrier than a tick on a teddy bear!" Hunter reached in front of me and opened the door, holding it so I could pass.

We were seated on the patio. It was getting dark now, but the night was warm and balmy.

"May I get some drinks started for y'all?" our waiter asked.

"Mint julep, please," we both said at the same time. I looked at Hunter and laughed. He smiled a shy smile at me.

"Very good, I'll be right back with those," the waiter said, leaving.

"They really make a good mint julep here," I said, feeling a little shy myself. Why did I feel like I was on a date in high school?

"Yes, ma'am, nothing like it on a warm summer day. Or night now, I s'pose."

I reached out to pick up my menu and Hunter grabbed my hand. He gazed at me while he held my fingers in his. I felt a flush come to my face. I couldn't remember the last time that had happened.

I cleared my throat and pulled my hand away, hiding behind my menu. Hunter chuckled.

"What're you doing back there?"

"Just looking at the menu. Don't you want to eat?" I asked, not coming out from behind my shield.

"Already decided."

I put my menu down and looked at him. "And what will it be then?"

"Eggplant parmigiana. I *will* have to look at the dessert menu after, though. I've got a bit of a sweet tooth." He winked at me again.

"No steak?" I asked, surprised.

"I'm a vegetarian. I know. You're wondering how I even get back across the state line to go home. Believe me, they don't get it either. But after I watched Bambi I just couldn't anymore, you know?"

I was stunned into silence. I wasn't sure if he was putting me on, but he seemed sincere.

"Wow, I'm a vegetarian, too," I said.

"Except for raw fish?" he smiled.

"Well, yes, except for fish. And not *always* raw."

Hunter talked a lot during dinner, mostly about home, and I learned a lot about him. He loved his family, and he spent several times a year with them, helping with the harvests. There were six of them; Hunter was the second son, then four little sisters. When he talked about home his whole face lit up. He loved Charleston, too, especially the beach.

But Hunter was also a very good listener. I found myself opening up to him in ways I hadn't even done with Chad after almost two years. I talked about home and realized I missed my parents. I made a mental note to go home for a visit after this case was over.

After dinner, and several desserts, which he insisted on trying, Hunter convinced me to walk on the beach with him. The moon was high, and the city was quiet for a Saturday night. He held my hand in his and pulled me into the water.

"Hey!" I said, trying to push my way to the dry sand. It was like trying to move a brick wall. The wave hit my ankles and splashed up to my knees. I squeaked.

Hunter let go of my hand and wrapped his arms around my waist, lifting me until my face was level with his. "That better?" he whispered.

"Mmm-hmm," I said, staring into his eyes.

"Can I kiss you, Daphne?" he whispered, almost touching my lips.

"Ye-," I said, and his lips met mine before I got the whole word out. His kiss was soft as before, but this time it deepened and a slow burn began to grow in me, starting at my lips and moving down my body.

Hunter held me to him in a way that made me feel almost weightless. My feet dangled in the air and I had a hankering to wrap my legs around him. But then he stopped, his face just inches from mine. His eyes soft and warm again.

"Take me back to your place," I whispered. Hunter smiled.

5

Caught

Hunter walked me back to my car and I drove us to his place. It wasn't far from the restaurant where we'd run into each other. He had me pull over in front of a very nice little house. Not what I was expecting. It looked like two kids and a dog would come running out at any minute. I'd half expected him to take me to a college dorm room.

"This is it?" I asked, skeptically.

"Yep, come on in," he said, hopping out. He ran around to my side, but I was already out of the car. He took my hand and closed the car door behind me, pinning me to the car and kissing me softly. "Come on," he whispered, pulling me along.

Inside, the home was decorated nicely. Plush furnishings, neat and tidy.

"Who lives here?" I asked. I'd never seen a man's home so orderly, aside from David's. His home was always neat as a pin. The thought of him made my stomach knot. I wondered what he was doing right now.

"I live here, really. You think I'm breaking into someone's house to impress you?"

"No, it's just so, nice."

"Well, I'm nice, or hadn't you noticed?" he laughed. "The maid came yesterday. She comes a few times a month. I can't take all the credit."

"Oh."

"So, can I get you something? Beer, Coke?"

I stepped into him and Hunter gazed down at me. "How old are you really?" I asked.

"Twenty-four," he said quietly.

"Mmm, younger man. I hope you're not too innocent still." I reached my arms around his neck and pulled him in to kiss me.

"Maybe a little," he whispered on my lips.

"What?"

"I've never had a woman back to my place before."

He had to be kidding. Now I knew he must be lying. The man was gorgeous. "What about Kelly? From high school?"

"Sure, Kelly, but that was high school, and mostly in the backseat of my car. Not my momma's house, ever. Maybe once in her house, when her family was gone. But I wouldn't call Kelly a woman. Not like you," he whispered, and kissed me again.

"So, you haven't been with anyone since her?" I asked.

"I've had a couple girlfriends, but not in my place. Never really lasted long enough. I travel so much, and all. Only just moved into this place. Before that I was living with a bunch of men. Couldn't bring a lady back there."

"I see," I said. "Well, sounds like I got here just in time. Can't let a gorgeous thing like you go to waste like that." I kissed him again. "Take me to bed."

"Yes ma'am," he whispered, kissing me. Then he scooped me up in his arms and carried me to his room, laying me on the bed.

This was more what I expected. Wildcats banners hung on the walls. A basketball hoop was set up over the wastebasket, and baseball caps were hung on the closet door. I was happy to see a king-sized bed and not a twin, at least.

Hunter was on top of me, pressing me onto the neatly made bed. He kissed me deeply, his lips working slowly on mine, stoking the fire. My lips parted and my tongue slipped in to meet his. He moaned.

"Oh, Daphne," he moaned against my lips, then moved his kisses down my neck. I ran a hand down his back and grabbed his t-shirt, pulling it up and running my hands over his smooth back. He stopped and pulled his shirt up over his head.

I gasped. He was beautiful. All long, lean muscle, and smooth, golden skin. No farmer's tan for this country boy. He must spend a lot of time with his shirt off at the beach.

Hunter smiled down at me and kissed me again. His hand came up to my chest and he spread my suit jacket open. Slowly he unbuttoned one button at a time, looking at me with those soft eyes. When he had all the buttons undone, he spread my blouse open and ran a finger from my collarbone to my navel. His eyes followed his hand and he lowered his head to kiss my stomach softly. It drove me mad.

His arm came around my waist and he pulled me up into a sitting position and kissed me hard. He slid my blouse and jacket back over my shoulders and I wiggled out of them. Then I saw it. On his shoulder, right where Trevor had his, the same tattoo of wings and crossed hammers. My heart sped up.

Shit, Daphne? What are you doing? They're friends for goodness sake!

"Aviation structural mechanic, Navy," he said when he saw me staring at his shoulder.

Oh shit.

"So, when you said you lived with a bunch of guys..."

"Aircraft carrier. Like I said, couldn't really bring dates home."

"So, that's how you know Trevor." It was a statement, but he took it as a question, poor, innocent boy.

"Yeah, he was an AM, too. Taught me everything I know."

"So, you're out now?" I asked.

"Yeah, served my four years, but then my dad got sick. He needed me more than my country. And my momma. Still have two little sisters at home. I just couldn't be there for them when I was out to sea for months at a time. Besides, always thought I'd move back someday, take over the farm... I'm sorry, I really can't concentrate when I look at you. You're just so incredibly beautiful."

Hunter pushed me back onto the bed with his body. His skin was hot against mine and I forgot everything as he buried his face in my neck. Soon he'd worked my bra off and unzipped my skirt, sliding it down and off. "Oh Hunter," I moaned when his hand found my breast.

I couldn't stop. I didn't want to stop. He was so tender, and moved so slowly, taking his time with every inch of my body. I felt worshipped and comforted and most of all, aroused beyond the point of self-control.

Hunter slid down my body and pulled my panties off. He kissed my bare hips, down my inner thigh and back up the other side. Slowly he spread my legs apart and softly sucked my lips into his mouth. "Mmm!" I moaned, rending the pillow next to me.

His tongue pushed my lips apart and found my clit, moving there in lazy, slow circles. "Uuuhhhh!" I moaned again. Gently his finger found my wet spot and slid its way in, slowly moving in and out.

I ached inside and the ache was growing until it was almost painful. I needed release or I would die. Suddenly the ache became a throb and my pussy clenched down in one long, wonderful contraction. "Aaaahhh!" I screamed. Another pulse followed, then a third more quickly until my orgasm erupted full force. Slowly Hunter pulled out of me and began kissing up my abdomen. I quivered under his lips.

When he reached my face, I kissed him, hard, tasting myself on him. I pushed him over onto his back and straddled his hips. I slithered down his long body, delighting in the feel of my nipples running down his hard chest. I got to his belt and made quick work of his pants, freeing his manhood.

He was long just like the rest of him. I couldn't wait to take him in my mouth. I ran my tongue up the underside of his hard cock and around the tip, closing my lips over him and sucking. I caressed him with my tongue, up both sides before taking him all the way into my mouth. He was making sounds that drove me on and made me drip again. There was nothing I loved more than having this power over a man.

I took him in, all the way into my throat, sticking my tongue out at the base to lick him there. He all but screamed my name. Juices ran down my leg. Up and down his shaft I went, sucking him hard, swirling my tongue around the ever-swelling head of his amazing cock.

I couldn't take it anymore, I needed him inside me. I slid my body up his, running my hands up the length of him, straddling his hips again. Taking his face in my hands, I looked into his eyes, which were burning with anticipation, and I slid back onto him, taking him into my body.

"Daphne," he whispered, and I kissed him as I pressed him deeper inside me, until he was all the way inside. So god-damned deep inside! I moaned as I slid up and down the length of him, grinding on him with every stroke.

I grabbed his wrists and pinned his arms over his head. The muscles in his chest and arms stretched and bulged. I held him there and rode the length of him. Seeing him there, under me, my body giving him so much pleasure, made me cum again. It came out of nowhere this time, making me cry out. "Oh my god, Hunter!" I screamed, writhing on him.

He broke away from my grasp and wrapped his arms around me, pulling me down to him and whispering in my ear. "Oh Daphne, you're incredible!"

I knew it, but I would never get enough of hearing him say it. The way he said it, in total and complete awe, was like a drug to me. I squeezed my muscles around him and made him cry out again. I knew he would cum soon. And I wanted to feel him cum in me more than anything.

I rocked my hips and slammed onto him and he held me even tighter. I felt him swell and then start to throb. "Oh Daphne!" he choked and then I felt him burst inside me, hot and deep. My moan joined his and I squeezed him again, savoring every throb of his dick.

I laid on top of him, listening to his heartbeat slow in his chest. He had the heart rate of an athlete. So strong and steady and slow. Hunter stroked my hair and my arm, sending tingles through me.

"You have the most beautiful hair, Daphne," he mumbled, kissing the top of my head. "You have the most beautiful everything."

"Mmm, thank you," I said, stroking his chest. I reached over to the nightstand and grabbed a tissue out of the box there, then extricated myself from him. I grabbed another tissue, cleaned up, then shot them right through the basketball hoop and into the can.

Hunter whistled, low and long. "Darn, girl, where'd you get that arm?"

"I played a little," I said.

I'd never been what you'd call sporty, but I reached my adult height of 5'9" in junior high and I'd been hassled so much to play on the girls' basketball team that I'd finally given in by sophomore year. It also looked great on my college applications.

"I may have to challenge you to a little one on one," he said, smiling.

"I thought we just did that," I smiled back at him.

Hunter blushed. Funny what made him suddenly shy. He closed his eyes and pulled me into his arms. I lay there thinking, hoping this wasn't going to cause too much trouble between him and Trevor. Maybe they wouldn't even compare notes. Maybe my name would never come up.

Yeah right. I started to feel guilty again. Hell's bells, they'd been two of the most amazing lays I'd ever had. I wasn't sorry for spending that time with either of them. But Hunter was so sweet. I didn't look forward to hurting him.

Soon his breathing changed, and I could tell he was sound asleep. I unwrapped his arm from around me and rolled off the bed. I dressed quickly and looked at the boy on the bed. One long, muscular arm was flung up above him. His face was so peaceful and pure, almost angelic, except for the rugged beard, which I now longed to reach out and stroke.

But I didn't. I gently pulled the covers over him, grabbed my shoes and purse, and tiptoed out of the room. The hall was dark, but when I emerged into the living room, the TV was on. Reed Butler sat in an armchair, watching some documentary.

"Leaving so soon?" he said, his eyes never leaving the screen.

"Yes, sorry, I didn't realize anyone else was here." What on God's green earth was he doing here?

"Just got home. You know, Hunter's gonna be real upset when you're not here in the morning."

Oh, cheese and crackers! He lived here? All the hours we talked, and Hunter never mentioned he had a roommate?

"Yes, well, I have a breakfast meeting tomorrow. Let him know I said goodbye."

"So that's it, then? Why don't *you* tell him goodbye? Not even leaving him a phone number, are you?"

"It's really none of your business." I was getting annoyed now. What was it to him?

"Hunter is my business, and I think you should treat him better than that."

"Oh, I treated him real nice, trust me," I growled, and stormed out the door. It was like having to talk to his dad, or something. I hadn't taken his virginity, for Pete's sake. He was a grown man.

I drove home and was asleep as soon as my head hit the pillow. Guess all I needed was a couple nights of good loving and everything was right again.

6

Camile

I woke up as the sun was beginning to lighten the sky. Outside birds called and I could smell the sea air. I felt wonderful, exhilarated, and ready to crush this case. I got to work right away. After an hour I started texting David the relevant information. I was deep in work mode.

It was going to be a long day for a Sunday, but sometimes that was necessary. We had a client breakfast this morning, followed by a lunch, followed by a dinner, after which we still needed to figure out what we were doing with the witness protection issue. The FBI was ready to take him. We just weren't sure if he wanted to go.

I dressed for the long haul and grabbed my attaché. My phone rang. It was an unknown number. I sent it to voicemail and ran out the door.

The day seemed to fly by. David and I were both on fire. We managed to shock and awe our first two clients and I was riding high come dinner. I felt the rush of knowing we had those two cases in the bag. It was only a matter of time now.

Dinner went just as well. Spending the entire day with David and watching his brilliant mind in action was ambrosial. When dinner was done, and the clients had left, I sat at the table with David, enjoying my first drink of the day, as I'd been trying to pace myself until now. I raised my wine glass to David.

"To us," I said. David touched his glass to mine.

"To everyone we've helped today. Daphne, you impress me more every day. How did you come up with that Lankin argument? It's absolutely brilliant. And they'll never see it coming. I know I don't tell you enough but thank you for coming on with me. I don't think I'd be where I am without you. I know I wouldn't, actually."

A heat ran down to the pit of my stomach, and it wasn't just the wine. "Thank you, David. Your opinion means a lot to me. I really enjoy working with you. And you're right about that. You'd never make it without me." I winked at him and he chuckled.

"Listen, Daph, I need to go make a phone call, and then we need to figure this thing out with Ibi."

"I know. I talked to him again just before dinner, while you were at the bar with Mr. Taylor. He's spooked. Looks like we're probably going in."

"Alright. Excuse me for a moment, and I'll be right back and we can get that started."

David stood and walked out of the dining room. Another mysterious call? I swallowed my wine. Then I got a very interesting, very stupid idea in my head. I desperately wanted to know what David was saying on that phone call.

I made my way out of the dining room and looked down the hall. He probably went toward the restrooms. It looked dark and quiet that way. I crept down the hall and heard his voice around the corner. I pressed my back to the wall and listened.

"Oh, my darling, please, have breakfast with me. I'm going to be stuck here for hours. I'm not sure when I'll be done. I need to see you, Camile. Come to my place. How early can you make it? I'll be counting the seconds."

I ran back to the table before I heard any more. Camile. Cute little name. I poured another glass of wine and David was back. My mood was not as chipper as before.

"Alright, let's get on the phones," David said, sitting down. We both started dialing. But before I finished dialing a text popped up on my screen.

I stopped and froze. It was from Trevor. Oh no. I wasn't really expecting to hear from him or Hunter again. At least as soon as they compared notes. But my heart pulled in my chest. Eagerly I opened the message.

-Hi angel eyes. Back in town and hoping to see you.-

Didn't sound like they'd talked yet. I felt a heat in me when I thought about Trevor. Maybe I could see him once more before he hated me...

-Hi there. Wish I could but stuck at work. Can I text you when I get off?-

He replied almost immediately.

*-I was hoping you'd call me **before** you got off.-*

-Sorry, bad joke. Yes, text me.-

I laughed and David looked over at me. I cleared my throat and made my phone call.

Four hours later we finally wrapped things up. It was almost three in the morning. The FBI had transported Ibi to an unknown location. Any further communication before the trial Monday would have to be through them. David and I had moved from the restaurant to my car, neither of us feeling like driving to the office. I made a final note and sighed.

"I'm wired, David. You wanna do something?" I asked.

"Oh, Daphne, I'm beat. I really need to get a few hours of sleep, sorry. Don't bother calling me in the morning. I'm turning my phone off. I'll text you."

Tears threatened my eyes, but I pushed them back. "Alright, David, I'll see you tomorrow then."

He climbed out of the car and I watched him walk away through the parking garage to his car. I sighed and typed into my phone.

-You still up?-

I waited a few minutes, but no reply. I supposed it was too late for him to still be up waiting. Or maybe he'd talked to Hunter. I turned my car on and put it in gear. I drove home and fell asleep with an unsettled feeling in my stomach.

7

Reed

I woke late the next morning. I still felt tired. This wasn't physical anymore, I realized. I was emotionally drained.

I picked up my phone. No text from David, yet. Oh, shoot! There was still a voicemail on there! I'd totally forgotten about that. I hoped it wasn't something important. I called my voicemail and listened.

"Morning sunshine. This is Hunter. Sure was sorry not to see your pretty face when I woke up. You could've stayed. I mean, I wanted you to. I just hope you didn't feel like you had to go. Sorry, I'm rambling. Just wanted to tell you how wonderful last night was. Call me when you can. Bye."

Oh lord, he was adorable. He was just so honest about his feelings. It tugged at me a little. In the story in my head I imagined myself as a pretty little housewife on the farm, with a pretty little baby. No doubt a child created by Hunter and me would be more than beautiful, but the picture wasn't what I wanted. I mean, it was, but it wasn't complete. I wanted more. I just didn't know what, exactly.

Maybe what was missing was David. I thought about the life David and I could have. Penthouse apartment, dinner and dancing every night, working together side by side. But David would want children, I knew that about him. He longed to have a child. It was hard for me to picture myself with a baby, even with David. We would both be at work all hours, who would raise the child?

Ugh, Daphne, stop listening to your biological clock. It's not telling you truths, just pushing its own agenda.

I smiled and decided to text Hunter. I owed him at least that much. My phone buzzed. It was a text from Trevor. My heart sped up. This was just getting too confusing.

-Hey, just getting up, sorry. Fell asleep last night. Hard to keep up with you.-

Damn straight, Trevor. I decided to let him sweat a little. I opened a new message and started writing to Hunter.

-I'm so sorry, I was trapped in work until the wee hours this morning. I just got your voicemail. You were amazing, by the way. I really did have to leave, early morning meeting. On my way to another meeting today. I'll text you when I'm free.-

There, nothing too committal, but should stroke his ego a bit. Didn't want the poor boy to lose confidence. Not with his talents and endowments. That would be a shame.

I showered and dressed and started gathering the things we needed to go over. David was going to have to prep Ibi to testify next Monday. That gave us one week exactly. Not much time, especially when your witness was hard to get to. It looked to me like David was going to need to go with him for at least a few days. And I wouldn't be able to talk to David while he was away.

But neither would Camile, I realized. Hmm, this presented a unique opportunity for me. Maybe I could get Camile out of the way quickly. David would come back, she wouldn't be there, but I would...

My phone rang. It was David! "Hi David."

"Daphne, get down here now. You know where I mean. It's hitting the fan."

"Be there in ten," I said and hung up.

I grabbed my briefcase and ran to my car, speeding down to the garage the FBI had chosen as a rendezvous point. When I got there David was leaning against his car and a black SUV was stopped in the middle of the lane. I parked and jumped out of my car.

"What's going on?" I asked.

"They need me to go to Ibi now. Some possible security breach. Have you got everything with you?" David asked. He was talking fast and was disheveled for him.

"Yes, here." I grabbed several files from my case and David transferred them to his.

"Thanks, Daphne, you're a godsend."

"Mr. Monroe, we need to leave now," the agent said.

"Of course," David said, stepping into the backseat. He pulled out his phone and started typing, but the agent reached his hand out.

"These can be traced, sir, you'll have to leave it here."

"Don't worry, David, I'll take it." I ran over and grabbed the phone.

"Thank you, Daphne. Please, call Camile, explain the situation to her. I know you can't tell her what I'm doing, but please..." he was being hustled into the SUV.

"Sure," I said, and watched him drive away. "I'll be sure to call her right away," I whispered after he was gone.

I got back in my car and looked at David's phone. I knew his passcode. I knew all his passcodes. We updated each other with these things just in case. If something happened to one of us the business would be screwed if the other couldn't get critical info.

I unlocked his phone. I opened his photos. There she was. Short and slim. Dark hair and eyes. That seemed to be David's type. Nice skin. But I thought I could compete. I put the phone down and headed to the office. I needed to get to work with David gone indefinitely.

I didn't look up from my desk for hours. David's phone buzzed and I grabbed it. A message from Camile. Dare I? Of course I did. I had to keep her informed, after all.

-Miss you already. We've broken down somewhere just south of the Florida border. Looks like our plans may be a little derailed. Call me if you can. Sitting in this mechanic's shop isn't as entertaining as it sounds.-

I put the phone down and went back to work. A few hours later another message came through from Camile.

-Staying the night in Jacksonville. Car should be fixed tomorrow. What are you up to?-

I wondered how long she would keep texting before she got the hint that he wasn't going to respond. A few more messages about her mundane vacation arrived at regular intervals. Later, as I was having dinner, she called. I sent it to voicemail.

"Hi David, we've got an adorable little beach house for the night, but I'm not enjoying it at all without you. Call me."

She sounded upset. I felt a little bad. But not that bad. This was the game and I was playing to win. She'd get over it. But a few hours later, as I was wrapping things up for the night, she called and left another message.

"Hi again, really hoping everything is ok. Just text me if you can so I know you're ok. Bye."

Talk about clingy. She wasn't giving up easily. If a man hadn't texted me back after the first time that would have been it. Multiple messages and voicemails seemed excessive to me. I didn't know how David could be into someone like that.

While I'd been eagerly reading and listening to David's messages, I'd been avoiding mine. Trevor and Hunter had both texted me. I hadn't read the messages, but I'd have to face them sooner or later. I picked up my phone and leaned back from my desk.

2 p.m. Hunter -*Hey there. It was nice to get your message. Hope you're not working too hard. Have dinner with me?*-

4 p.m. Trevor -*Closing up the garage soon. Dinner?*-

Well, at least as of four p.m. they still weren't mad at me. Or maybe they didn't care. It was after ten. They'd both probably eaten. Good. We could get down to what I really wanted to do. But who to call?

I thought of Trevor's black curls and dimples, and a heat pulsed in me. His dry wit and quiet intelligence had excited something in me. Whatever it was had me thinking about him all day, and I was surprised at the longing I felt now.

But then I pictured Hunter, and a warm glow started up in my heart. He was home and comfort and so adorable. I had called my parents after being with Hunter and I realized I didn't call enough. I missed home and now I missed Hunter.

Suddenly my phone rang in my hand. Unknown number. I sent it to voicemail and waited until the message icon popped up. I dialed and listened.

"Hello Miss Williams, this is Reed Butler. I need to talk to you. I'm guessing you're going to say no, that's why I'm outside your office right now. I'm not leaving until you talk to me. I'll be waiting by the front door."

He was really starting to get on my nerves. If he wanted to talk to me, he could make an appointment and I'd bill him for hours, just like everyone else. Let him sit out there. But, darn it, that ruined my plans. I had to go out the front of the building to get to my car and go home. Fine. I'd let him have his little chat so I could get home and maybe return one of those texts.

I walked out of my office and through the dim lobby of the office building. I could see Reed through the glass doors, planted there like a tree. He was wearing some sort of military flight suit and had his arms crossed in front of his massive chest.

"If you insist upon visiting me at my place of business, please call and make an appointment during normal business hours. If I didn't want to go home desperately right now, I would have let you sit out here all night," I said, opening the door a crack.

Apparently, he took that as an invitation and walked right in the door, pushing it open. I stepped back quickly.

"Which cell is yours?" he asked gruffly.

"Sure, come on in," I said sourly.

Reed continued to walk, looked at the directory, and made a beeline for my office, disappearing through the door as I jumped to catch up. As I came in, he was already taking a seat in the reception area.

"Have a seat, ma'am." He motioned to a chair beside his.

"Why don't we go into my office," I started.

"I'd prefer to discuss this here."

"Fine," I said, sitting next to him. "What is the emergency?"

"I want to know what you're playing at. Are you serious about either of them? Or is this a game for you? If so, I hope you're done playing." He looked at me sternly, awaiting my reply.

"I really don't see how this is any of your business. And I think it's mighty inappropriate of you to come down here in the middle of the night and harass me like this."

"Look, you've kind of turned things upside down in my home and I am only asking when it's going to stop so I know how to proceed."

"Upside down? How's that?"

"Both my friends are in love with you, that's how. I don't see it, but that's the way it is. For the time being neither of them knows about the other, but that's probably going to change soon, and when it does, what are you going to do about it?"

"In love with me? You're kidding, right? And how do you even know I've been out with Trevor?"

"So, that's it, then? You're done with both of them?" He sounded almost relieved.

"I said nothing of the sort, and I'll thank you to leave my office now and never speak to me again," I said, standing. Reed didn't stir.

"I can't do that ma'am. Now, Trevor, he'll get over you, but Hunter is gonna take this real hard, especially when he and Trevor compare notes,"

I cut him off, "Stop talking about my love life like you know anything about it! Please leave now or I'll call security!"

Reed smiled at me. "I know *all* about it, unfortunately. My brothers and I share everything. It just so happens that right now each of them thinks he's sparing the other one's feelings by not telling him you chose him. But they've both told me everything. Nope. I don't see it."

"Stop saying that! What don't you see? And really, whatever they told you, just forget it. I never said I was going to be anyone's girlfriend." Oh, my lord, why was he getting under my skin like this?

"I don't see why either of them would want to be with you," he stated simply.

I was taken aback. "Really... how's that, now?"

"Do you want me to tell you what you want to hear, or how I really feel?" Reed asked.

"Oh please, tell me how you really feel. You've been so reserved until now," I sniped.

"Well, you've got the body, and the face, I'll grant you that. But you play too many games. I don't care for games. Or people who don't know what they want."

"You're a fool, then. Everyone plays games. Only some of us can win. Sounds like sour grapes to me."

"Miss Williams, whatever game you're playing, you're not winning. Now, all I want from you is to let my boys down easy and never speak to them again. Find another mechanic. Take your games somewhere else."

I'd never had someone speak to me like that before. I was absolutely livid.

"Leave now, and I won't press charges. As for your request, I will do as I please in my personal life. I'm not the cold-hearted bitch you seem to think I am, however. I don't want to hurt them. And I think you're overestimating how beholden they are to me after one date."

I walked into my office and closed and locked the door. I fell down into my chair and stared at the desk, gripping the edge in both hands, trying to crush it. How dare he? He didn't know anything about me.

So why couldn't I get his words out of my head?

8

Sabotage

I'd tossed and turned all night. When light began to seep through my window I finally gave up and went to take a shower. I turned the hot water up to scalding and tried to get my head on straight. I hadn't been able to get Reed out of it all night.

I needed to think about work. Today was Tuesday. On Monday Ibi would testify. I would spend this afternoon, and most likely the rest of the week in court. I wondered when David would come back. Probably not until Monday. He'd want to make sure our witness had all the support he needed. It wasn't good to leave him stewing in a motel room alone.

I spent the morning in my office, somehow avoiding any thoughts of my personal life. When I was working, I was focused. I had just grabbed my things to head down to the courthouse when David's phone rang. It was Camile. I decided I should take care of this now.

"Hello, David's line," I answered. Silence. "Hello?"

"Um, hi," she stammered. "May I speak with David, please?"

"I'm sorry, he's not available right now. May I give him a message?" I said in my sweetest voice.

"Uh, yes, tell him Camile called, thank you. Wait, when would be a good time to call back?" she asked.

"He will be... occupied... for the next several days, dear. I wouldn't expect to hear from him. Is this regarding a case? I would be happy to help you if I can. I'm Daphne Williams, David's partner. We work the cases together. I'll be with him tonight if you'd like me to discuss it with him." A little fib, but I thought it would get the job done.

"No, please just tell him I called, that's all." Camile ended the call, sounding like she was about to cry.

I felt a momentary twinge of something. It couldn't be guilt. No. David and I belonged together. I shook my head and headed to court.

Late that night, as I wrapped up for the evening and came down from the mania of the day, Hunter suddenly appeared in my head. His puppy dog eyes, the feel of the soft stubble on his cheek. I closed my eyes and sighed.

Of course, thoughts of Trevor soon followed. My mind ran over him from head to toe. Playful black curls, deep hazel eyes, those dimples. The arms that felt like they could crush me, but wrapped around me like they would protect me from anything. His dry wit. He kept me on my toes, for sure.

Then Reed was back in my head. Arrogant, obtrusive, presumptuous ass. He was probably saying the same things about me right now. I hadn't responded to Trevor or Hunter. In my defense work always came first and I was deep in it right now.

But I wanted to respond. I picked up my phone and started a text.

-Hi Hunter. Sorry I've been out of touch. Work has a hold of me right now. I'll be in court all week. I need to see you. Saturday?-

Then Trevor

-Sorry for the radio silence. Court all week. Big case. I'll understand if I don't hear back from you.-

There. If they'd already talked that gave Trevor an easy out. I thought it might be better to explain things to Hunter in person. If he wanted to. Maybe Reed had already talked him through it.

I fell asleep and dreamed. I never dreamed anymore. My dreams were twisted together. Different futures I might live, with different people. I woke Wednesday feeling even more determined to make David mine by week's end and stop all this madness in my head. He was what I wanted, right?

Camile didn't seem like she was going to give up after one failed attempt. I decided it was time I called her and gave her David's message. He did ask me to explain, after all. But it would have to wait for lunch recess. I needed to get to court early today.

Things were going very well so far. I could feel the jury seething at the oil company already, and falling in love with me. David would be thrilled. All the better for me.

As soon as lunch came, I raced to my car. I needed a quiet place for this call. I pulled up Camile's contact information and hit the green call button.

"Hello?" she said, breathing like she was running and sounding hopeful.

"Hello, this is Ms. Williams. David has asked me to contact you."

"Yes?" she said weakly.

"He would like you to know that he will not be contacting you. Please don't bother to call or text, he won't be available."

There was silence for a moment, and then she spoke quietly. "Oh. Ok. Thank you."

"Of course," I said. "Goodbye."

I didn't think she'd be bothering me anymore. It was over. I took a deep breath. So why didn't I feel victorious? I hated the idea of hurting David, but it was for his own good, really. I was the one he should be with.

After a few more minutes of reasoning with myself, I went back to prepare for the afternoon session. But I felt tired now, the rush from the morning all but gone. My phone buzzed and I pulled it out. Hunter.

-Hi beautiful. Saturday it is. Can't wait.-

His response had me flustered. Did he really have no idea yet? Did he not care? Or maybe he thought I was choosing him. Darn! I should have worded it differently. I kicked myself. Oh, but I wanted to see him! I missed him. No, I didn't have time to deal with this right now. Head in the game, Daphne, head in the game.

9

Red Roses

Friday evening, I flew out of court. The week had been incredible. The jury was primed for Monday, and so was I. I'd worked a few small miracles in there and was busy patting myself on the back when I got to my car and stopped short.

Trevor was standing there, leaning against the back of my car, a huge bouquet of red roses in his hand. He was wearing a suit and had one hand in his pocket, looking the playboy part again. I set my jaw and strode toward him.

He stood and raised his free hand up in the air in a gesture of surrender.

"I know, I know, you're not the old-fashioned type. But I'm tired of texting with you, Daphne, and you really didn't seem to like the daffodil, so..." He held the bouquet out to me.

I stopped in front of him and stared him down. "How did you find my car? You didn't put some tracking device on there so you could stalk me, did you?"

"You know, we're going to have to do something about your mistrust of humanity," he smiled, and the dimples appeared.

"Comes with the job," I said, not moving.

"Look, I drove around the courthouse for half an hour to find your car, ok? Will you accept these from me?"

I closed the distance between us and took the flowers from him. "Thank you."

"You're still mad at me for falling asleep, aren't you?"

"What?"

"Sunday night. It was jetlag, I swear. I won't let it happen again. Forgive me?"

I didn't know what to think. I'd all but forgotten about Sunday by now. But apparently, he'd been thinking about it all week. I sighed.

"I'll take that as a yes. Now, would you allow me to feed you dinner? I assume you haven't eaten yet."

"Well, you know what they say about assuming..."

"Yes, and it's you and me to a T," he smiled devilishly. Lord he was sexy. "So, you free? Or are you stuck in court all night, too?"

"Do you really want to take me out, Trevor?"

"Why wouldn't I?"

Oh, no reason. "It's just, I didn't think we had thing."

"Maybe we did, maybe we didn't. But I'd sure like to find out. Come on, you drive." He took the flowers from me and walked around to the passenger side door.

He'd practically ordered me to drive. Normally I'd rebel against that, regardless of the fact that I would have insisted on driving anyway. But I had no desire to disagree with him. Somehow, Trevor's calm control turned me on. I unlocked the car for him, and he put a large box in the backseat.

"What in tarnation are you putting in my car?" I asked, slipping into the driver's seat.

"Dinner," he said, simply.

I looked back and realized it was a picnic basket.

"And where, exactly are we going to eat this dinner?"

"A little place I know."

Trevor gave me directions and I followed them, not sure what I was doing. This was crazy! I should be breaking it off with him, but I just couldn't seem to do it. My mind was spinning.

"So, Daphne Olivia, what's your favorite color?"

"That's the silliest question I've ever heard. Who cares about colors? They're all fine, aren't they?"

"Ok. What's your sign?"

I burst out laughing.

"First question isn't so silly now, is it?" he laughed.

I glanced over at him and he smiled at me. He had a fitted dress shirt under his sport coat, the top few buttons open. I swallowed.

"Gemini," I said.

"Oh, that explains everything," he laughed. "How did you get into law?"

"You want the long version, or the short?" I asked.

"Tell me everything."

So, I did. I couldn't remember the last time I'd talked so much about myself. Talking came naturally to me, but not about my personal life. But whenever I stopped, Trevor would ask me to go on, and I would.

We pulled down a little street on Sullivan's Island. I hadn't been out here in years.

"Park right there," Trevor directed.

There was still an hour until sunset and the day was warm. Out here on the island a cool breeze blew, and it was delightful after a week in a stuffy courtroom. I took off my suit coat and threw it in the car. Trevor grabbed the basket from the backseat and walked around, grabbing my hand. Soon we were at the sand.

"Alright, give me those torture devices you call shoes," he said, bending and slipping my shoes off my feet.

"You don't like them?"

"They're fine and all, but I happen to think your legs look pretty good without them."

"Wait! I don't want to get holes in my stockings!"

"You can't walk on the beach in heels."

"Let me take them off," I said, lifting the hem of my skirt and unhooking a garter.

"Good night a living, woman!" he said, sucking in a breath and staring at my legs.

"What, darling? There's no one around," I teased him.

"You're playing with fire, missy. I haven't seen you in a week and you go and put on a show like this."

I smiled to myself. I wobbled rolling the first stocking down my leg and sliding it off my foot. Trevor caught my elbow and steadied me. Soon I had them both off and stuffed them in my shoes.

"Come on then, fire," I said in a throaty voice.

"Yes ma'am."

Trevor led us to a secluded cove with a wide stretch of sand. It was sheltered from the wind and so peaceful. He dropped the basket and wrapped his strong hands around my waist.

"Kiss me, Daphne?" He said it like a question, but there was no question there. He was going to kiss me, and he knew I wanted him to. My heart threatened to jump out of my chest. He looked down into my eyes and slid a hand up my body and into my hair, pulling my lips to his.

Trevor's kiss was pure desire. My body melted into him until I thought I might disappear entirely into his scorching embrace. I felt small in his arms and I reveled in the feeling of being completely and absolutely protected. In these arms I felt nothing bad could ever happen to me.

Trevor's kiss softened and he stopped and looked into my eyes. His eyes were burning; blue circles of pure crystal ice surrounding warm ebony centers. I stared into them and I wanted to know what was behind them. What drove this man? Who was he?

Trevor loosened his hold on me and kissed me softly once more. "Hungry?" he asked.

"Starved," I said, my eyes locked with his. Then he broke away, turning to pull a blanket from the top of the basket and spread it out.

"My lady," he said, motioning for me to sit.

I sat and Trevor began pulling things out of the basket. As he opened the packages my mouth began watering. It all smelled so good.

"Greek food?" I asked. "You cook?"

"No," he laughed. "I wish I could claim I made all this, but I picked it up on the way over. I hope you like it."

"It looks like all my favorites, actually. Is this vegetarian?" I asked, holding up a dolma.

"Yep. All of it."

I took a bite. "This is incredible," I said. "You'll have to tell me where you went." Then I stopped chewing. Something had been nagging at me and I realized then what it was. "Why no meat?" I asked.

"A little birdie told me you didn't like it."

I choked as I swallowed. "Really. Are you sure you're not stalking me?" I had no idea what to make of him. If he'd talked to Hunter, he was being awfully cool about it. If not, I wasn't going to ruin this, after he'd gone to so much trouble.

"No, I'm not stalking you, jeez. Try this," he said, lifting a fork to my mouth. I let him feed me and whatever it was tasted like heaven.

"Mmm, wow," I said.

"My thoughts exactly," he whispered, watching me. The fire was back behind his eyes.

"Trevor, what's your favorite color?" I asked.

He smiled the biggest grin I'd seen from him and I couldn't help myself. I reached up and stroked his dimple. He grabbed my hand and kissed my finger.

"Blue," he said. "Same shade as your eyes."

My breath rushed in a little. It wasn't something I hadn't heard before. But the way Trevor said it, so sincerely, like he wanted me to know, it hit me hard.

"And your sign?" I giggled.

"Libra."

"Well, that explains everything," I laughed. "That's actually kind of perfect. The scales. Very balanced. So, Mr. Balance, what is your dream?"

"My dream?"

"Yes. You do have one, don't you? If not, just make something up, because I am really attracted to you right now, so don't ruin it by telling me all you ever want to be is a grease monkey."

"I'm flattered and offended in the same sentence. You do have a way, Daphne."

Oh. My. God. My foot was in my mouth again. But I was less concerned about that than what he had just said. It was exactly what David had said to me one week ago. David.

"Daphne?" Trevor asked, looking at me.

"I'm sorry, Trevor. I don't know why I keep doing that when I'm around you. I really didn't mean it that way."

"It's alright," he said, looking at me quizzically. "Do you still want to hear my answer?"

I was staring at the cliff behind us, I realized, my heart being pulled in too many directions at once. But I did want to hear his answer. I desperately wanted to hear it.

"Yes, please. I'll try not to ruin it."

"Where did you go just now?" he asked, instead of answering the question.

"Nowhere, really. Trevor, I..." I didn't know what to say. Part of me wanted to tell him everything I was feeling, all the swirling thoughts in my head. But my rational side knew it would be pure folly.

"It's alright, Daphne, whatever it is. You can tell me. Something's bothering you," he said softly, tucking my hair back behind my ear.

"No, it's nothing. I'm just not used to saying the wrong thing. Please, tell me."

"Ok. Simple answer. I'm living my dream. Well, almost. I do enjoy fixing things, though I much prefer planes over cars. It's the reason I joined the Navy. I enjoy helping people. And I enjoy doing it all with my closest friends. Hunter, Reed, and I, we're like brothers. We've been to Hell and back together and there's nothing we wouldn't do for each other. I don't have any family, other than them. But there's one thing I'd like that I don't have."

Trevor stopped talking and took a few bites of food. I waited for him to go on, but he didn't. I felt tears sting my eyes. I hadn't known. How could I? I didn't want to be in the middle of breaking up his family. I had to end this.

Trevor looked up and concern covered his face. "Daphne? What's the matter?"

"I..." I couldn't say the words.

"Oh, what'd I say?" He wrapped his arms around me and held me tightly. He stroked my back and I breathed deep, inhaling his scent.

"Oh, Trevor, I'm in love with someone else!" I blurted out. I regretted it the minute the words were out of my mouth.

Trevor stopped rubbing my back and released me, sitting back on his heels, his hands dropping to his sides. He just looked at me. I waited, but he didn't speak.

"I'm sorry, Trevor..."

"No, no. I thought as much. Thank you for being honest with me. I just have one question for you. And please answer me truthfully and don't beat around the bush. Do I have any chance?"

"What do you mean?"

"I mean, is there any chance, at all, that you could fall in love with me, too?"

Too? I didn't know what to say. So, I closed my eyes and I thought. I thought of David's face, and voice, and smell. So familiar to me. Desire sprung up in me. But then I thought of Trevor, and I knew the answer was yes. Yes, he had a chance. Maybe, if I'd met him sooner, before I realized how I felt about David. If I'd not met Hunter, or not slept with him, at least.

But I couldn't be in the middle of them. I couldn't do that to them. I had to end this now, before he invested more than a take-out meal and a dozen roses.

"No," I said quietly, opening my eyes. But the tears rolled down. I couldn't stop them. Trevor reached out and wiped one off my cheek.

"I don't believe you," he said.

"Well believe it. We can't ever work out, Trevor, don't you see that? You don't know what I've done. What I'm really like. You'll be happy about this one day, trust me."

He looked into my eyes as if trying to read something there. He sucked in his breath.

"Then tell me," he said.

"No."

"Then let me tell you what I think. I think you do love me, but you're holding back. Holding onto some idea of what you're supposed to do, or be, or who you're supposed to be with. But that's the thing, Daphne. You're not *supposed* to be with anyone. You should be with whoever you want to be with. And I think you want to be with me."

We were both kneeling in front of each other, sitting on our heels, our knees almost touching. Trevor wrapped his hand in my hair and pulled my lips to his. He kissed me hard, claiming me with his mouth. Shocks of electricity raced through my body and I wrapped my arms around him. His other arm came around my waist and he pulled me into him.

I could feel his chest, hard and warm. His heart pounded so hard I could feel it in my own chest. Tears streamed down my face onto his.

"Trevor, we can't do this. I love him."

"I don't care," he said, sliding a hand up my skirt. "I want to be with you, Daphne, however you want it to be."

I couldn't stop then, not when he held me like that. Not when everything he said was true. My conscience stopped telling me no, or I stopped listening. My body took control and I gave myself over completely to Trevor.

I let him dominate me; allowed his hands to rove over me. I kissed him hard, our tongues tangling with each other. I reached down and unbuckled his belt and unzipped him. I grabbed hold of him, and his chest rumbled.

His hand moved under my skirt, pulling my panties to one side as he sat back on the blanket. His other arm held me firmly around my waist, lifting me onto him. He held me there for half a second before I couldn't wait any longer.

"I need you, Trevor. I need you inside me," I whispered to him.

He loosened his arm just a little and I slid down onto him, taking him in one long motion. "Uuuhhh!" I screamed.

"Daphne!" he moaned into my breasts, kissing my chest.

I wanted his mouth on me. I ripped open my blouse and unhooked the front of my bra, freeing my breasts. Trevor took a nipple in his mouth and flicked his tongue. My nipple hardened and he grabbed my breast in his hand and bit down gently. Molten lava shot down my body and I felt my pussy spasm.

"Oh Trevor! Trevor!" I yelled as my orgasm burst around him. Both of his hands came down to my waist and he pulled me down onto him, pressing his hard cock deep inside of me while I spasmed.

My orgasm peaked and I pulled his body to mine, not able to get close enough.

Trevor's arms came around my back and I felt like they covered my entire body, wrapping me in his protection. I longed to stay there, to never let go.

"Daphne," he moaned, low and quiet. I felt him throb and he came in me, pulling me tighter, kissing my neck. His chest heaved as he held me, and my tears burst out again. Trevor pulled back and wiped the tears from my cheek.

"Don't cry, angel eyes," he said, kissing me softly. "I'm not going anywhere."

But I thought he didn't know what he was saying. I stopped crying and we were still for a few moments, just looking at each other.

I turned my head and tried to move, but he gripped me in his arms. "Don't go, not yet."

"We have to leave sometime. Please, Trevor, let me go." I didn't mean let me go from his arms, I meant let me go from his life. And I could tell he got it. He released me, pain clear in his eyes. We began packing things up.

We didn't speak as we walked back to the car, or as we drove back to the courthouse. I pulled into the parking garage and Trevor pointed to the old compact he'd been working on the day I met him. I stopped my car and he got out, loading his things into his car.

I pulled away and didn't look back.

10

Goodbye

That night I cried myself to sleep. I don't think I'd ever cried that much in one day before. Not even as a child. I'd never had much to cry about. My head was a mess of emotions. It wasn't supposed to be this way. I knew what I wanted. I had goals and I had plans to achieve them. Why did I feel so mixed up?

I woke with the sun and headed to the shower. I glanced in the mirror as I went by. I almost screamed. I looked terrible, deep circles under my red-rimmed eyes. I looked like the Devil I felt like.

I tried to wash away the feelings of guilt and remorse in the shower. But it didn't work. I knew what I had to do today, and I was even more terrified than I had been before. And even more confused.

I toweled off and took my time with breakfast, chewing every bite slowly, deliberately. When I was done, I washed the dishes like a zombie and crawled back into my bed, squeezing my pillow. I could be working. There was still a lot to do before Monday. But I couldn't bring myself to do it.

My phone buzzed on the nightstand. It was from Hunter.

-Good morning. Have lunch with me today?-

Sure, why not get it over with as soon as possible. I typed a reply.

-Pick me up at noon, Gadsdenboro St.-

He replied a few minutes later.

-See you soon!-

I cried again. Why did Trevor have to show up last night? I was a wreck now. It would have been so much easier if he just took the hint the first time.

Somehow, I got a few things done before spending half an hour fixing my face. It was almost noon. I walked out to the street and stood on the curb. Soon a white pick-up came around the corner and stopped in front of me. Hunter jumped out and ran around to the sidewalk. Before I could even say hello, I was lifted off the ground and spun around in a circle. I clung to Hunter's neck for dear life.

"I sure missed you, darling!" he said. He set me back on the ground and smiled down at me with those coffee-colored eyes and I softened.

"Hi Hunter," I smiled back. I couldn't help but smile with him. My bad mood evaporated faster than ice in a skillet.

"Hi Hunter? Shoot, that's all I'm gonna get, huh?" He winked at me, pulling me in close. He kissed the top of my head and reached out to open the door for me.

"Oh, come here," I said, feigning exasperation. I ran my hand down his soft stubble and leaned in and kissed his cheek. He grinned from ear to ear.

"Hoo!" he hollered, and I climbed in the truck.

I giggled despite myself as he closed the door. Hunter's happiness was infectious, and I wasn't immune. I rarely felt as happy as he seemed to be over the littlest things. I envied him.

Hunter took off down the road at breakneck speed. I guess there was one thing he wasn't slow about.

"Are you a race car driver on the side, or is someone chasing us?" I asked.

Hunter laughed long and hard as he slowed his speed.

"Hunter, could we just go to the park? I'm not really hungry," I said quietly.

"You want to go on the twisty slide, don't you," he laughed. I laughed, too.

"No, goofy goose. I just want to talk. Just turn in over here," I said, pointing to a shady parking lot.

"If you want to, but you sure you wouldn't rather get something to eat first?" he said, parking.

"No, really."

Hunter killed the engine and turned to me, leaning back against the door and gazing at me. He looked even more like Indiana Jones today in a light linen shirt and khaki pants. All he was missing was the hat. If I were his girlfriend, I'd get him one, I thought.

But I wasn't his girlfriend and I couldn't ever be. Even if the farm and the beautiful baby were enough for me, there was still Trevor, and he wasn't something Hunter or I was likely to get over. No matter how I tried to make it work in my head, so I could have my cake and eat it, too, there were just too many obstacles.

"What's going on in there, beautiful?" Hunter asked, smiling.

"Hunter," I started. His face fell.

"No," he whispered.

"Hunter," I started again.

"No, don't say what I know you're gonna say." He sat up and gripped the steering wheel in both hands until his knuckles were white. He stared out into the empty park, his jaw flexing.

"Hunter, it's not that I'm not real fond of you, I am, really. We just don't make sense. I'm not a farm girl, and I never will be. I care about you or I wouldn't be saying this."

"If you care about me, you'd stay," he said quietly.

"Oh, honey, I wish it were that simple." A tear fell down my cheek. It was harder than I thought it would be. I didn't want to leave, but I couldn't stay.

"Daphne, why're you doing this?" he asked, looking me directly in the eye.

"Because I'm not a nice person, Hunter. I didn't mean for anything to happen between us, but I'm not sorry it did. It was wonderful. But you're a real nice person, and if you really knew me you wouldn't like me."

"You don't think I really know you? Daphne, I know you better than you know yourself, I think. Don't cry, darling."

Hunter reached out and took my hand. *He* was comforting *me*. I felt like a complete villain. And the worst part was, I wanted it. I wanted his comfort. I wanted him close to me, to lay my head on his chest and listen to his slow and steady heartbeat. I wanted to lie in the dark with him and feel his kiss tickle my neck.

"Don't you see I don't deserve you, Hunter?" I pulled my hand away and turned, looking out my window.

"Daphne, please," he began. I had to do it. I had to make him see.

"I'm in love with someone else," I said quietly. And, even without looking at his face, I felt like a knife had stabbed me through the heart. After a minute I worked up the nerve to look at him. He was just watching me. Our eyes met and the tears came again.

"I'll drive you home," he said and started the car. He drove slowly this time, but even so, he was on my street in a few minutes.

"I'm sorry. I wish it was different," I said as he stopped. I got out of the truck and closed the door. I stood there for a moment and we looked at each other through the glass. Then I turned and ran inside.

A few hours later I was able to pick myself up off the bed, my pillow soaked with tears. I went to the kitchen and poured a glass of wine. I raised the glass to my lips, then dumped it down the drain. I went to my desk and began to work.

11

Crushed

I stood anxiously in the courtroom, awaiting Ibi's and David's arrival. The bulk of our case hinged on what happened today. The doors opened and they appeared, along with three FBI agents. David's eyes met mine and he smiled his brilliant smile. My heart skipped a beat.

Everything went better than we ever could have hoped. Ibi's testimony even shook up opposing counsel, and the jury had seen it. I watched David's face and thought I'd never seen him so happy before. As soon as I could I ran out of the courtroom.

I drove like a flying demon to David's condo. I keyed the code in and ran inside, throwing his phone in a corner in the kitchen. I'd prepped everything yesterday. I grabbed food and threw dinner together. Then I unbuttoned my blouse and popped the champagne.

David was at the door not a minute later. He walked in absolutely beaming. Welcome home, lover.

"Daphne! I couldn't figure out where you could have disappeared to after court. Wasn't that the best thing you've ever seen!"

"Yes," I said, handing him a glass of champagne. "I wanted to celebrate, so I made us a little victory dinner."

David took the champagne and we toasted.

"Thanks, Daph. And thank you for holding everything down around here while I was detained. Clearly you did an amazing job. That jury was primed."

"It only took a few miracles," I laughed.

"This all looks delicious, especially after a week of cheeseburgers. I am in serious need of a real shower. Go ahead and start eating if you're hungry. I'll be out in a flash."

David disappeared into his bedroom, closing the door behind him. I walked over and listened at the door. When I heard the shower turn on, I opened the door a crack. I peeked in and could just see the corner of the shower. I started to pull my blouse off.

There was a knock at the door. I looked through the peephole. Was she serious? I would put this issue to rest once and for all. I opened the door and took a sip of my champagne.

"Hi, I'm Camile. I would like to see David, please," she said firmly.

She was all dolled up. Red dress, ruby lips. Not bad, sweetie, but you're still not ready for the big leagues.

"He's in the shower. It's nice to finally meet you. I'm Daphne. So, you're the one that had my David distracted the last few days. Well, don't worry, I've got him back on track. I'll tell him you stopped by."

I closed the door firmly. I looked through the peephole and watched her go. I walked over and turned on the stereo, selecting something low and soothing. I sat down on the sofa and had another glass of champagne.

David came out, his wet hair a little wild. I wanted to run my hands through it.

"Come sit with me David. Let's celebrate." I patted the sofa beside me. David straddled the arm of the sofa.

"Do you have my phone, Daph?" he asked. "Did you talk to Camile while I was gone?"

Her again! "Yes, I talked to her and gave her your message. She didn't call again. Now, come sit over here and toast with me."

I picked up another glass and held it out to him. He didn't move. It was time to make my feelings very clear. I stood and moved directly in front of David, giving him a good view through my open blouse. I leaned down and placed my lips to his.

David jumped up, knocking the glass out of my hand. I stepped back.

"Daphne, please. I don't want this. I am serious about Camile. You are a great partner, but that is our relationship. Business partners, nothing else. I think you should leave now."

My heart shattered. "Fine, David, but we could have been great together. Much better than that mousy little brunette."

"When did you ever even meet Camile?" he said with shock in his voice.

Anger surged through me now. What was so great about her? "Oh, she was here a little while ago. I sent her away. I don't think she'll be back."

"Get out Daphne," he snarled through clenched teeth. "Just go. I don't want to look at you right now."

I was crushed. I grabbed my purse without another look at him. I couldn't. Everything I'd been dreaming about was ruined. In one fell swoop I'd managed to ruin my love life and my career. There was nothing left now.

I flew through the lobby of David's building and out to my car. I jumped in and started to drive aimlessly, tears pouring out of my eyes. Finally, I couldn't go any further. I pulled over somewhere near the marina and rested my forehead on the steering wheel. I cried my heart out.

When I finally looked up, I saw I was parked in front of some little bar. A drink or ten sounded good right now. I flipped my mirror down and looked at my face. I wiped a little mascara off with a tissue and figured I was presentable enough for a dive like this.

I got out of the car and looked down at my unbuttoned blouse. I quickly buttoned it back up and went inside. It was dark and noisy inside. Perfect. I sat on a barstool and the bartender immediately came over.

"Bourbon, neat," I said. He placed a shot glass in front of me and poured. I downed it and motioned for another.

"You might want to slow down, there," a gruff voice said from behind me. I turned and met ice blue eyes.

"Oh, hellfire and damnation!" I yelled, a little too loudly. "Are you here to lecture me some more? Please, just leave me alone."

Reed Butler took a seat on the barstool next to me instead. I downed my shot and waved for another.

"Really, Miss Williams, that's strong stuff."

"You trying to be my daddy, or something? Well don't. I got a daddy back in Kentucky, and he's a real nice man, too. I think I know a little something about drinking bourbon, *Ace*." I drank the third shot and was starting to feel it.

"No disrespect intended, Miss Williams."

"You know, why can't you just leave me alone?"

"Hey, you walked into my bar. And I have something I'd like to say to you."

"Oh, this is your bar? Well excuse me, I didn't know. And please don't give me any more advice about my love life. Your advice stinks."

"Actually, I was just going to thank you. I didn't think you would be so kind to my brothers. Didn't think you had it in you, to be honest. They both came home broken hearted, but still talking about you like you were the sweetest peach in Georgia. I owe you an apology, Miss Williams. I thought poorly of you, but you proved me wrong."

Reed stood and walked away. I stared at the bar and had one more shot. I thought I should stop now. I was already going to have to call a car. I pulled out my phone and it slipped out of my hand and fell to the floor.

Reed picked it up and handed it back to me.

"I thought you finally took the hint. Shoo. Give me my phone back."

"Miss Williams, will you allow me to drive you home, please? I don't think you're even sober enough to load into a taxi."

I laid my head on my arms and started to cry uncontrollably. How did I get here? Me. This should not be happening. I felt Reed's hand on my back, rubbing firmly. It felt good, friendly.

"Come on, Miss Williams," he said, lifting me up. I went willingly with him. I had no fight left in me tonight.

"Where's your car? Ok, hand me the keys."

I did as he said, and he loaded me into the backseat. I fell over on my side and sobbed. Reed got in and started the engine.

"Address, ma'am?"

I told him and he began to drive. I watched his eyes in the mirror. He glanced back at me from time to time. He sailed over the streets, complete control over the vehicle without even seeming to try. Or else I was very drunk and not seeing things straight. He pulled into my parking garage and parked right in my space. I thought for sure all of them were stalking me now.

"Ok, come on then, you're gonna have to help me a little. Just stand up now."

I stood and leaned on him. He was as solid as a wall. My head lolled on his shoulder. We made our way slowly to my door and he unlocked it and dragged me inside. I was almost dead weight at that point.

Reed had one arm around my waist and plopped me on the bed. He fussed a minute with the pillows and pulled my shoes off. Then he covered me with the comforter. I rolled over and curled into a sobbing ball. He rubbed my back again.

"Miss Williams, I'm going to stay with you for a while, make sure you're alright, ok?"

"Fine you overbearing, meddlesome, impertinent man!"

Reed chuckled. "You've got a fire in you, that's for sure. You want to talk about it?"

He had to be kidding. But I did want to talk about it. And who else could I talk to? I didn't care if Reed Butler judged me. He already thought I was the worst person in the world. I could tell him anything and his opinion couldn't get lower.

The whole story poured out of me. Everything about Chad. Everything about David. Everything I'd done. Everything I'd thought and felt. I talked and talked until my voice gave out and I slept. When I woke I was alone.

12

A New Friend

Thank the heavens we didn't have court today. We were on recess until Thursday, which at least gave me a day to regroup. I forced my eyes open and the light hurt. I looked around, trying to remember what had happened last night.

The memories of David were etched in my mind and I tried to ignore them, to bury them somewhere deep inside. But pieces seeped to the surface and tears sprang up again. I felt so dry, like I'd cried out every last bit I could. My throat was scratchy.

I looked at the nightstand and there was a glass of water and my phone. I never put water by the bed, that was so strange. But I grabbed it and took a long drink. My stomach revolted. I made a mental note to never drink four shots of bourbon after half a bottle of champagne again.

I picked up my phone and started reading the news. Maybe the rest of the world's misery would keep me company. I should be working, talking to David, strategizing for Thursday. But I couldn't call him, not today. Maybe tomorrow. After all, tomorrow was another day.

A lot of good that thinking did for Scarlett. Rhett hated her as much as David hated me in the end. Why had I never realized that before? He hated her. It was too late. She'd been too selfish, and for all the wrong reasons. None of it had helped her, really. She had a string of husbands she didn't love and children she didn't want. And for what? Maybe I didn't want to be like Scarlett, after all.

I crawled out of bed, literally. My head was spinning too much to stand. I made my way into the bathroom and climbed into the tub, tossing last night's clothing in a trail behind me. I turned on the water and poured bubbles in. I sat and tried to soak the smell of liquor out of my skin.

I emerged smelling like a rose, if not feeling like one. I wrapped a satin robe around myself and combed my wet hair. I looked in the mirror. "What are you going to do with yourself, Daphne?" I asked my reflection.

There was a loud knock on my door. I near jumped out of my skin. My head still pounded. I walked out and looked through the peephole. My stomach churned. I opened the door.

"Morning, ma'am. Hope I'm not waking you," Reed Butler said, standing there in his flight suit. "I was just on my way to work, and I thought I'd check in on you. Make sure you were ok."

"Thank you for your concern, *Ace*. I'm just fine," I snapped at him. Why was I being such a bitch? None of this was his fault. He just got under my skin and I couldn't stop myself.

"Good." He nodded to me and started to turn away.

"Wait, Reed, I'm sorry. Thank you for coming. Do you have time for a drink?"

"You really think that's wise after last night?" he asked, surprise on his face.

"No, no, I meant coffee or orange juice. You really do think poorly of me, don't you?"

"No, ma'am, I really don't, actually," he said quietly.

Suddenly memories of last night flooded back. Reed here, rubbing my back. Me babbling on and on, lord knows what kinds of secrets. Heat rose to my face and I turned my head, but there was nowhere to hide.

Reed watched my reaction and then stepped in the door. "Coffee sounds good," he said.

I turned my back on him and walked quickly into the kitchen, glad to have an excuse to hide my face. "Have a seat," I said motioning to the sofa. "I'll be right back with that."

Oh, god! What had happened last night? It was all a blur. Did I sleep with him, too? Good job, Daphne. Might as well have all three of them, I mean maybe you'd finally be satisfied. But it didn't feel like we'd slept together. I was fully clothed this morning. Damn you, bourbon.

"Do you take milk or sugar?" I asked, setting a tray on the coffee table.

"No, just black, thank you," Reed said. He picked up his mug and took a long sip. "That's pretty good."

"Coffee is probably my best friend. I take a lot of care with it." Maybe I should apply that more to people.

The look on Reed's face made me think he was having the same thought.

"Reed, can you please just tell me what happened last night? I'm not gonna beat around the bush with you. I can't remember."

"Nothing untoward, if that's what you're worried about."

"It's not really. I mean, not that I wanted anything to happen, I mean I would care if it did, and it would be bad. Not that you're bad, I mean..."

Reed cut me off, "I know, Ms. Williams, relax."

"What did I tell you?" I said, squaring my shoulders and looking straight into his eyes. For just the briefest moment I saw something I'd never seen in him before. Vulnerability. Then it was gone, and he was the same solid, controlled, stolid man again.

He cleared his throat. "Well, it was a lot. I feel like I know Chad and David pretty well now. Though I would have been happier without knowing Chad," he said, a bit disgusted.

For some reason that made me burst into laughter. I sipped my coffee and it was like liquid heaven. I decided to try the toast.

Reed watched me. "Really, I don't know how you were with him as long as you were. If you ask me, Elena was a gift to you."

I grimaced at her name.

"I'm sorry, I overstepped. That was insensitive."

"No, no, it's alright. It's good to talk to someone who doesn't sugarcoat things. You're probably right. You seem to be right about a lot of things."

"Not everything, though," he said ponderingly.

"So, you know my life story. I think you should tell me your darkest secrets so we can be even," I said, only half-kidding.

"Not for all the tea in China," he said.

"Ok, then tell me what you do? You work at the garage, too?"

"No ma'am. Navy pilot. I'm much more comfortable *in* a cockpit than under one."

"Ah. Ok, Ace makes sense now. So, you've been around the world?"

"A few times, yes."

Dragging information out of him was like pulling teeth. Maybe I should only be asking name, rank and serial number.

"And your family?"

"My parents are retired in Boca. I'm an only child. Have a few cousins hanging around, but we're not close. You've met my real family."

Met them, so that's what we were calling it. Over the next hour I managed to draw out more information about Reed. He admitted to me finally, under much coercion, that he was one of the Navy's top pilots. He'd trained Carrier Strike Groups all over the world. He'd graduated top of his class at Top Gun. Now his chosen path was as a Radar Intercept Officer. I wasn't sure what that entailed, but his drive and commitment really impressed me.

In our discussions it became clear that he, Trevor, and Hunter had been through something terrifying and life-altering. He never spoke of it directly, but I got the impression that he owed them his life. No wonder he was so protective of them.

"Don't you need to get to work?" I asked, after an hour of talking with him.

"I'll be honest with you, now. I don't need to be in for another hour." He smiled sheepishly at me. "I was hoping you'd tell me more of your interesting stories, but looks like I did all the talking today. I'll bring bourbon next time."

"Please don't!" I laughed. Next time?

We talked for another thirty minutes and it helped me. When he left, I didn't feel like life was hopeless anymore. Maybe if Reed could forgive me, and even like me, David could be swayed, too.

13

Birthday

Twelve days later was June nineteenth. My thirtieth birthday. It was not a day worth celebrating. Saying goodbye to my twenties made me feel more like throwing a funeral than a party. My twenties had been good. Really good. My thirties were not starting out so well.

It wasn't all bad, though. David had accepted my apology without any hesitation. Things were mostly back to normal between us. We fell back into our old rhythm and it was comfortable. I hid my broken heart under a hard facade. It hurt even more that David believed it.

Or maybe he just didn't notice. His full attention was devoted to Camile. They were getting closer than ever since my interference. It crushed me.

One thing kept me hanging on. Reed. We had become close friends in these few weeks. We saw each other every day. He got off late at night and it worked well with my schedule. While the rest of the city slept, we talked.

It was never small talk. In the dark of the night, sometimes with bourbon, sometimes not, we shared our deepest desires, fears, and secrets. In all my life I'd never shown my dark side to anyone like that. If Reed had wanted to blackmail me, he would have plenty of ammunition. But he told me his secrets, too.

Reed was a few years older than me, closer to forty than not, though he didn't look it. His square jaw and ice-blue eyes gave him an ageless look; not old, not young, but incredibly handsome. Reed had lived several lives in those years. He'd experienced much more than I had, and he shared that knowledge with me.

Reed forced me to look inside myself. It was uncomfortable at times, but it helped me come to terms with a lot about myself. And I helped him in my own way, too.

His walls came down with me. I looked inside and what I saw was a beautiful person who had been broken by trauma. But he was healing. I wanted to help so I listened; really listened. The more he poured his pain out to me, the more his wounds began to heal.

The sun was setting low in the sky as I wrapped up some research I was doing for a new client. It was Saturday, and it was my birthday, and aside from a phone call from my parents I'd spent the day working alone. I stood and stretched my legs. I walked out from behind my desk and placed my hands on the edge. I spread my legs and bent over, stretching my back.

I heard my office door open as I stood there, my legs spread and my ass sticking out. I spun around and Reed was standing there, a smirk on his face.

"Waiting for me, or someone else?" he laughed. "Please say me," he winked.

"Oh, stop it, you cad. What are you doing here, anyway? Shouldn't you be at work?"

"Took the evening off so I could celebrate with you. Brought us dinner." He held out two bags and looked at me questioningly.

"Oh, thank the lord, I'm starving. But what are we celebrating?"

"Your birthday, honey. Happy thirtieth!" He pulled out a party blower and blew it. It squeaked in my face.

"Knock it off. Did you decide to become a birthday party clown instead of a pilot now? Anyway, that's not something to celebrate."

"Oh, come on now, it's not that bad. I survived it, so will you."
He set the bags on my desk and began taking little boxes out of one.
Sushi. I felt a pain in my chest.

Reed looked up. "What's the matter? It doesn't mean anything, really. I'll pull one of the candles off your cake if you want and you can be twenty-nine again, ok?"

"How is Hunter?" I asked.

Reed pressed his lips together and sighed. "I'll be honest, not great. He's taking everything pretty hard. I'm glad he's going home next week. Think he needs it."

It was agreed between us that Trevor and Hunter shouldn't know about our friendship. At least not now. Maybe never. In all the things we talked about, we almost never talked about them. On my part it was just too painful. I missed them both, desperately, and I cared too much about them to come back in and mess things up.

"I'm glad," I said. "That he's going home, I mean. I wish I could make the rest of it go away."

"I know," was all he said.

We ate mostly in silence. It was unusual for us. My mind was occupied with thoughts of Hunter and Trevor.

After we ate, Reed pulled a cupcake out of the bag. He put a little candle on top and lit it with a lighter he produced from his pocket.

"Don't make me sing, please," he smiled. "Just make a wish. And make it a good one."

I blew out the candle.

"What'd you wish for?" he asked.

"Wouldn't you like to know," I teased.

"I would," he said softly.

"Well, then it wouldn't come true. So, I'm not gonna tell you."
He looked disappointed. "How long will Hunter be gone?" I asked.

"Six weeks. Apparently, they have a lot of peaches." Reed searched my face. "What are you thinking tonight, Williams?" he asked, tapping my temple.

"Nothing. It's just the sushi made me think of him."

"Hunter? He hates sushi!"

"I know. I suggested it to him once." The memory made me laugh.

Reed laughed, too. "Yeah. I can imagine how that went over."

Reed sat barefoot and cross-legged on top of my desk. It was strange to see him in his 'civvies'. I was so used to the uniform. I liked him like this, though. Soft t-shirt and shorts. I sat directly in front of him, barefoot and cross-legged as he was. I felt like we were re-enacting a scene from an 80's movie when he placed the cupcake between us. I had an older cousin who'd forced me to sit through every Molly Ringwald movie at least three times when she babysat me in the summers. Lately I felt a little like one of those characters where everything goes wrong. Then Reed came in and made it better. I felt a pull toward him that was more than platonic.

I pulled the candle out of the cupcake and sucked the frosting off. I didn't mean to be seductive about it, but I looked up and his eyes were on my mouth. He quickly looked away. I tore the cupcake in half and held out one side to him.

"No, that's for you," he protested.

"You know I don't like sweets that much. Don't make me eat cake alone on my birthday."

He took the cake and bit into the dark chocolate, eating half of it in one bite. I tasted mine. It was quite yummy. I finished it off and licked the frosting from a finger. Reed was watching me again. But when my eyes met his he looked away, reaching for his water.

"Makes you thirsty," he said, taking a sip.

"Thank you, Reed," I said, holding his gaze this time.

"You're welcome, Daphne."

I was a little surprised.

"You used my name," I said. He never called me by my first name. It was always ma'am, Miss Williams, or just Williams, like I was one of his Navy buddies. He smiled a small smile.

"Reed, would you do something for me if I asked you to?"

"You know I would," he said.

"Good." I leaned forward and kissed him softly on his lips.

"Daphne," he said, pulling back, but his eyes locked with mine and there was a look of longing in them.

"Reed, just for tonight, can we not be friends? Can you just kiss me?"

Reed looked into my eyes and then I saw him make his decision. He leaned forward and kissed me deeply, his hand stroking my neck and jaw. His lips were soft and tentative, but he pulled my face in and held me there while his lips pressed into mine.

I uncrossed my legs and wrapped them around his waist, crawling onto his lap. His arm came around my back and held me tight. He kissed me until my breath was coming in short gasps. I could feel him pressing onto me through his pants and I reached down to unbuckle his belt.

"I don't want to sleep with you, Daphne," he whispered to me. I stopped and looked at him.

"What?"

"I mean, god! I do want to sleep with you! But I'm not going to sleep with you."

"But it's my birthday," I pouted.

"Oh, put that little lip away," he said, grabbing my bottom lip and pinching it lightly. "You don't really want to sleep with me right now, either."

"I don't think you're paying attention," I said, kissing his neck.

"Daphne, stop. Let me ask you one question. Are you in love with David?"

I stopped. I fell back until my bottom was on the desk again. He knew the answer to that. He knew how much it hurt. Why was he bringing this up now?

"You know I am."

"That's why we're not going to do this. Daphne, I need to tell you something and you need to listen. David is your Ashley Wilkes. He loves you, but he'll never *love* you. He has his Melanie. They belong together. Don't make Scarlett's mistakes and hang onto that fantasy until it's too late."

"And I suppose that makes you Rhett," I said angrily.

"I didn't say that."

"Good, because Reed Butler isn't quite the same as Rhett Butler, is it? It's missing something." I was angry and hurt. I was lashing out. Reed grabbed my hand and I pulled it away. "Stop, I don't want to hold your hand right now," I pouted.

"Frankly my dear, I don't give a damn," he said and grabbed my hand again. He squeezed it between his and looked at me. I refused to meet his eyes.

"Why can't he love me?" I began to cry. Reed jumped off the desk and stood next to me, still holding my hand. He spun me to face him and pulled me into his arms.

"The question is, why do you insist on looking at him while ignoring what's right in front of you? You'll realize it someday, Daphne, what it is you really want. And it's not David Monroe."

14

An Accident

"Daphne," he choked when I answered the phone. Something was wrong with his voice.

"Reed? What's wrong? Aren't you at work right now?" He never called me from work. I hadn't expected to hear from him for a few days, in fact.

Yesterday we'd had a fight. He came to my place after work as usual. I was in a mood. I'd just gotten David's wedding invitation in the mail. Two months he'd known her, and he'd proposed. And they were getting married three months from now. I'd torn it in half, and it sat on the coffee table next to the half-empty bottle of bourbon.

Reed had refused to understand. He'd called me a child. I'd thrown him out. Maybe he was calling to apologize.

"There's been an accident," he said.

"Oh, lord! What?"

"It's Hunter. He's in the hospital. I don't know how bad it is, only that he hit his head and they can't wake him up. Me and Trevor are leaving now to catch a flight to Cincinnati." His voice caught.

"No!" I cried. "I'm coming," I said, hanging up the phone. I pulled up plane tickets and booked the fastest flight I could. I threw things in a bag and raced down to the airport. There was a flight leaving in two hours.

As I drove, I called David first. I hadn't thought I'd be able to talk to him yet, but now the wedding invitation was all but forgotten.

"Hello?" he answered.

"David, I'm leaving town now and I'll be gone for a few days at least. I'm going home. A friend has been in an accident. I'll try to keep up remotely with what I can."

"I'm so sorry! Please, don't worry. And I really hope everything is ok."

"Thank you, David. Goodbye." I called home next.

"Well darling girl! So nice to hear from you!" my momma gushed.

"Momma!" I cried. "Oh, Momma, something bad has happened." Tears poured out and I had to slow my speed.

"Deedee, what is it?"

"Hunter's had an accident, down in Paris. I'm going to the airport right now. I'll be home in a few hours, but I'll get a car and drive down to Paris. I don't know when I'll come home, but I need to be with you and Daddy, Momma." I began to sob.

"No, no, baby, you stop that bawling while you're driving! We don't need two accidents. We're gonna come get you and drive you down. Is he in the hospital, baby?"

"Yes. They said he won't wake up, Momma!"

"Well then, they probably took him down to Lexington. I don't want you driving like this. Send me your flight number. We'll be there."

Momma was always calm during a crisis. I knew I got my cool head in the courtroom from her. I felt the tears stop and my heartbeat slow down. I pulled into the airport long-term parking lot.

"Ok, Momma," I said. "I'm going to get on my flight now. I'm texting you the information. I love you."

"I love you, sweet pea. It's going to be alright, now, you hear? You just get yourself here safe and sound."

"Bye, Momma."

I grabbed my briefcase and rolling case out of the trunk and ran to the terminal. I found a kiosk and got my boarding pass. The security line inside snaked around at least ten times. I ran through the TSA pre-check gate, which was empty. Thank goodness I'd done this for all the business travel I did.

I checked the board and found my gate. Forty-five minutes before takeoff. They'd probably start boarding soon. I made my way to the gate. The only thought in my head was to get to Hunter, to hold his hand. To tell him everything was going to be alright.

"Daphne!" Reed called out. I turned around and he stood from where he had been sitting. I'd walked right by him.

I dropped everything to the floor and ran into his arms. He held me in his arms, and I buried my face in his neck. I began to tremble. Reed held me tighter.

"Daphne?"

I opened my eyes and Trevor Bond stood looking at me with wide eyes. I hadn't seen him in over two months. My heart leapt in my chest. Reed released me.

"Trevor," I said, twisting my fingers awkwardly in front of me. "Hi."

"Hi? Ace gets a hug and I get a 'hi'?" He looked over to Reed and his face fell. Reed looked at him seriously.

"Trevor," I began.

"What the hell is this? Reed?" Trevor said, his eyes darting between the two of us.

"We're friends, Trevor," I said.

"Friends? Like you and I were friends? Why you hypocritical son of a..."

"Stop!" I screamed. "This is why we didn't tell you! This is why I can't be in your life, Trevor! I ruin everything."

"So, all this time, Reed was the one you were in love with? Not me, not Hunter..." he shook his head.

"No! It's not like that. We're really just friends. Say something Reed!" I yelled. People were looking at us now. I didn't care.

Reed walked quietly behind me and picked up the things I'd dropped, carrying them to a seat. He looked Trevor in the eye, "Just friends."

"Wow, Daphne, so there's another guy? How many of us are in this club, just so I know? Maybe I'll find some long-lost brother and it sure would be nice to know if you're dating him or not before I get real close." Trevor sat down in a chair and looked out the wall of windows.

I sat down next to him. "That's not fair," I said quietly.

"What about this whole thing is fair? Is it fair that Hunter is lying in some hospital bed right now? Is it fair that you're here rubbing salt in my wounds? Fair... shit."

Reed stood to the side and watched us. He watched my face as the tears began to stream down again. Trevor kept his back to me. I stood and picked up my things, ready to move to the other side of the gate.

"Don't go, Daphne," Reed said. He took me in his arms again. I was still shaking. I felt him raise one arm and move it about. Then he was releasing me and handing me into someone else's arms. Trevor's.

Trevor grabbed me fiercely, holding me to his chest. His massive arms covered my body and my shivering stopped. Oh god, I'd missed this! The calm, warm, safe feeling of Trevor Bond's embrace. I reached around his neck and pressed myself to him, resting my head against him, listening to his heart. My tears soaked into his shirt.

"I'm so sorry, Trevor," I whispered.

"I know." He held me and my tears stopped. In his hold my breathing slowed, and my head cleared. I breathed him in and stroked the back of his head with one hand, running my fingers over the short waves there.

"Now boarding flight 2461, direct service to Cincinnati. First class passengers and those requiring assistance, please board now."

I looked up into Trevor's eyes. He just stared; his eyes full of pain. "Come on, let's get on the plane," he said.

"It's first class only right now," I said.

"Sorry, I assumed you'd be in there," Trevor said.

"Business class."

"Ah."

I felt Reed behind me. He pressed himself to my back and reached around me, grabbing Trevor's shoulders and squeezing. We were all terrified of what we'd find when we got off that plane.

"Now boarding flight 2461, direct service to Cincinnati, business class passengers, please."

"Now can we get on the plane?" Trevor asked, looking at Reed. They broke apart and I felt suddenly cold and alone. I picked up my things and we filed onto the plane.

"I wish you'd told me she was coming," I heard Trevor whisper to Reed behind me.

We stepped inside the plane and I stepped to the right, expecting Trevor and Reed to follow. But they stepped to the left, headed into first class.

"Mr. Bond! It's so lovely to see you again," a stewardess gushed. "You just let me know, whatever you need. I'll be sure to take good care of you."

What the hell?

"Sorry, Daphne, our seats are up here. We'll see you after the flight," Reed said, a look of concern on his face. "You going to be ok?"

"Yes, yes, fine. But...?"

Reed made a gesture indicating we'd talk about it later. Damn straight we would.

I fidgeted through the whole flight. I didn't drink a drop. I was too nervous even for alcohol. The plane landed and I waited to deboard. As I came out, I saw Trevor and Reed waiting for me.

"You want to drive down with us? We've got a car," Reed said. Trevor shuffled his feet. I didn't think he wanted me to come. We walked out of the gates and my parents ran up to me.

"Oh, my baby!" Momma yelled, throwing her arms around me. Daddy came up behind her and wrapped us both in his long arms.

"Real sorry to hear about Hunter, Deedee," he said.

I held Momma in a vice grip. It was so good to be home. Then I saw Trevor and Reed standing there, looking a bit surprised.

"Momma, Daddy, this here is Trevor Bond and Reed Butler," I said breaking away. "These are my parents, Roger and Edna Williams."

"Real pleasure to meet you gentleman," my father said, shaking their hands. "Daphne speaks very highly of both of you. We were real sorry to hear about Hunter. We sure hope he's ok. You let us know if there's anything we can do."

Trevor and Reed stood there for a moment, then made all the proper noises of greeting. Momma hugged them both and I think they blushed.

"Momma, I'm going to ride down with Trevor and Reed. They've got a car. No need for y'all to go driving all that way."

Momma looked me up and down. "So long as Reed does all the driving, I'm fine with that. I don't want to hear about you getting behind the wheel. Not the way you were crying and carrying on."

"Momma!" I whispered. "Don't worry, Reed will drive."

"Alright, you be sure to text us as soon as you get there. If you need anything you just let us know. Love you, dumpling."

Momma and Daddy hugged me and walked out. I turned to my men. "So, I hope you meant it when you invited me along."

15

The Hospital

I climbed in the back of the SUV, insisting they take the front. I
wanted to be in between them as little as possible. I felt like I was
driving them apart enough already. Maybe I shouldn't have come.

Reed took the wheel and sailed out into traffic. I barely felt the
car move. Soon we were merging onto the highway. We were flying
past the other cars, but it barely felt like we were moving. I looked
at the speedometer. Ninety! Momma would probably have second
thoughts if she saw that. But Reed maintained perfect control, like
he was part of the vehicle.

"Real nice folks you got," Trevor said, glancing back at me. "Sure
was nice of them to come all the way down to see you."

"This is my hometown. We only live a few miles from the
airport."

"Oh. You and Hunter grew up pretty close. You ever go to the
same places?"

"No. Probably would have been hard considering he was still in
junior high when I went away to college." I saw Trevor smile in the
rearview mirror.

"So, you talk about us often?"

"Yes, actually," I whispered, dropping my eyes. It was true. I did.
I'd talked to my parents a lot lately, and mostly about Trevor, Hunter,
and Reed. And I was never going to hide anything from Trevor
again. I wanted him to know.

I looked out the window at the familiar scenery. I didn't want to see Trevor's reaction. It didn't matter what it was. How could it change anything? I bit down on a red painted fingernail. Please, God, let Hunter be alright.

We drove in silence. After a half-hour or so I glanced up to the rearview mirror again. Trevor's eyes met mine and he looked away. I took my finger away from my mouth. I'd chewed the nail up something awful. I was going to have to cut my nails shorter now.

Soon we were pulling up to the hospital. Reed slid into a space and we made our way to the front desk. They directed us to his room.

We walked into a room full of people. Hunter lay on a bed in the middle, tubes and machines all around him. An older couple occupied the space by the head of his bed. At the foot a slightly older version of Hunter sat in a chair, along with four very blonde, very lovely young women. This must be his family.

I stood just inside the door. Trevor and Reed walked up to the tall, slender man in overalls and he jumped up when he saw them.

"Boys! You made good time." He stood over the bed. "Hunter, the boys are here." He placed his hand on Hunter's in the most gentle manner. I was going to cry again. But then the small, wiry woman with graying hair approached me.

"You must be Daphne," she said quietly.

"Yes, ma'am," I said. "How is he?"

Suddenly she threw her arms around me. She was so small her head barely came up to my shoulder. I put my arms on her shoulders, not sure what to do.

"Hunter's been missing you something awful. Come on over here and talk to him. I'm sure it'll help him," she said, dragging me to the bed.

"I'm not sure that's such a good idea," I said.

Reed turned to me then from where he stood at Hunter's head. "Talk to him, Daphne, it's alright."

I felt every set of eyes in the room on me. It didn't faze me; I was used to performing to larger audiences than this. But when I looked at Hunter's peaceful face, memories poured back of our time together, and a pressure settled in my chest. I reached out and stroked his soft cheek.

"Hunter, it's Daphne. I came to see you." Something beeped and I jumped back. Everyone stared at me. A nurse came rushing in.

"Is he waking up?" she asked. "There was a spike in brain activity and heart rate. Whatever you were doing, keep doing it. He's responding." She checked a few things and made a few notes and left shortly.

All eyes were on me again. The tall man, whom I assumed was Hunter's father, spoke softly to me. "Go on, girl. We need to pull him out of this. Doctor said longer he's asleep, the worse it could be. Please."

Hunter's father bowed his head and squeezed his eyes shut, still holding onto Hunter's hand. I bent down to Hunter's ear and hoped no one would hear me.

"Come on, Country. You need to take me to the playground again. We still haven't tried out that twisty slide and you did promise me. Wake up and show me around your town."

The machines beeped again, but this time I didn't jump. My cheek was resting against his and the feel of his beard sent shivers through me. Not of lust, but of true, deep, honest love. Hunter wake up, I love you. I loved him. I said it in my head. I knew it in my heart. But what could I do about it?

I pressed my face more firmly to his. I put my lips right up on his ear until I could feel them brushing his skin as I spoke. "I love you, Hunter Falco." A tear rolled out despite my closed eyes.

I stood and looked once more at his beautiful face. Even in sleep he looked happy. Please wake up, Hunter. His eyelids fluttered and I ran out of the room. I stopped outside the door and leaned my back against the cold wall. I was gasping, unable to get enough air.

An eruption of voices spilled out into the hall from the room. A doctor rushed past me through the door. I laid my head back against the wall and closed my eyes. I still couldn't catch my breath.

"Not even gonna tell him you're here?" Reed asked, appearing by my side.

"You know I can't."

"I don't know that. I think you can do anything you set your pretty little mind to, Miss Williams."

"So now we're back to Miss Williams? And you want me to go in there and break his heart all over again? Who are you and what have you done with my best friend?"

"I'm your best friend?" Reed asked, smiling at me.

"Oh hush, you know you are. So, he's ok in there? He's awake?"

"Right as rain. Or seems to be anyway. Doctor's checking him over now. And I don't want you to break his heart. Quite the opposite."

I looked at Reed. He was serious. What was he trying to do to me?

"You're a fool, Reed Butler, when you know I'll always love another man. Or have you already forgotten our fight yesterday?"

Reed's face contorted in anger. He grabbed my arms and pushed me against the wall. He glared at me. He put his lips to my ear and his breath was hot as he hissed the words at me.

"Stop it! Do you hear me, Daphne? Stop it! I know you. I know your deepest depravities, your darkest desires. If you're really in love with David Monroe, then I'm the king of Siam. Don't push us away because you're afraid."

He released me and walked back into Hunter's room. I slid down the wall to the floor, hitting my bottom, hard. I hung my head in my hands and sat there, sobbing quietly.

Someone sat down beside me. I looked to the side and quickly wiped my tears.

"I'm sorry, I just..." I didn't know what to say to Hunter's father.

"Don't worry. I just needed to get some air, too. It's a lot in there, right now. Name's James Falco." He held out a hand to me.

"Daphne Williams," I said, taking it.

"I know who you are. We all do. Hunter never stops talking about you."

"Oh." I didn't know what to say to that.

"Yes, ma'am. He goes on and on until we're sick of hearing about his big city lawyer friend, how all her cases are going, who she's fighting for now. How she's the smartest, most beautiful, sweetest girl he's ever known." James stared across the room looking thoughtful.

"That's incredibly flattering. I think Hunter's just about the kindest person I've ever met," and I hid my face in my arms again, unable to stop the tears.

"Hush now, he's going to be ok. You both will. I hope you won't get mad at me for interfering, but I've just got to say my piece. Don't waste it. Don't worry about what might happen, what could happen. Just jump. Life don't hand you happiness too often. Take it when you can get it, even if it means cutting a new path."

If this was happiness I trembled at the idea of misery. I didn't understand his farm metaphors. What did 'cutting a new path' mean? Then I had a terrible thought.

"What about the orchard, Mr. Falco? Who's looking after the farm right now?"

"Well, tell you the truth, don't really know what'll happen now. Really depended on Hunter's help since I got the cancer. Haven't been able to do the heavy stuff. Ryder helps, but he's still only one man. Even got the girls out there, but it won't be enough. If we hire anymore outside labor, it'll break us. And no one knows the place like Hunter. He was born to be a farmer. You know he's a vegetarian? I don't know where he gets his ideas sometimes. But he's stubborn as a mule once he sets his mind to something. Never gives up on it. Still, he won't be back this season. I've been thinking of selling the peaches anyway. They've still got ten good years left. Could probably get enough to save the house at least."

"There must be something else you can do. Hunter talks about those peach trees like they're his second family." I said.

James laughed. "He sure does. I don't know. I'm not much of a businessman. Just love the quiet life, growing green things in the warm sun, and feeding my neighbors good food. Now we'll be bogged down with insurance for years. They don't like it when someone gets hurt. Even if he *was* being a darn fool operating that tractor when I specifically told him..."

I cut him off. Something he said had my curiosity peaked. "Insurance? What kinds of insurance do you have, Mr. Falco?"

"Whatever they told me I needed when I got the loan to invest in the peach trees. Not cheap to start, but it's a crop that lasts twenty years, so..."

I cut him off again. "Mr. Falco, would you mind if I took a look at your insurance? I mean, give me all your information and let me deal with the insurance companies?"

He looked at me like I was an angel from heaven. "Why, ma'am, I'd be grateful to you! So grateful. Do you really think there's something you can do?"

"Hunter wasn't exaggerating when he told you how good I am at my job. Let me take care of it, please. But I do have one condition."

James looked at me.

"Don't tell Hunter."

From the room I heard a laugh. That same loud, wonderful laugh that had caught my ear at Nathaniel Eldritch's party. It felt like a lifetime ago. My heart faltered. This wasn't going to be easy, was it?

16

Revelation

I left the hospital before anyone could stop me. I called a ride and went to the nearest car rental agency. I got a car and drove home. It was peaceful and dark, and my mind reeled as I drove, trying to make sense of everything that had happened today.

What was I going to do? Hunter would know I'd been there. But what would he make of it? Reed was pissed at me. Again. Trevor; I had no idea what to think about Trevor. But my body sure did. Just the thought of him and I trembled deep inside.

Then I thought of David. No tremble. I felt something, though. What was it? I let the feeling come out of its box, the place I had packed it down into when it wasn't convenient to feel it. And soon I could name it. Vanity. The moment I named it, I owned it.

I loved David, yes. But I didn't *love* him. I loved the *idea* of David, the brilliant mind, the flashy lifestyle, god, those gorgeous green eyes. But I didn't love him. Not like that. My ego had been badly bruised, and it still hurt, yes. But my heart... my heart had remained intact. Not until I saw Trevor at the airport, did I realize what true heartbreak was.

And now it was hitting me full force in the gut. I pulled the car over just a few streets from my house, unable to breathe. My head was spinning. I laid the seat back and closed my eyes, trying to slow my breathing. It didn't help. There was nothing I could do to make this ok.

I was in love with three men. There was no going back from it. I'd finally admitted it to myself; opened the box and shook it out, dirty spiders and all. And it only made things worse.

David had been my shield. He *was* my Ashley. My Captain Butler, Reed Butler, had been so right, as he always seemed to be. I only wanted David because I couldn't have him. If he'd given in, if he'd slept with me the first time I'd turned my eyes in his direction, I'd have used him and thrown him away by now. I knew it was true.

Yes, David and I were great together. We were the dream team of litigators. But David had been right, too. That's all we were; and all we would ever be. And it was more than enough. David helped me live my dream every day. With him I could go all the way. Anywhere I wanted to go. I toyed with the idea of the Supreme Court for a moment in my head. Justice Williams had a nice ring to it.

But now that the box was open, it felt like my heart had been flayed into three raw, bleeding sections. And it hit me like a hurricane.

My sweet Country. The one who could make me laugh at myself, laugh at the world that usually made me spit fire. The true center of my heart, where all the goodness that was in me was stored. I had it locked tight away, but Hunter held the key. How could I ever go back to the harsh grayness that existed without him? Without those hot-chocolate eyes that only saw the good in me?

And my very best friend. My real-life Captain Butler. I liked calling him that. I thought I might start. It would irritate him. He would tell me that captains in the Navy manned ships, not jets, and I was confusing it with the Air Force, or some other such silliness. I smiled. He could tease me and be teased and see every dark corner of my soul and he still loved me. There was nothing I hid from him, and nothing he hid from me. We knew each other completely, warts and all, and we both wanted it. We wanted to be together forever, our souls connected in darkness, but also in light. For Reed and I pulled that darkness out of each other and held it up to the light, where it could fade away. I needed him and he needed me. If he left it would be like cutting out a piece of my soul.

Then there was Trevor. Trevor, with his sharp mind and razor wit. The man who I could never say the right thing to, but it only endeared me to him more. The only person I'd ever known who gave me faith in humanity. Truly. He saw the good in everyone, even me. He was trusting and caring and when I was with him, he made me that way, too. He made me better. He made me a complete person. And he didn't take any of my shit. Trevor pulled me out of myself and made me take a good, hard look. He held my face to that mirror until I didn't flinch. No one had stood up to me that way in my entire life. No one had ever seen me the way Trevor did. And I had looked down on him for something as trivial as his job. Not anymore.

How could I live without any one of them? Could I be happy with one of them? Reed would be my friend, no matter what, I knew that. He'd all but said as much. But how could I pick between Trevor and Hunter? Even if I could, I wouldn't do that to them.

I sat up in the car. "I can't think about that right now. If I do, I'll go crazy. I'll think about that tomorrow," I said out loud, quoting Scarlett.

I drove back to my house and went inside. It was late and my folks were already asleep. I snuck into their bedroom and kissed them both. They didn't stir. I went back down to the kitchen to have some warm milk. I never drank it at my house, but somehow, when I was home, nothing calmed me like a warm glass of milk.

I heated the milk in a pan on the stove and poured it into a mug and stirred it with a spoon dipped in honey. I sipped it and felt a little better. I took it up to my room and sat on my bed, sipping.

I wasn't happy. I wasn't peaceful. But a weight had been lifted off of me, and it felt good. I knew what my feelings were now, at least. And Hunter was going to be ok. I couldn't lose him. I just couldn't.

Something hit my window with a plink. Must be a June bug, I thought. Stupid bugs. Another plink hit my window, followed by another. What in tarnation? I peeked out the window to the yard below, illuminated by the porch light. Trevor was standing on my lawn throwing rocks at my window. My heart skiddered.

I padded down the stairs and opened the front door. He ran over and grabbed me in his arms, holding me in an iron grip.

"What are you doing, silly boy? Trying to break my window? We have a doorbell, you know." I sounded bitchy again. Why did I do this?

"Aren't you at all happy to see me, Daphne?"

"Come inside before the neighbors see you," I whispered. I pulled him in and shut the door quietly. He looked at me with pain behind his eyes.

I threw my arms around his neck and pressed my lips to his. I jumped up and wrapped my legs around his waist, knocking him off balance. He wobbled but found his footing and crushed me in his embrace.

"I'm so happy to see you; you don't know how happy. Oh, Trevor," I sighed and closed my mouth over his again. Trevor took four large strides and sat down on the sofa with me still wrapped around him. I looked down into his gorgeous face and smiled.

"Oh, Daphne," he whispered, stroking my face and running his fingertips through my hair.

"Trevor, I have to tell you something important. I've had an epiphany tonight."

"Have you, now?" he said, gazing at me with dreamy eyes.

"Yes, and it's very important that you listen and don't make any judgements or interrupt me until I tell you everything. Is that clear?"

"Yes, ma'am," he said in that way that meant he was going to get exactly what he wanted. But I wasn't as sure as him.

"I love you, Trevor Bond. I love you so much my heart is aching."

"I love you, Daphne Olivia," he interrupted me. I was going to scold him, but the way he said it sent a shiver through my body. I trembled in his grasp and he felt it. He pulled my body into his, kissing me with a fire I thought would burn right through me.

"Wait, please," I breathed, not really caring anymore if he heard the rest. But he stopped and gazed at me patiently.

"I'm sorry, angel eyes. Tell me more, please." He smiled and I almost couldn't think. I ran a finger over his dimpled cheek.

"Uuuhhh, you are such a naughty boy!" I smiled. Then I let my smile drop. "I'm still in love with someone else, though."

Trevor's face became an unreadable mask. I hated it when I couldn't read a person. It was one of the things I was most talented at. But with Trevor I never could seem to get it right. Was he angry? Hurt? Interested? Why did I read 'interested' on his face?

I plunged ahead. "It's Hunter. I love him as dearly as my own heart. As dearly as I love you, my darling." I looked at him, searching his face for his reaction.

He smiled a small smile. "Is that all? There's no more?"

I sighed and squeezed my eyes shut, drawing up the courage to spit out the rest. Praying he wouldn't stomp on my heart too badly when he ran out the door. I opened my eyes and looked back down into his. I knew I had to tell him.

"And Reed," I whispered, holding his face in my hands and looking him right in the eye.

"Anyone else?" he asked, his voice soft and devoid of emotion. What was going on in his head? The man had the patience of Sisyphus to sit through this list.

"No," I whispered.

"Well, alright then," he said, flashing those dimples at me.

"Alright then?" I asked.

"You know, I'm just glad I don't have any other brothers, or a father, or maybe an uncle that I have to worry about sharing you with." He smiled at me devilishly and tickled me in the ribs.

I yelped and slammed my hand over my mouth. What would my Daddy think if he saw me straddling a man on his sofa in the middle of the night? But Trevor was laughing! Laughing?

"What ever is so funny about this?" I asked.

"Darling, the three of us have known for a long time how you felt. But I really enjoyed watching you squirm while you told me."

"You have? How could you? I didn't know until tonight!"

"Well, it took us a little while to work it all out. I mean, after all the punching was over and all."

"Punching?! Oh no, you didn't!"

"Calm down, I'm just teasing you. But really, it was rocky there when everything first came out."

"Reed. I'd like to punch him," I mumbled.

"Oh, no, it wasn't him. He kept his mouth shut. I wanted to punch him for it then, but now I'm kind of grateful. If I'd known any earlier how Hunter felt about you, I would have backed off right away. But as it happened, it was too late for anything like that."

"But you did back off. I mean, I haven't seen you in ten weeks!"

"I know. We didn't figure it all out until after you'd dumped both of us and we'd been hanging around the shop like a couple of depressed sloths. Seriously, nothing was getting done. Hunter spilled his guilty guts to me one day after we closed up. He hadn't wanted to tell me because he figured he was stealing you from me and I'd seen you first."

"Just what a woman loves to hear. Men making claims on her without consulting her opinion at all."

"It's really not like that." He looked into my eyes and tucked a strand of my hair behind my ear. He was always doing that. It was a caring gesture. Like he wanted to make sure I was comfortable. And also touch my hair. It comforted me and turned me on at the same time.

"What's it like, then?" I asked.

"Well, we all sat down around the kitchen table and spilled everything. After Hunter and I came clean with each other, Reed shared what he'd learned after your little meltdown in the bar, thank you Maker's Mark."

I playfully punched him on the shoulder.

"Ow!" he smiled and tickled my ribs again.

"Stop it, my Daddy'll wake up!" I hissed through the giggles.

"Anyway, between the three of us we pretty much had you figured out. We decided to wait for you to figure it out for yourself. And lucky me, I got to be the one here when you did. So, how heavy of a sleeper is your daddy?"

Trevor lifted me off his lap and laid me down on the sofa, pressing himself on me and kissing me like I'd never been kissed. The fire spread from my lips, down my chest, through my belly and settled deep in my pelvis. I felt a flood hit my panties.

I reached around his back and grabbed on, my hands delighting in every curve of hard muscle. I ran my fingers through his curls and over his dimpled cheek. His lips moved on mine and I completely gave in. Whatever he wanted, whatever he needed, I would give to him.

"Daphne Olivia, I love you," he whispered on my lips.

"I love you, Trevor." I moaned a quiet moan as his hips nestled in between my legs. I could feel him straining in his pants. God, I wanted him.

But he stopped and sat up, pulling me up with him and sitting me sideways across his lap. I wrapped my arms around his neck and kissed him, but his kiss was tentative.

"So, you're ok with it?" he asked, pulling back from my kisses.

"Ok with what?" I asked, confused.

"Ok with being our girlfriend."

Our girlfriend? I wasn't thinking clearly. I wasn't thinking at all. It was a hazard when I was in Trevor's arms.

"Are you speaking with the royal 'we' now? Since when did you become royalty?" I teased him.

Trevor shifted uncomfortably. "Daphne, I came here tonight to see if you would be open to dating all three of us. We wanted to talk to you together, but you ran off so fast... and one of us wanted to stay with Hunter..."

My jaw dropped open and I stared at him. Was he really saying what I thought he was saying?

"Daphne, don't get scared. It can be whatever you want it to be. For us, all we want is you, however, whenever, whoever you want. I can speak for all three of us when I say we have fallen in love with you. With everything you are. We've worked it out on our side. No jealousy. We've shared everything in our lives. It really wasn't that much of a stretch for us to consider this."

Trevor looked at me and now I saw doubt in his eyes. He really didn't know what I would say. But I'd already told him. How could he think I would hesitate now?

"Yes." I smiled shyly at him.

"Yes?" he said, his own smile breaking across his face and his eyes widening in surprise.

"Well, don't look so shocked. Did you think I'd say no?"

"I didn't know what you'd say. I hoped, but... guess I owe the guys twenty each."

"What! You better tell me you're not betting on me like I'm some horse in the derby!"

"It's really not like that," he smiled at me.

"You keep saying that. Sounds like my first task as your girlfriend is going to be to put you in your place. No more betting on me or making claims on me, you hear?"

"Yes ma'am."

17

Sushi

"There she is! Get over here! You sure do keep a fella waiting!" Hunter beamed at me from his hospital bed. He looked good. Real good.

Four angelic faces turned to me and giggled. Hunter's sisters were all sprawled on the small bed with him, heaped up like a pile of puppies. I didn't know how they all fit on that narrow bed. They rolled or jumped off the bed and stood in a row as I made my way over.

My eyes locked with Hunter's. I felt my heart melt when I looked into those warm chocolate pools. His eyes didn't leave my face as I bent down and kissed his cheek.

"Hi there," I whispered.

Hunter reached up and grabbed my arms, pulling me so quickly I didn't know what had happened. Suddenly my lips were on his and he was kissing me. I sank onto the bed, my knees trembling. Four little giggles filled the room.

"Hush, now all y'all," Hunter mumbled, breaking the kiss and staring into my eyes again.

I smiled at him and then turned my head to his sisters. "Hi, I'm Daphne," I said, holding out a hand.

"Piper."

"Aster."

"Heather."

"Summer," they said, shaking my hand one by one.

"Pleased to meet y'all," I said.

Summer, the youngest, turned to her sisters and said, "See! She is as pretty as Hunter said. Pay up now!" and she held out her hand.

Hunter laughed his infectious laugh. "That'll teach y'all not to trust your big brother! Now, get out for a while." He shooed them away with his hand and they smiled at him indulgently. When they had gone, he turned his eyes on me and smiled his soft smile.

"Trevor was here first thing this morning. You're really staying?" he asked.

"I am if you want me to," I said.

"I want it more than anything," he said quietly.

"Can't say as I understand it all yet, but Hunter, I don't ever want to be apart from you. I love you."

Hunter's face flushed and he smiled. But then the smile disappeared, and he looked at me seriously. "I love you, too."

I leaned down and placed my lips against his, softly, gently, feeling the curve of his mouth. His hand moved up my arm, over my shoulder, into my hair, his fingers exploring every inch, while his lips moved slowly on mine.

I felt the fire burn in me, slow and hot, and dying to break free. My breath sped up and Hunter stopped, looking into my eyes.

"I'm going home tonight. Doctor said I'm all cleared for light duty. Not sure what you're doing to me right now qualifies." He smiled at me mischievously.

"Oh, Hunter," I said, laying my head on his chest. I listened to his steady heart, so happy that he was ok. Happy beyond words that he was laughing and teasing and that he wanted what I wanted, and I'd finally said it. He stroked my hair and sighed.

"I have some business I need to take care of in town today," I said. "Then I'll need to get back to Charleston. When will you come back?"

"Soon. Doc says no farm work for at least six months. Not much to do around here until the spring after that, anyway. Won't you stay a few nights here with me?"

"Of course I will, honey," I said lifting my head to kiss him again. "You gonna take me back to your momma's house?" I laughed, but he looked horrified, which made me laugh even more.

"No! Oh, I see, you're teasing me. Naughty girl."

"You don't know the half of it," I said slyly.

"Oh, I think I do, actually," he said. And to my surprise he slid a hand down and grabbed my bottom.

I moaned and kissed him. "Do you think you'd come visit me if I got a hotel room in town tonight?" I whispered. Suddenly a cacophony of beeping sounded around us and I sat up, startled. Hunter took a deep breath.

"I told you doc might not like that... But I would."

"Alright now, Mr. Falco, I brought your lunch," the nurse said, bustling in with a tray. She adjusted the table and set the tray in front of Hunter, then checked his charts and took his blood pressure. She seemed satisfied, although she did give me a sideways glance when she looked at the heart monitor.

Hunter opened his lunch tray and sighed. "Not enough to feed a mouse," he said.

I laughed. "Don't they know growing teenagers need more?"

"You're not really worried about that, are you?" Hunter asked, looking worried.

"About what, honey?"

"Our very little age difference. I don't even think about it. I hope you don't."

"Sweetie, when I'm with you I feel thirteen, too, so no, I don't think about it." I kissed him again. Then I reached over and grabbed my briefcase. "And, I brought you something," I said, opening it. I pulled out three little boxes and set them on his tray.

"Presents?" he asked.

"Sort of. Something to make you feel better, I hope. Here, open this one first." I handed him one of the boxes.

He opened it and when he looked inside his face screwed up. "Sushi? You have a lot to learn about what makes me feel better." I laughed again. "Do I, now? Take it out of the box." He reached in and took out the little cake. "Now try some." He bit into it tentatively and his face lit up. "It's chocolate cake!" he said, and finished it off in two bites, a big smile on his face.

Hunter promptly opened and devoured the other two boxes which contained a small cherry pie and lavender lemon bars. I'd stopped by the bakery on my way, and when I saw the little petit fours shaped like sushi I couldn't resist.

Hunter wrapped his arms around me and pulled me tight. I rested my cheek against his and whispered in his ear, "Eat your lunch now." Then I bit his earlobe. I sat up.

"You leaving?" he said, disappointed.

"I have to go get some work done. But I promise I'll be back. As long as you really want me." I still didn't believe it.

"I really do," he smiled at me.

18

The First Time

I drove straight over to the farm. Mr. Falco and Ryder met me there. We sat down at their huge dining table and I got right down to work. They handed me stacks of insurance information, all on paper. It took me a few hours to go through it all. But in the end, I knew I had what I needed.

"Mr. Falco, this looks much better than I'd expected. I can assure you right now that you won't need to sell anything. I'm going to work on getting you compensated for the extra labor you've had to hire so far, as well. I'll take this back to Charleston with me but expect to hear from me by next week with numbers. In the meantime, if you're comfortable with it, go ahead and hire a few more hands here. I can guarantee you at least two men's salaries will be covered, but I'm fairly confident I'll be able to get you more."

"I... I just don't know how to thank you, Miss Williams. You're a real blessing, a real blessing. And please, call me James."

"Yes sir, and you call me Daphne. And this is nothing, really. I'd do anything for Hunter, I want you to know that."

James teared up a little and Ryder laughed just like Hunter. "Miss Daphne, you are everything Hunter said you would be. Looks like I owe Summer, too."

"Well, I oughta take a cut of all the action around here. Your family has a bit of a gambling problem, I think," I said, laughing.

"It's just that none of us quite believed the stories he came back with. We thought the city must've got to his head. Summer'll believe anything he says, though. She's followed him around since she could crawl. We all thought it would be easy money," he laughed.

"Well, then, Summer and I should get along just fine." I glanced up then, and saw Reed standing in the doorway watching me. My heart fluttered. "Reed!"

"Hi Daphne," he said in his staid voice. Oh no, maybe he was still mad at me.

"Where have you and Trevor been? You weren't at the hospital, so I expected to see you here."

"Trevor's there now. We were out running errands for Ginny. Lord, she's a small thing, but she's tougher than a drill sergeant in bootcamp." James and Ryder laughed.

"Gentleman, thank you for the lovely lunch. It was mighty nice getting to know you both. I have some business with Reed now, if you'll excuse us."

"Surely. And thank you," James said.

"You have a minute?" I asked Reed as I walked past him and out the front door. He turned on his heel and followed me out.

"What was all that? What are you doing here anyway?" Reed asked me.

"Are you still mad at me or something?"

"No ma'am. Not at all." He looked at the ground as he said it and I realized what he was feeling.

"Come on, darling, there's something you and I need to do." I led him to my car and motioned for him to get in.

"Don't you think I should drive," he said, pausing at the door.

"No, I do not. I like to drive. Get used to it." Reed smiled and got in the car.

I turned the car on and cranked the AC. I pulled out my phone and looked around for a few minutes.

"What are you doing there?" Reed asked, trying to peek at my screen. But I held it away from him.

"Don't you worry your pretty little head about it."

"And why are you here? You planning on moving in with all of us? The house is pretty crowded as it is with the three of us in Ryder's room and all Hunter's sisters. How many of them are there again? They all look so much alike and they're like a tornado in the bathroom in the morning. There must be enough girly stuff in there for eight women."

"No, I am most definitely not staying in Ginny the drill sergeant's house," I laughed.

I drove down the long dirt driveway and out onto the road into town. In a few minutes we were at my destination. I pulled into the property.

"Where are we?" Reed asked.

"A place with a little more elbow room."

"For who's elbows? Goliath?" Reed gaped as I pulled up to a historic mansion on sprawling, willow covered grounds.

"I figured if I'm going to stay the night in town, I'd like to do it right. And there isn't a decent hotel closer than Lexington. This place is more my style."

"Guess so," Reed said, stepping out of the car.

"Come on, let's go exploring!"

I ran up to the front door and keyed the code into the lockbox. I popped the key out and unlocked the door. I pushed the heavy double doors open to reveal a southern home worthy of Scarlett and Rhett.

I grabbed Reed's hand and pulled him inside, leaving the doors open wide. I dragged him from room to room, the great hall, the kitchen, the living room, the formal dining room, the four bathrooms that were on this level. Then I headed for the stairs.

"Let's go see the bedrooms. There's eight of them" I said, smiling at him wickedly. Reed hesitated, then followed me.

Upstairs was as opulent as down. Everything was hardwood, marble, satin, and lace. I pulled Reed into what looked like the master suite. I kicked my shoes off and leapt onto the enormous, raised four-poster bed. Reed stood, hands clasped in front of him, looking like a soldier even out of uniform. I patted the bed next to me.

"Come on, I'm not gonna bite. Unless you want me to." A few days ago, we would have teased each other like that and thought nothing of it. Now everything was different, and Reed just stood there, indecision clear on his face. Finally, he kicked his shoes off and sat down on the bed next to me.

"I have to apologize to you," I said. Reed looked at me in surprise. "I know, it doesn't happen often, so enjoy it while you can. Yesterday, in the hall, you were right. I was afraid. I was terrified, actually. What you said, it made me think. I went home last night and realized it all then. I love you, Reed. You're my best friend. I've never held anything back with you, you know that. But I was holding it back from myself. How I really feel about you. And I'm sorry."

Reed looked at me with longing in his eyes. "Daphne, you are the most incredible woman I have ever met. Your friendship means more to me than almost anything. You know I'll be with you, no matter what. As a friend, if that's what you need."

"I do. I do need you as a friend. More than I've ever needed someone like that. But, Reed, I want more. I want all of you. And if you're really ok with this whole, crazy idea, then I'm ok with it, too."

We looked into each other's eyes and I was lost in his crystal blue irises. I reached up and ran my hand over the soft, short hairs on the back of his head. His hand slid up my arm and around my shoulder, caressing my skin.

Then Reed grabbed me and crushed me to the bed with his body. His hand tangled in my hair and he found my mouth, moving his lips over mine until I couldn't breathe. He moved down my neck and I gasped, sucking air in, my body pulsing under his.

Reed's carefully constructed walls came crashing down, releasing a furious passion that I'd only glimpsed before. His hands moved over my body with purpose and speed. My silk tank was swiftly removed, my arms pinned over my head, and Reed's lips came down on my wrist, down my arm, down my side, his teeth grazing my waist.

He straddled my hips and knelt over me, his eyes locked on mine. Desire burned behind them. He tore off his shirt and my body spasmed. Every inch of him was covered in muscle. Hard, smooth edges of powerful flesh that I wanted to sink my teeth into. But before I could move, he was on top of me again, his arm around my back and his hot skin pressed to mine.

My bra was whisked away faster than I could see and now my tender flesh was melded to his. I felt my nipples harden with the contact and Reed kissed me. My lips parted and his tongue slipped in to touch mine. His hand roved up my side and found my breast, his fingers closing over the sensitive nipple. I moaned in pure ecstasy.

"Reed! Oh, my love!"

Reed moaned against my lips and forced his tongue in again as he reached behind him and his hand made its way up my skirt. His hips pinned me to the bed, and I couldn't move as his hand slipped into my panties. One finger slid down my dripping slit and back up, circling my swollen clit. Then he plunged it into me, sliding it in and out and back up to circle my clit again.

"Uuunnnhhh!" I cried as his mouth left mine and he bit into my neck. His hands were everywhere, and every touch sent spasms through me. His finger plunged into me again and I could feel my orgasm coming.

Reed pulled his hand out from under my skirt and unbuckled his belt. I watched with hungry eyes as he unzipped his pants and pulled his cock out. It was wide like him, pale pink with a huge head. Oh, god, I wanted it!

I propped myself up on my elbow and reached out and grabbed him. He looked surprised for a moment, but the fire burned behind his eyes as I ran my tongue around the tip of him, swirling the sticky pre-cum over the whole head. I looked up into his face as I took him in my mouth, sucking hard, watching him groan with pleasure. I ran my hand over his scrotum, cupping him as I sucked. I grabbed the shaft and held him firmly, moving up and down on him, my eyes never leaving his face.

I couldn't take it anymore. My pussy throbbed with the need for release. I let go and laid back. Reed stood and removed the rest of his clothing as I slid my skirt and panties down my legs. He grabbed my ankles and spread them apart, running his hands up my thighs and pulling me to the edge of the tall bed. I squeaked in anticipation.

Reed bent over me and chuckled. "Do you want this Daphne?" he whispered, smiling wickedly at me.

"I need you, Reed," I moaned.

"I love you, Daphne," he said.

"I love you," I whispered, and he sank his cock into me.

The whole world began to spin. I cried out. He filled me to the edge of madness. Every nerve-ending lit up like a Christmas light. He fucked me hard, his chest pressed to mine, his hands gripping me and sinking into my flesh.

I wrapped my legs around him and bucked against him, taking him into me until he screamed my name. It sent me over the edge. I burst on him, my muscles throbbing and squeezing so tight around his thick shaft I thought I might pass out. He grabbed me and fucked me even harder, peaking my orgasm, making me cry out.

As the throbbing slowed, so did Reed. He looked into my eyes and kissed me as he slowly slid in and out. The rocking of my body and his lips moving gently on mine was complete nirvana. Reed stood upright and pulled out, grabbing my leg and flipping me over. My feet slid down to the floor and he bent me over the bed. I wasn't used to be handled like that, but before I could even think, he was behind me, pressing into me, continuing the same slow rhythm.

Reed reached up and took hold of my breast, squeezing and caressing until I was mad with arousal. His hands seemed to know every place to touch, every spot to caress. He grabbed my hip with his other hand and pulled my ass up, slamming into me. I moaned as he hit that secret spot, sending an ache through me. He slid in hard again and I knew I would cum again.

"Oh, Reed," I moaned into the bedspread.

He bent over me and slammed hard into me. "Daphne! God, you're incredible!"

I squeezed him and he moaned in my ear, slamming into me again and again until I came on him, writhing and wobbling, my knees weak. Reed held me until I finished, then slipped out again, turning me back to face him.

He kissed me and whispered, "Lie down on the pillows."

I wondered how long he could last. I laid back on the cool bed, my body slack. Reed climbed onto me and looked into my eyes. He slid into me and I moaned again. He was so damn thick. Holding me tenderly he moved slowly, kissing my jawbone, my neck, my shoulder. He was so tender tears came to my eyes. I ran my hands over his back and held him to me.

"Oh, Reed, I love you. I love you!" I whispered. "Cum inside me. I want you to cum in me." I needed it, needed to feel him, to take part of his body in mine.

"Oh, Daphne," he moaned, and I felt him swell. He pressed into me, deep, and I felt the throbbing, the pulsing as he came. He held me to him, and I held him, too, our bodies becoming as close as our souls.

We lay there, our bodies connected, our breath slowing. Tears spilled out of my eyes. But they were tears of joy. Never had I made love to someone like this. Never had anyone been able to break through my shield and know me like Reed knew me, inside and out, physically now, as well as emotionally.

Reed raised himself up and looked at me. I smiled and he wiped the tears away. He kissed me and I closed my eyes, savoring the feeling of his lips, of his body inside mine. Every inch of skin touching me. I was finally happy.

19

The Estate

Reed held my hand as we walked into Hunter's hospital room. It was crammed full of people; Mr. and Mrs. Falco, their five other children, the doctor. And Trevor. He looked up and his eyes met mine. I dropped Reed's hand.

"Where did you two get off to?" Trevor asked, stepping up and taking me in his arms. He hugged me and punched Reed on the shoulder.

"Daphne was just showing me the house she's rented for the night. Although, 'house' might not be quite the right word for it," Reed said. There wasn't a hint of tension in his voice. I looked to Trevor's face and he seemed relaxed, too. I felt as nervous as a turtle crossing the highway.

"Hunter's been released, doc's just giving him his marching orders. Then we can all get out of here. Ginny's cooking up something and it smells just heavenly. I can't wait til Hunter's out of this place and back home. And I know he's ready for a real meal," Trevor said.

"Oh, that sounds lovely. I'm starved!" I said.

Trevor smiled conspiratorially at Reed. Reed actually blushed. "I bet you are," Trevor whispered to me.

"Alright, who's driving the getaway car? Get me out of here!" Hunter laughed.

"Daphne, why don't you drive him?" Reed said loudly. "I'm sure he'd love a tour of the mansion you've rented. You should see it Hunter, it's insane. It has *eight* bedrooms."

"There's still a few hours before supper," Trevor chimed in, grinning.

I wanted to disappear into the wall. I glared at Reed. "I'm sure he's seen it before. This is his town after all," I said.

"You rented the Bluegrass Estate?" Hunter said, eyes wide. "I've always wanted to see inside that place! Let's go, Daphne! I need to stretch my legs. Been stuck in bed too long."

I heard Trevor and Reed stifle laughs behind me. They were just being too much now. I spun around and stared them down, my back to the rest of the room. I mouthed 'you're in trouble' at both of them and gave them the eyebrow. They tried not to laugh again.

"Sure, honey, *anything* for you," I said in my sweetest voice. Let them chew on that. If they wanted to be cavalier about this whole thing, I could too.

"Momma, Momma, can I go, too, please?" Summer begged.

"Hush now, girl, no," Ginny said, shooting a look at her daughter. "You two have a good time and be back by supper."

Hunter grabbed my hand and we strode out of the room, a line of people behind us like we were leading a parade. I felt a little ridiculous. But Hunter caressed my hand as we walked and it felt so familiar, so comfortable, that soon I forgot about everything but us.

Outside everyone dispersed and we walked in silence to my car. It was unusual for Hunter to be quiet like this, and I wondered if he was having second thoughts. If any of them would, it would be him. He was young and handsome and homespun. He could have any girl in the county, probably, and most of them would be a more likely match than me.

We got into the car and I put the key in the ignition. I turned to Hunter and he was gazing at me with those puppy dog eyes. My heart melted.

"You sure you wouldn't rather go home? Aren't you tired?" I asked, hoping he would say no, but wanting to give him the out.

"Tired of being inside. Tired of being away from you. But not tired, no," he smiled.

No second thoughts then. Oh lord, what was I getting myself into? I pulled the car out of the parking lot, distracted by my own thoughts. I felt something on my knee and looked down. Hunter was running a finger up my leg and taking my skirt with it. My breath rushed in. But then he pulled the hem of my skirt down and smoothed it, putting his hand back in his lap.

"Your garter was showing," he said, smiling at me. "You dress up just for me?" he said in a lower, sexier voice.

"You know I did," I flirted.

"So, tell me everything I missed in the last ten weeks," Hunter said, sitting back in his chair and smiling that adorable grin at me.

I told him about everything I'd been working on and he told me everything he'd been doing. By the time we pulled onto the property it felt like we'd never been apart. My heart was glowing in the happiest way. The way only Hunter could make me feel.

"Whooo!" he yelled as he got out of the car. "It's amazing! You sure don't go halfway, do you?"

"I sure don't," I said, thinking how true it really was.

"I'd like to scoop you up right here and carry you in, but doc says no heavy lifting."

"Hey now, what's that supposed to mean?" I said, mock hurt in my voice.

Hunter turned vermillion as he backpedaled his way to China. "Oh, Daphne, I didn't... I mean, no... That's not what I meant..."

I let him sweat and then I turned my smile on him. I stepped into him and pressed my body to his, pushing him against the porch wall. I stared up into those brown eyes and I pressed my breasts into his hard chest.

"Don't worry," I breathed, "there's plenty to do that doesn't require any lifting at all." I kissed him softly and I felt his body relax and go slack under mine. When I opened my eyes, he smiled at me.

"Go for a walk with me?" he asked.

"There's no playground here, sorry, if that's what you're hoping for."

He laughed. "I just want to hold your hand some more, that's all."

"Alright."

"So, Daphne, I was wondering, what are we gonna tell my family? About us, I mean," Hunter said as we strolled along the pond on the huge estate.

"I hadn't really thought about that." And I hadn't. What were we going to tell them? What were we going to tell everyone?

"I've been thinking about it, and I'd like to tell them you're my girlfriend, if that's alright with you."

I stopped walking and pulled his hand so he would look at me. "Hunter Falco, that's just about the nicest thing anyone has ever called me. I'd like that very much."

He smiled down at me and kissed me softly. We kept walking.

"What have you told them already?" I asked.

Hunter blushed. "I got caught, didn't I? I couldn't help it, Daphne. You're all I've been able to think about since I met you and you were wearing that green dress. Couldn't keep my mind on anything else, even after you broke it off. I still loved you. I had to tell them something. I told them we were friends, that's all. That we were all friends, you, me, Trevor, and Reed."

"We are, aren't we?" I asked. "I mean, you know the only reason I left was because I loved you and I didn't want to see you lose Trevor.

I couldn't come between you like that. And I need to know that it's not going to be a problem now."

"It's not going to be a problem at all. We've worked it out. We know where we stand. And all we want is to be with you." He stopped and pulled me into his arms. "I love you, Daphne, and I want the world to know it. I LOVE DAPHNE WILLIAMS!" he hollered into the sky. The horses in the stable nearby went wild.

"You're scaring the animals, you silly boy!" I laughed.

"There're horses here? Come on!" He took off in the direction of the stables.

I had to run to keep up. Thankfully I'd worn flats today. Hunter reached the stables and peeked into one of the stalls. A huge brown head came out and sneezed at him. Hunter laughed.

"Hey there, girl, what's your name?" he said quietly, stroking the horse's face and neck.

"How do you know it's a girl?" I asked.

"Can't you tell the difference between girls and boys, Daphne? Shoot, and I thought I was the innocent one." He laughed.

"Well, she likes you, I can tell that. Guess it *is* a girl, then."

"And you're a real beauty, too, aren't you darling?" he said. The horse nuzzled him.

"Hey now, I'm gonna get a little jealous."

"Sorry, come here and let me see your teeth, we'll see who's prettier," he teased.

Hunter had to pet every horse in the stable before we walked back to the house. When we got inside, I glanced to my left and remembered something.

"Wait here, one second," I said, running down the hall. I closed the door to the study and ran back. "Ok, let me give you the tour."

I led Hunter through the downstairs, except for the study, which had a large stag head mounted on the wall. I didn't want him to think of Bambi. It would kind of ruin the mood. Then we began the tour upstairs. I skipped over 'Reed's' bedroom and instead we ended up in a sweet little room with a rustic theme and a quilt on the bed. It was cozy and warm. Perfect.

"Well, that's the whole house. Now you've seen it, what do you think? As good as you expected?" Hunter gazed at me.

"Better," he said, stepping toward me and taking my face in one large hand. He lifted my face and bent his head down to kiss me. "I love you, Daphne," he said, looking into my eyes.

"I love you, Hunter." I wrapped my arms around his neck and wriggled against him. He was so warm and long. Rarely did I feel small, being as tall as I was, but with Hunter I felt so feminine and diminutive, especially in flats.

Hunters arms came around me and he lifted me like he had that night on the beach. I melted into his arms and pressed my lips to his.

"Oh! Put me down!" I shouted.

Hunter jumped and released me, setting me gently on the ground. "What's wrong?" he said.

"You're not supposed to lift me, remember?" I was frantic. What if something happened to him and we were all the way out here messing around on this estate?

Hunter just laughed and tickled me in the ribs. "You are not heavy lifting. I didn't even have to try. But I'll leave you on the ground if it makes you feel better. Now, stop scaring me like that!"

Hunter took me in his arms again. "I'm sorry, honey," I said.

Hunter ran one long finger down my neck, over my collarbone, my breast, my waist, his eyes following the movement. He continued down to the hem of my skirt, wrapping his hand around my thigh and gently sliding the silky fabric up until he could see my garter again. His breath quickened.

I stepped out of his embrace, back one step, and began to unbutton my dress. I'd showered and changed before the hospital, putting on something I thought Mrs. Falco would approve of at dinner, and maybe Hunter would like after. I slid the sundress off my shoulders, and it floated to the floor.

Hunter's eyes were dark and intense as he watched me. I stood before him in a white satin bra with black lace, and matching garter belt and thong. As he watched I unhooked the bra and let it slide to the floor. I stood, offering my body to him. He reached out and ran his hand down my arm, taking hold of my waist and pulling me back to him.

Hunter spun me around and laid me down on the bed. I stretched out on my back, grasping a breast in my hand, squeezing the nipple while I watched him. Slowly he removed his shirt. Seeing his bare chest, the long, lean muscles and golden skin made me ache. My nipple hardened under my hand. He dropped his pants and stood before me in all his glory. He was hard and ready, and I wanted him so badly.

He laid down on the bed next to me and I rolled to my side, facing him. He ran a hand along my hip down to the garters. He leaned his head down and took my hard nipple in his mouth, moving his tongue firmly against it and sucking. I moaned. His mouth moved up my neck, across my jaw, finding my lips. Kissing me, Hunter pulled my hip into him and his manhood pressed onto me, so hard it almost hurt.

Slowly his lips moved on mine, teasing me, sending me into a tempest of arousal. Hunter began unsnapping the garters, one at a time, his mouth continuing to explore mine. When he was done, he rolled the stockings down with one hand, tossing them aside. He unhooked the belt and tossed it away, too.

Hunter looked into my eyes as he slid my panties down. It felt like the first time. Like we were teenagers, exploring our own bodies as much as each other's. I felt my own innocence, long ago lost in a box deep inside me. It came to the surface now, and I was shy and timid, and basking in the tender gaze of my lover.

His eyes never left mine as he slid inside me. My eyes went wide as I felt him there, pressing, opening my body to him. I threw my leg over his hip and pulled him to me. His hard length slid slowly into my wet slit, so slowly I could feel every inch of him as he penetrated me. A low growl erupted from his chest and my breath rushed out in a whisper, "Hunter!"

He began to move, every stroke long and slow, still looking in my eyes. My hands were pressed to his chest and his long arm was wrapped around all of me, holding me to him as he pushed in and out. A slow aching began to build in me. I slid a hand up to caress his cheek and run my fingers over his brow, around his beautiful eyes.

I felt my arousal reaching its peak. My mouth fell open and a high cry ripped from my chest. He watched my face, his eyes burning with desire, as my orgasm burst. My hand grasped his face and I held him there, staring into his eyes, as I throbbed around him. He thrust into me then, forcing the whole length of his shaft deep, deep into me. I screamed again, my orgasm erupting with a whole new intensity.

Again and again he thrust, until every muscle ached with intense pleasure. Then I felt him swell and I looked in his eyes as he shot into me, hot and hard. His eyes were almost black with rapture and the pleasure of release. I pulled him into me, wanting him deep in me, my leg clasped around him like iron.

We both remembered to breathe at the same time. Our breath rushed out and we both laughed. Hunter's eyes left mine as my shaking laughter squeezed him again.

"Oh, darling," he whispered, stroking my back. He placed his lips softly on mine and kissed me for a long time.

"Oh, Hunter, you are incredible," I moaned.

"Sweet thing," he smiled.

"No, really. I've never... twice like that. How?" I was truly in awe.

"I'm a good student. May not have a lot of practice, but I remember everything I'm taught. And your body is teaching me a lot, beautiful."

"I think you just got an A+."

"Are you grading on a curve?" he laughed.

"Why, you naughty boy! I can't believe you just said that!" I smacked his chest and he crushed me to him, kissing me deeply. I clenched down on him.

"Mmm, darling! Quit that now. We have got to get going. If we're late for supper Momma's gonna get the switch out."

My stomach growled. I giggled and Hunter's eyes closed again against the wiggling of my body. "Sorry," I smiled.

"You are something else, Daphne," he said, handing me a tissue and sliding out of me. "Something else."

20

Dinner and Dessert

"Bless us, O Lord, and these thy gifts, which we are about to receive, through thy bounty. In a world where so many are hungry, may we eat this food with humble hearts. In a world where so many are lonely, may we share this friendship with joyful hearts. Through Christ our Lord we pray. Amen." James finished the prayer and a cacophony erupted around the table.

I had never seen food disappear so fast before. Rolls were passed, then butter, then mashed potatoes, then roasted squash and peppers and mushrooms. A salad that had been picked that afternoon. There was cheese for everything, and gravy. There was prime rib, which Hunter and I passed up, much to Ginny's disapproval. I almost ate some, despite fifteen years as a vegetarian, just to appease her.

I liked Ginny very much. She was smart and sassy, and despite her size, quite commanding. She ruled the house and I admired her. And I desperately wanted her approval.

I was seated between Hunter and Summer. Hunter had pulled out a chair for me, and Summer had swooped in to sit next to me. Reed and Trevor were directly across from me, sly smiles on both their faces. I hoped they would be gentlemen during dinner at least.

"Daphne, how do you get your hair to look like that?" Summer asked me. She reached up and stroked my hair.

"Tell you what, Summer, tomorrow I'll bring my things and I'll teach you. You have the most lovely hair. But you have to promise you'll braid mine. I love having my hair braided."

Summer's whole face lit up. "I love braiding! I wish I had a horse so I could practice on its mane. My friend Sally has a beautiful Palomino. She lets me braid her hair sometimes. I just love horses, don't you?"

"I sure do. I have a horse. His name is Theo. He's an old man now. Can't ride him anymore, but he's still a good friend."

"You do? How do you keep a horse in the city?"

"He lives here, with my parents," I laughed.

"Ohhh. Daphne, will you bring your lipstick, too? You have the best color."

"I'm not wearing lipstick."

Summer's eyes were wide, and she stared up at me adoringly. She had just finished the eighth grade this year. I remembered that year. It was the year I had gone from being a little girl to being something else. Not a woman yet, but not a child anymore. I thought I was grown then, but boy did I have a lot to learn. Here I was at thirty and I knew less now than I did then.

I looked up to see three other sets of eyes watching me. Hunter's were just as adoring as his sister's. Trevor's sparkled, and Reed's looked speculative. The picture of me with a beautiful baby in my lap leapt into my mind. I pushed it out.

"Will you do my hair, too, Daphne?" Heather asked eagerly. She was three years older than Summer, and the only other child still living at home. Piper and Aster were both in college. They flanked Reed and Trevor, each with moon eyes that didn't leave their respective dinner neighbor. I would have been jealous if Reed or Trevor had noticed the attentions of the beautiful young women. But their eyes never strayed from my face.

Hunter held my hand in his lap. He was left-handed, so it didn't pose a problem for him to eat and stroke my skin at the same time. It was a problem for me to keep from running that hand up his thigh, though.

After dinner Ginny brought out two beautiful peach pies and homemade ice cream. The woman was a diva in the kitchen. I even had a piece, and it was the best pie I'd ever tasted. I said as much and Ginny seemed pleased, finally.

After finishing off two entire pies, Hunter and his siblings all stood and began clearing and washing dishes. It was the most organized ritual, almost military. I tried to help, but I mostly just got in the way. Dishes weren't my forte.

Summer had brought out her brush and a few hair accessories and had me sitting on the floor in the living room. She didn't want to wait until tomorrow. She had a book of braids on the sofa next to her and she was doing something elaborate on my head.

I watched the men, drinking beers after dinner, except Hunter, who was not allowed alcohol yet. Hunter, Trevor, and Reed were in a corner, in a tight little circle like they had been that night I'd met them. Trevor was telling a story, Hunter was laughing loudly, and Reed sipped his drink, a reserved smile on his face.

My men, I thought. My sexy, sweet, strong men. I sighed in pure bliss.

"You love him, don't you," Summer whispered in my ear. She had seen me watching them. "It's ok. I'm glad you do. He loves you, too. You make him so happy."

She sat up and pushed one more pin in my hair. "There! I'm done. You look lovely, if I do say so myself."

I turned around and hugged Summer, kneeling on the floor in front of her. She squeezed me tight. This family had so much love. It made me a little sad I was an only child.

"I knew we would be best friends," Summer whispered.

"Best friends," I said, smiling at her.

"Well, hallo fraulein," Trevor said in his best German. "Nice hair."

"Thank you," I said. "My stylist is very talented."

"I can see that. You ready to head out? Reed and I thought we might be able to get a room at your place seeing as you have one or half a dozen extra. I think Ginny is getting a little tired of us."

My heart beat. They were *both* going to stay with me? What did that mean? How was that going to work? Trevor must have seen the look of terror on my face.

"Or not. We can stay here, it's not a problem."

"No, no, of course you can stay with me. That big house is probably spooky at night, anyway. I'd be glad for the company."

"Good. We're ready whenever you are." He walked back to the little huddle and they all began discussing something. Probably their invasion of Germany later tonight. I smiled to myself.

"Would you like to come see the house tomorrow?" I asked, turning back to Summer. "There are a whole mess of horses."

"Oh, Daphne! Yes, please!" She threw her arms around me again.

"Alright, then. I'll see you tomorrow." I stood and gathered my things. I thanked James and Ginny and said my goodbyes. Hunter grabbed my hand and led me onto the back porch. It was a warm night and the moon was bright. The only sound was the crickets.

"Wish I was going with you," he whispered, leaning his head down to mine. "Momma would throw a fit, though."

"I know. But you'll come up in the morning, right?"

"You know it! I sure love you, Daphne." He kissed me chastely, holding my hands in his.

"I love you, too, Hunter."

He walked me to my car and Trevor and Reed were already waiting. Hunter opened my door and I slid in.

"Goodnight, beautiful," he said, and closed the door. I sighed and started the engine.

Reed and Trevor followed behind in their SUV. It was only a few minutes to the estate, but by the time we got there my mind had gone all sorts of wild. I parked the car and took a deep breath.

"Sweet baby Jesus!" Trevor yelled, getting out of his car. "You weren't kidding, Reed. Only eight bedrooms? You sure? Looks like at least a dozen could fit in there."

I unlocked the door. "Don't you think eight is enough?" I asked.

"I think one is enough, but then, that's never enough for you, is it?" he whispered in my ear. My hand shook and I dropped my keys. Trevor chuckled, picking them up and dangling them in front of me, a wicked smile on his face. "Ma'am," he said.

We all walked in and I gave Trevor the tour, including the study. He laughed when I told him not to let Hunter in there. It was getting very late and I was exhausted. The emotional stress of the last thirty-six hours was catching up to me.

"Y'all ready to go to bed?" I asked, yawning, as Trevor explored the walk-in pantry. Reed had been leaning on the kitchen island and he stood straight up, he and Trevor passing a look between them.

"Are you?" Trevor asked with an inflection that made me jump out of my skin. I'd meant the comment innocently enough, but they had taken it in a very wrong way. I backed away from them a few steps toward the door.

"I'm going to go brush my teeth," I said, and fled the room. Oh, lord! What was I doing? This was not something I had ever really considered.

But wasn't it, though? Two men, both bent on pleasing me, at my beck and call? My heart raced and my breath came in short gasps as I ran up the stairs and locked myself in the bathroom. Oh, god.

I brushed my teeth furiously, flossing meticulously. I looked in the mirror. My hair was adorable, up in two braids roped over my head like a headband. I could have graced an Austrian beer label. I tore my clothes off and jumped in the shower.

It was possible I was reading the situation completely wrong. Trevor delighted in leading me to false conclusions. Maybe they wanted me to choose who would share my bed tonight. But that would leave the other to sleep alone and that hardly seemed fair. I supposed it would be Trevor's turn, really, since I'd sent him home last night with only a few passionate kisses on my front porch. He was probably boiling over by now.

But Reed and I had only been together once, so if we were talking about number of hours, then it would be his turn. Oh, god, stop analyzing it Daphne! I toweled off and slipped my satin robe around myself. I opened the door, not sure what I would find on the other side.

I'd chosen a pink, frilly room with its own en suite as my own. I peeked out the door. No one was here. I'd half-expected to see them naked and sprawled across my bed. I was a little disappointed. Maybe they had gone to bed. But then there was a knock on my door.

I opened the door and Trevor stood there, a magnolia flower in his hand. So, it was going to be him tonight, then?

"I brought this for you, angel eyes." He stared down at me and his eyes burned.

"Thank you," I said, taking the flower.

"May I come in?" he asked.

"Yes, of course," I said, opening the door wider. Trevor walked into the room and leaned against the edge of the dresser.

"You got the pink room, I see," Trevor said.

"Yes, I didn't think you or Reed was going to want this one."

"Mmm. You gonna stand all the way over there all night, or are you gonna let me kiss you?"

I felt a spasm deep in my pelvis. Trevor's hands gripped the edge of the dresser and his biceps bulged as he leaned back. I wanted those arms around me desperately. It had been so long since we were together, and my body craved him.

I closed the door and stepped over to him. I threw my arms around his neck and his lips crushed mine. He was hungry for me; I could feel it. Pure lust seeped out of him. His mouth devoured mine, then moved down my neck biting and sucking. The exhaustion I felt moments ago melted away and every fiber of my body went on high alert.

"Take your shirt off," I breathed, wanting to feel his skin on mine. He obeyed and soon his ridged chest was bare before me. I ran my hands over him and reached for the tie on my robe. I opened it and let it fall to the floor.

Trevor sucked in a breath as I pressed my breasts to his hard body. My tongue explored his mouth while my hands ran over every bulging muscle. I felt my juices dripping down my leg as Trevor's hand squeezed my backside pulling me in closer.

I dropped to my knees and grabbed his belt, tearing it open and unzipping him. Soon I had him free, his incredible cock hard and ready for me. Looking up at him and smiling, I took him in my mouth, running my tongue around and around his smooth head. He moaned and pulsed in my mouth. I took him all the way in, deep in my throat. I gently squeezed the base with my teeth, then sucked my way back to the tip. Trevor gripped the dresser until the wood groaned.

There was a knock on the door, and I froze. Trevor looked down at me and smiled salaciously.

"Can Reed come in?" he asked. Oh god!

"You're ok with that?" I asked, unsure of how much they had really worked out between themselves.

"I am if you are."

"Ok," I said. My stomach did a little flip. "Come in," I said loudly.

Reed opened the door and his eyes met mine, and I suddenly realized I was on my knees with Trevor's dick in my hand. I wasn't sure what to do, but Trevor cleared it up for me real quick.

"Don't stop," he whispered, turning my face back to his with gentle fingers on my jaw.

I looked up into his eyes, pretending Reed wasn't watching me for the moment, and took him back in my mouth. I watched his eyes roll back in his head and my pussy dripped again. He was mine and I could have my way with him, make him scream my name. I moved my tongue on him and he moaned loudly.

I heard movement behind me and was momentarily startled. Reed was taking off his clothes and watching every move I made. I wasn't self-conscious anymore. I wanted him to see. Wanted him to see what I was doing to Trevor, what I was going to do to him soon.

I stood, never taking my mouth off of Trevor, and spread my legs, sticking my ass in the air. I reached one hand out to the dresser to steady myself. I grabbed Trevor with my other hand and squeezed, sucking and licking him hard.

"Uuuhhh, Daphne!" he screamed my name. My pussy spasmed.

And then his tongue was on me and I cried out. Reed was on his knees behind me, spreading my lips apart and thrusting his tongue into me. He ran it down and tongued my clit hard, sending shockwaves through me.

I'd fantasized about this many times. I'd wanted it, never thinking I'd actually do it. It was hotter than I'd ever imagined. I wanted Trevor to cum in my mouth. I wanted to make him scream again. I deep throated him and wiggled my tongue on the base of his shaft. I cupped his balls, coaxing him. I felt him getting close.

I felt myself getting close. Reed's hands moved over my backside, his fingers sliding in and out of me, touching me in all the right ways, while his tongue worked my clit into a swollen, throbbing tempest of pleasure.

I took Trevor in deep once more, sucking hard as I moved back. I felt the head of his cock swell in my mouth and the pumping under his skin as his body prepared for its release. I knew one more stroke and he would be mine. The knowledge sent me over the edge.

I sucked him hard and I felt him explode in my throat. At the same moment my muscles clamped down and I burst in a torrent of throbbing, aching ecstasy. Reed grabbed my hip and slammed his fingers into me, thrusting me forward harder onto Trevor's cock. Small squeaks escaped me in between panting and swallowing. I took all of him. Reed slid his fingers out and over my clit, causing me to drop Trevor and cry out long and low and loud.

Trevor stood and moved away, but I couldn't move, staying there bent over the dresser, my eyes closed. Then I felt Reed behind me. Gently he caressed my back, his hands running over my skin, a trail of sweet bliss in their wake.

Reed bent over me, his body pressed to mine, and whispered in my ear. "Do you still want more, Daphne?"

When he said my name, it felt like nothing else in the world. "Yes, Reed, I want you," I whispered. "I need you."

He pressed into me, sliding into the dripping mess he had made. His thick shaft filled and stretched me, and I cried out, a guttural sound that came from my throat. Reed was pressed against my back, his face next to mine and he bit my neck, kissed my shoulder, as he sank his whole cock into me.

He held me firmly, one arm around my waist as he pressed into me. My body opened to him, clasping him, sheathing him. His hand came up to my large, round breast, and he gently caressed it, my nipple hardening under his palm.

His hands were like magic. Every touch sent new filaments of pleasure through me. My arousal began to build again. His thick cock made my pussy ache deep and slow. Reed stood upright and ran his hand down my back, grabbing onto both hips now and thrusting into me.

"Aaahhh! Reed, oh, god Reed!" I screamed as he slammed against me. He was deep inside me now, rubbing that spot over and over again that only a hard cock from behind could reach. I could never get to it myself and it drove me mad with pleasure now.

I felt him swelling inside me and I knew he was getting close. The thought of him cumming inside me drove me even more wild. I felt new slickness as I got closer to orgasm. Reed felt it, too.

"Make me cum, baby!" I breathed. Reed grabbed me tighter and rammed deeper. I cried out. "Yes! I'm going to cum on you!"

"Daphne!" Reed cried. My pussy clenched down on him and started to throb. I screamed and he burst into me, hot cum dripping and spilling out of me as I felt him pulsing inside me. I could feel every muscle aching and releasing on him and I almost fell to the floor. Reed held me steady, pushing into me and moaning my name.

He slid out of me and I stood, straightening my back. I could barely see straight. I fell onto the bed and lay there on my back, panting. Two hot bodies pressed up against me on either side, hands exploring my body.

Trevor was back, his mouth pressed to mine, his tongue finding its way in and tangling with mine. Reed lay by my other side, kissing and stroking my shoulder, my breast, my waist. It was pure heaven. Every inch of my skin was being stimulated. I never wanted it to end.

Trevor rolled on top of me, kissing me deeply. I knew from our first night together that he wouldn't be satisfied with a blowjob and a goodnight kiss. He needed it almost as much as I did, and I was ready for him again.

He was soft and gentle as he lay on top of me. He ran a hand up my thigh and pulled my hips into position. Looking into my eyes he pushed himself into me and I moaned. I reached my arms around his neck and kissed him softly, making love to him languorously.

Slowly my hips moved with his, up and down, wet sounds coming from us, making me giggle.

"Something funny?" Trevor whispered. "You know, it doesn't do much for my ego to watch you cry Ace's name, but then laugh at me." He was trying to act hurt, but his voice was full of teasing.

"I'm laughing at me. I'm a bit of a sopping wet mess, or hadn't you noticed?"

"Oh, I'm noticing. Dear lord, I'm noticing," he said, pumping deep inside me, making me moan. "That's more like it," he whispered.

Trevor pushed deeper, my moan becoming a choke as he caught me off guard. He moved his hips, hitting me just the right way. He was longer than Reed, almost as thick, and he filled me with a delicious pressure.

Trevor buried his face in my neck and kissed me as he pumped into me. Reed still lay by my side, holding my hand, sucking my fingers now, watching his friend make love to me. I pulled my hand away and reached down to grab Trevor's cock as it slid out of me. I rubbed my hand on it and dipped my fingers into myself until my hand was covered. I reached to my side and began stroking Reed, his cock hard from the show.

I wrapped a leg around Trevor's back and bucked into him. He groaned into my neck and squeezed my ass. I thought about him cumming in me. Having two men cum in me in a row. I started to throb again.

And now I wanted to feel Trevor's cum in my pussy. I wanted it so badly. I clamped down, rising up to meet his thrust, taking him deeper. Trevor moaned again and I was almost undone.

"Oh, Trevor! I want you to cum in me, baby!" I whispered. "I want to feel it inside me."

Trevor moaned, almost a wail, into my neck. I squeezed him tighter and felt my release coming soon.

"Trevor, I'm going to cum on you," I whispered in his ear. "Make me cum, baby!" With a cry my orgasm hit me, pulses shooting through me. Trevor screamed into my neck again and I felt him throbbing in me, shooting it into the depths of my body, and my orgasm rocked me.

In my hand I felt Reed start to throb, too. He came, shooting onto my hip. I milked him until his release was complete.

We lay there, panting, sweating, dizzy with gratification. My eyes closed and I began to drift. I don't think I'd ever felt so safe, so warm and protected and sated as I did at that moment.

I felt Trevor sit up beside me and then his fingers in my hair. I opened my eyes and watched as he pulled the pins out and set them on the nightstand. When he had them all he loosened the braids and ran his fingers through my hair until it was spread on the pillow around my head. He laid back down beside me, whispering in my ear.

"Didn't want you to get a headache," he said, kissing my cheek. I smiled.

"How do you want to work the sleeping arrangements, Daphne?" Reed spoke softly in my other ear.

"Mmm, can we stay just like this all night?"

"We can, but can we move to a bigger bed? One without puddles?"

I laughed. "Picky," I said.

I walked down the hall, stretching and running my hands through my hair as I decided which room I liked best. I could feel Trevor and Reed watching my ass and I liked it.

"This one," I said stopping in front of a room. Inside was a massive king-sized bed with a Tiffany-blue satin comforter. The walls were dark wood paneled, and it was cozy like a cave. I crawled in under the covers and Trevor and Reed took their places.

I rolled over to Trevor and took his face in my hands, kissing him. "Good night, tiger," I said. Then I turned to Reed and whispered in his ear, "Sleep tight, lover."

Two massive arms were flung over me, one around my shoulders, one around my waist. I held them to me and was asleep in minutes.

21

The Secret

We spent two more nights in the magic mansion, as I had come to think of it. Hunter came over during the days and we rode the horses, walked the grounds, and made love in the warm, still August afternoons. My other lovers left us to ourselves during the day, going over to help out on the farm. At night they came back and fulfilled every one of my fantasies.

To Hunter's family, I was Hunter's girl, and his friends were merely looking after me for him on those warm summer nights. I was good, and chaste, and lord, if they'd only known what was truly going on.

It was like living in a dream for sure, but reality had to be dealt with at some point. I was getting no work done. A few more days out here would mean dropping the ball for too many of my clients and I wasn't going to let that happen.

Reed had to go back, as well. He was shipping out soon and would be at sea on a training exercise for almost four months. I was going to miss him desperately.

Trevor was going to stay with Hunter another week and then they would both head back to the city. Hunter's momma refused to let him go any earlier than that. And so, we all stood in front of the farmhouse saying our goodbyes.

Summer hugged me and I squeezed her. "Can I come stay with you in Charleston, Miss Daphne?" she asked.

"Can I come, too, please?" Heather chimed in.

"Of course you can," I said. "We'll have our own little slumber party, no boys allowed." I winked at Hunter. He laughed his uproarious laugh.

Reed and I drove back to the airport together by way of my folks' house. We visited with them for a few hours before catching our flight. Reed had gotten the plane tickets, insisting on doing it. So, it was a surprise to me when he guided me into first class.

We were seated and served and fussed over until it was finally time to take off. I turned to Reed. "Alright, Mr. mysterious, are you really a spy, or terrified of coach, or a secret millionaire? What is with the first-class travel?" I thought I saw something in his eyes as I was asking the question that led me to believe I'd hit the nail right on the head.

"No," he said in his stoic way.

"Well then?" I prodded.

"Look, Trevor insists on it, and that's all I'm going to say. You'll have to ask him." And the way he said it I knew it would be futile to ask anything further.

"Trevor is keeping something from me?" I asked, hurt.

"I'm sorry, Daphne, he's asked me not to tell you. It's nothing, really. He wants you to know, but he's afraid you won't look at him the same way. I've told him it won't matter to you, but he's insistent. Please, just drop it for a while, ok? He'll tell you when he's ready."

Fine. I thought we'd moved past all that, but if Trevor wanted to have his little secret, what difference did it make to me? I tried to tell myself that, but I was angry. And I got angrier as I sat in silence the rest of the flight. Reed reached over and held my hand, but I stewed.

When we landed, I stood and gathered my things in silence and stormed off the plane. Reed ran behind me, following me to the parking garage.

"You can go home now, I'll be fine driving back to my place," I sniped at him.

"Daphne, please," he began.

"Don't 'Daphne, please', me, Reed Butler! I can't believe you've been keeping this from me, after all your talk about being honest with my feelings. Well listen to this! My feelings are hurt and I'm angry!" I slammed the trunk and yanked my car door open. Reed grabbed my hand and spun me around, closing the car door and pressing me up against it.

"I know," he said, his face inches from mine. "And you have every right to feel that way. But it's a waste of your energies, my little spitfire. Whatever it is really makes no never mind and you'll know soon enough. Now, I need you to focus all that fire on your work so tonight I can focus on you. I was hoping we could enjoy the next few days together alone before I'm stuck on an aircraft carrier in the middle of the ocean for fifteen weeks with six thousand men."

Reed kissed me, but I pulled back. In a move so uncharacteristic of his staid behavior, he reached up and grabbed my head, pressing his lips hard to mine. I resisted for a split second, but there was a fierceness in his kiss that made me stop. He wanted to protect me, to love me, to be with me, just he and I, and I wanted it, too.

He loosened his hold and slid his arms around me, holding me to him. I held him and melted into his broad chest. Reed was the only person I knew who could take the burning fire that raged in me and refocus it into a precision laser point. Whatever wild emotion was running through me, he could calm it, shape it, until I could use it for a force of good in my life instead of destruction.

"Oh, honey," I breathed against his lips, "there are a few women on those ships now, too."

"Is that a free pass?" he laughed.

I swatted his backside. "Don't even think about it!"

"Daphne, there isn't a woman on the entire planet who could compare with you." And I knew he meant it.

"Did I ever tell you I had a twin?" I asked.

"You mean there's another one of you? We don't have to share?" Reed laughed.

"There could have been, but she didn't make it. Might have been interesting," I said slyly.

"Oh, lord," Reed moaned.

"Alright, I really do need to get to the office now. David's been texting me since we landed. He's got all that wedding planning on top of everything and I've left him high and dry."

Reed looked into my eyes, searching for something. "I sure wish I wasn't going to miss his wedding. I'd like to be on your arm there."

"Wouldn't they talk at the firm if I showed up with three dates?" I laughed.

Reed laughed, too, and squeezed my bottom. I yelped. "Go on, then, get to work. I've got something planned for us tonight." He turned and strode away, leaving me hot and bothered and very curious.

I went straight to the office and got to work. I sat at my desk and plowed through emails, phone messages, faxes (yes, people still sent those), and files thrown on my desk. My assistant brought me coffee at regular intervals and after six hours I felt I'd made enough headway to go home for a shower. Air travel always made me feel sticky. I looked at the clock. Eight p.m. An early night for me, really.

I gathered my things and drove home. Being home felt so good. I fell down on the sofa, spreading my arms and legs wide and stretching. My phone buzzed. I picked it up. It was Reed.

-You home yet? Can I come over?-

I typed my response.

-Come on in, the door's open-

I began taking my clothes off and threw them in a trail leading to the shower. I stepped in and turned the water on hot until it scalded my skin. I washed my hair, then my body, then let the hot water hit my shoulders until the knots began to loosen. My eyes were closed, and I was adrift in my own thoughts when I felt Reed slide in behind me.

His skin was cool on my back after the hot shower. He pressed himself up against me and reached his arms around my waist. His mouth came down on my shoulder, just by my neck and he bit and sucked my sensitive muscle.

"Uuuhhh, Reed," I moaned. I felt him pressing into my back, hard and erect.

One hand came up to fondle my breast, slowly manipulating my tender nipple until waves of pleasure rolled down into my groin. His other hand slid down between my legs, his fingers deftly spreading me open, making me scream.

I reached back, grabbing him and guiding him into me. His hands continued their endeavors, ensuring I would peak in a matter of seconds. Never had someone had such complete mastery over my body. Reed's hands moved as if they knew every inch of me and how to make it scream.

His thick cock filled me, rocked me, made me ache with pleasure until I cried out his name, cumming on him, squeezing him, feeling him inside. Reed held me tight while I came, thrusting deep into me until I couldn't take any more. Then he flipped me around to face him.

Reed pushed me up against the cold tile wall and kissed me until I couldn't see straight. He lifted my body, his strong hand grabbing my thigh, wrapping my leg around him. In one long thrust he shoved himself into me, pressing me against the wall and making me cry out again.

Then he fucked me. Really fucked me. This was not sweet, tender love-making. This was raw, animalistic, hedonistic fucking. I knew he had a beast in him that he kept chained and caged. And as far as I knew I was the only one who'd ever seen it. Not Hunter, not Trevor, not anyone. But the beast was here now, screaming to be let out, to be unchained.

And I wanted it. I wanted to take all his rage, his pain, his lust and greed. Take it into me and burn it up, add it to my own raging desires, wickedness, perversions, until there was nothing left but ash. And so, I fucked him back. I rode him until he begged for mercy, until his legs almost gave out and he came in me with a wild howl of rapture.

We slid to the floor of the shower, neither of us able to stand any longer. The water poured down on us and we let it wash everything away. I laid my head against Reed's chest and he held me in his arms, and I cried. I cried from sheer exhaustion. From the fervid connection our souls had made. From the deep and true love I had for this man.

Reed kissed my forehead and I sighed. "What did you have planned tonight?" I asked him, my fingers playing over the ridges of his abdomen.

"Dinner and dancing at the Garden. Maybe tomorrow night instead?"

I laughed. My legs were not going dancing tonight. "Tomorrow sounds much better, yes. Oh, honey, I'm going to miss you so much!" I wrapped my arms around him and buried my face in his chest.

"Come on, now. Let's get out of this waterfall before we get all pruny." Reed stood and helped me up and shut off the water. We grabbed towels and dried off, then fell into the bed.

Reed pulled me in close and kissed me. "It won't be so very long. It'll fly by, I promise."

"I know, I know. I just don't know what I'll do without you."

"At least you know *who* you'll do," he chuckled.

"I can't believe y'all. You're so open about what we're doing, like it's perfectly normal, or something."

"Feels perfectly normal, doesn't it? It's strange, but it does. I never would have thought of having a relationship like this in a million years, Daphne, but it's right, you know?"

"I know."

"You hungry, baby?" Reed asked.

"Baby?" I snickered.

"What? Can't I have a cute little name for you, too. Trevor and Hunter do."

"Yes, but you, Captain Butler, when *you* say my name, it is the most precious sound in all the world to me."

"Captain? Not quite yet, my girl. Though, maybe someday," he said thoughtfully.

"Well, you're already *my* Captain, and you have full run of this vessel."

"In that case," he said, jumping on top of me, "all aboard!"

22

Deployed

Reed and I said goodbye in the early, pre-dawn hours with coffee-flavored kisses. He was wearing his flight suit and I sure did enjoy seeing him in it. I felt my heart become just a bit brittle when he left. Like it could be shattered a little more easily.

I wasn't used to feeling these things. My heart had always been carefully guarded, though I hadn't known it. And now I had laid it open and offered it up to three men, any one of which could take his piece and go, leaving me with a heart that would never work again. Seeing Reed leave threw that realization right in my face.

For the next five days, I threw myself into work. David was frantic to wrap up as much as possible before his wedding. We weren't taking on any more cases until after the holidays, which was fine with me, because he was taking a month off for his honeymoon and I was going to have to live in the office while he was gone as it was.

A month in the desert with his bride. I felt a stab of jealousy. Maybe it should have been me going on that honeymoon. What if all this was wrong and I was supposed to be with David? I snapped a pencil in half. "Daphne," I said in my best Reed voice, "you're being stupid. You don't love David. You're just afraid." I laughed at myself.

But it did make me feel better. I knew what he would say to me and he would be right. I had a serious fear of being left behind. Of not being or having or doing what I was supposed to now that I was thirty. Camile was just turning twenty-one. Compared to her I was practically an old maid.

And I had no prospects for marriage, did I? How could I marry three men? Would I want to were it even possible? Uuuuggghhh! I missed my boys. The late-night sexting was no replacement for the real thing. And Reed was out of communication completely for a while, leaving me to deal with my demons on my own.

Tomorrow Hunter and Trevor came back. I couldn't wait to see them. Five days on my own had seemed like an eternity, even working sixteen-hour days as I was. They had certainly done something to my head, those sweet, sexy little devils.

It was late and I was the only one left in the office, aside from the night watchman. I gathered my things and walked out the big glass doors in the front of the building. A white pick-up was parked right out front and it made me think of Hunter. Suddenly I was grabbed from behind and spun around in the air.

"Whooo! There's our girl!" Hunter yelled spinning in a circle.

"Stop spinning me before I throw up!" I yelled. He set me on my feet, and I turned to face him.

Hunter grabbed me in his arms and bent down to kiss me. I wrapped my arms around his neck, relishing the feel of his soft, sweet mouth. I slid one hand down to stroke his bearded cheek. I missed this.

"What about me?" Trevor said behind me.

"Wait your turn, I'm not done," Hunter mumbled against my lips, but he pulled back and I turned to face Trevor.

Darn, he looked good. What was it about him that always made me picture him standing on a yacht, aviator sunglasses on his face, drink in his hand, and a dozen bikini-clad women lounging around him? It must be that one black curl that always broke loose to fall across his forehead.

"Hi, angel eyes," he cooed at me. I jumped into his arms, mauling him with kisses.

"Oh, Trevor! I'm so happy you're back!"

"I can see that! Didn't Reed take care of you at all while he was here?"

"It has been FIVE days!" I said.

"Oh, shoot, Hunter, I think we're in trouble!" Trevor said, smirking at his friend.

"I'm not worried," Hunter drawled slowly, rubbing my shoulders with his huge hands. It felt so good.

"You have dinner yet?" Trevor asked, still holding me in his arms and gazing into my eyes. Lord, he was sexy when he wanted to take care of me.

"I ate at my desk. I'm really not hungry, just tired. Can we just go home and climb into bed?" I slapped my hand to my mouth, realizing what I had just said. Both of them looked at me with hungry eyes.

"Let's roll!" Hunter said, jumping behind the wheel. Trevor opened the door for me, and I climbed into the middle seat. He threw my $400 briefcase in the truck bed, but I didn't care. Trevor climbed in next to me and Hunter sped away from the curb. I grabbed onto Trevor's leg, fearing for my life. He chuckled.

"My house is that way," I said after a minute.

"Oh, I was going to our house. Didn't even think, sorry, beautiful," Hunter said.

"I do have to be at the office early tomorrow, but I can just go to my place in the morning. Let's go to your house. I haven't seen Trevor's room yet," I said, looking into his eyes. They burned for me. "What are you two doing here, anyway? You were supposed to come back tomorrow."

"We wanted to surprise you. Did it work?" Hunter asked.

"It sure did."

When we got to the house Hunter let me in and Trevor grabbed my things out of the back. I sat down on the sofa and stretched my arms up, laying my head back and closing my eyes. Trevor's mouth came down on mine and he bit my bottom lip. I moaned.

Hunter sat down on the sofa next to me, putting his long arm over my shoulder and playfully pushing Trevor out of the way. He came to sit on my other side. It was a strange dynamic. Not at all like it had been with Trevor and Reed.

On one side I had soft and slow, tender and sweet. On the other side was long and hard, fervor and heat. Plus, Hunter seemed anxious, not his usual laid-back self. It put me a little on edge.

"So, why don't you both tell me everything you've been doing," I said, trying to break the tension.

Hunter launched into a story right away. I could always count on him to talk a blue streak. Trevor looked at me questioningly. Maybe we should just do this, I mean, I was fit to burst for them, why was I hesitating?

I waited until Hunter was at a lull in his story and slowly ran my hand up his thigh, looking into his eyes. He swallowed and stared at me. I reached up and pulled his mouth down to mine. He only hesitated a moment, and then his lips were moving on mine in that slow, amazing way.

I felt Trevor tug at my jacket, and I put my arms back so he could slide it off, my lips never leaving Hunter's. I pulled the hem of Hunter's shirt up and over his head, revealing his beautiful torso. I kissed down his chest and he moaned. I moved back to his incredible lips.

Trevor had slipped off my heels and was on his knees on the floor in front of me. I felt his hands slide up my skirt and stop when they felt the garters there.

"Do you always wear these?" he asked.

"Lots of days, sure," I said, my mouth closing over Hunter's again.

Trevor's hands moved up, ignoring the garter belt and tugged the strings of my bikinis down until he had them sliding down my legs and off. His hands came back up under my skirt and I felt like a very naughty girl. I loved it.

Trevor hiked my skirt up and spread my legs apart with his strong hands. My breath rushed in with the anticipation of what he was going to do to me, where he was going to touch me. I felt his mouth on my thighs, sucking, running his tongue over me. I moaned into Hunter's mouth.

I reached down to Hunter's belt, unbuckling him. His kisses became more fervent and his hand slipped down my blouse, finding my breast. Now I had one man's hands down my top, and another man's hands up my skirt. It was absolutely, insanely hot.

There was one more thing I needed to make the teenage wet dream complete. I pulled Hunter's long cock out of his pants and started stroking him. Trevor's tongue found my clit and I moaned, my hand clamping down on Hunter. I felt him swell in my grasp.

I broke away from Hunter's mouth and moved my head down to his lap. Trevor pulled my hips closer to the edge of the sofa and I nestled in comfortably. His tongue flicked my clit and then pushed into me and I felt my orgasm getting closer.

I took Hunter in my mouth, just the head, swirling my tongue around and around. Then I sucked down one side and back up the other, running my tongue up the fat vein before taking him all the way in, deep throating him until he cried out.

Trevor slammed two fingers into me, stroking me inside. I moaned around Hunter's cock, sucking up to the tip before throwing my head back and screaming. I came hard, my thighs clamping shut on Trevor's head. I stroked Hunter while I came, probably a feeble attempt as every muscle in my body spasmed and refused to listen to my control.

I came down, panting and gasping. "Oh, fuck!" I said.

Trevor laughed. They weren't used to me using profanity. I slid off the sofa, onto my knees in front of Hunter. I stripped his pants off the rest of the way so nothing would get in my way. I was going to give him the best blow he'd ever had in his life. I just hoped Trevor was taking the hint as I stuck my ass up and wiggled it in his face.

I began working Hunter's cock. His long, beautiful dick, the same golden color as the rest of him, with a dark purple crown. I'd always loved penises. The variety of colors, shapes, and sizes. I loved the heads the most. The way they swelled and were so smooth, smoother than any other skin on the human body. And the way they felt inside of me.

Trevor had no problem with my non-verbal communication. I felt him behind me right away, his hands roving over me, and then his cock slammed into me. I lost concentration momentarily, breathing hard through my nose as he filled me. He slammed into me again and I took Hunter deep, savoring being filled from both sides.

Hunter's hands trailed over my arms and hair and back, while Trevor grabbed my hips and ass and breasts, playing with my nipples. I stroked Hunter, telling him I was going to cum, how good his cock felt in my mouth. Trevor fucked me hard, bringing me to orgasm again. I squeaked around Hunter's cock as I came around Trevor's.

"Daphne!" Trevor cried out as my pussy tightened around him again and again. He was close. I felt him swell in me. I wanted them to cum in me at the same time.

I primed Hunter, stroked him, licked him, took him deep and swallowed him, running my tongue around the base of him. He growled and swelled and one more stroke and he was cumming in my mouth. I felt Trevor swell and cum in me from behind and I almost passed out. It was incredible.

I milked and swallowed Hunter. I contracted and pressed against Trevor. They both panted and moaned their pleasure. We all collapsed in a heap.

I laid on the sofa, my head in Hunter's lap, and stroked Trevor's hair where he sat on the floor, his head resting against Hunter's knee. Hunter's fingers played over my waist and hip. It was sweet, and quiet, and good.

"Well, that was a first for me, Daphne," Hunter said quietly. I rolled my head over to look up at him. I met his beautiful brown eyes and they looked down at me with adoration and awe.

"What? Making love with your best friend watching?" I asked.

Hunter laughed. "Guess that, too. I meant what you did to me. Didn't think anything would ever be like that." He stroked my hair. I was flattered.

"Oh, my lord, Hunter. You mean I just took your oral virginity? I am a naughty woman. But I hope you'll let me do it again for you." I smiled up at him wantonly.

He blushed a very endearing shade of red and smiled a shy smile.

"Well, my lovely darlings, I am absolutely exhausted. And you only have yourselves to blame. I really do need to be up in a few hours, so where are we sleeping tonight?" I asked.

"Come on, angel eyes, let's bunk up in my room," Trevor said, standing and taking my hand to help me up.

"Alright, but first I'd really like to brush my teeth. Have a spare toothbrush?"

"You can use Hunter's," Trevor laughed. Hunter punched his arm.

I did use Hunter's toothbrush. Guess we were sharing everything now. I crawled into Trevor's bed, barely able to keep my eyes open. I tried to take it all in before my eyelids fell shut.

The room was sparse. Aside from one wall covered in books, a large bed, two nightstands, and one dresser were the only furnishings. A stack of books sat on the dresser. No pictures, no decoration. But neat and clean. And the softest sheets I'd ever slept in.

I nestled my hips into Hunter, and he curled around me. Trevor stroked my brow, facing me as I drifted off into a dreamless sleep.

23

Tensions

My phone rang. It was Hunter. Again. He'd been texting me all day. I told him I was going to be in court all week and working late. Guess he needed to hear it from my lips.

"Hello?"

"Hi, beautiful," he drawled. "I'm sorry I keep pestering you, but I want to take you out tonight, just you and me."

"Aw, sugar, you know I have to work late. I just can't get away today."

"Please, Daphne. I worked it out with Trevor, he's ok with it."

I got a little annoyed. "Well then, I suppose if the two of you decided then I just have to go, regardless of how I feel about it." I was using my mean voice, and I knew it. It hurt a little inside to use it with Hunter.

"I'm sorry, darling, I just miss you. I miss us."

My temper softened. "I do, too, sweet thing. Tell you what, I'll get out of here just as early as I can and you and me will have some alone time, ok?"

"Whooo! Love you," he said.

"Love you, too, sugar."

It had been over two months since Reed left and I missed him now more than ever. Things had been different without him. I was finding it harder and harder to deal with my dark side. Especially now that David's wedding was next week. I needed to talk it out, but Hunter and Trevor didn't understand.

My sweet Country got a hurt look on his face every time I mentioned David. I avoided that subject with him at all costs. He was still the same happy, sunny, goofy man I fell in love with, but lately he'd been more and more anxious. I knew it was hard for him to share me, even with Trevor. He longed for us to be alone, if only once in a while, but there just wasn't time right now.

There had been tension between Trevor and I as well. I'd asked him point blank what the big secret was that he was too afraid to tell me. He refused to discuss it. We'd fought a few times, always making up in the most passionate way, but every time I felt a little more distance between us. I loved him desperately and the piece of my heart that belonged to him was breaking just a little.

At least things on the farm had been going well. I'd gotten a very nice insurance settlement for them and they'd had one of their best seasons yet. There was no question the orchards were safe for years to come. Hunter still didn't know, and I wanted to keep it that way. No need for him to feel obligated to me for that. All it had taken was a strongly worded letter on *Monroe and Williams* letterhead.

I'd had Hunter's sisters down twice. All four of them, actually. Piper was almost morose when she found out Reed was deployed. But Aster was pleased as punch when Trevor came by unexpectedly. We were all in our pajamas, hair braided in ridiculous styles, when Hunter and Trevor had "stopped by". I knew they just wanted a peek at us.

Whenever I spent time with Hunter's sisters it made him ridiculously happy. And Trevor looked at me with a twinkle in his eye, conjuring up images in my head of me with that beautiful baby on my lap. But not one of them had ever hinted that our relationship might go further than what it was right now. Where could it go, really? I told myself I was fine with it. I didn't have time for more now, anyway.

I was able to get away that night a little after ten. I drove straight to Hunter's place, excited to see him. I parked and walked in the front door. I was scooped up before I could even let go of the handle.

"Oh, beautiful girl," Hunter whispered, nuzzling my neck. I'd been staying at my place the few hours a night I wasn't in the office for the last three days. It felt incredible to be in Hunter's arms. He lifted me up to kiss him as he always did and I wrapped my arms around his neck, popping the hat I was holding on his head.

"Got you something," I smiled at him. Hunter reached up and pulled the wide-brimmed sable fedora off, looking at it.

"A hat?" he asked, putting it back on his head.

"An Indiana Jones hat. I thought you might like it." I knew I did. He looked unbelievably handsome in it.

"I love it," he said and kissed me, sweet and soft. "Wanna go for a walk?"

I didn't really, I was tired, but Hunter loved to walk. And I loved to hold his hand and listen to his stories. "Sure," I said.

We walked down the dark, quiet streets, Hunter in his sexy hat, rubbing my hand and telling me a funny story about one of their clients at the shop. We ended up at a playground and Hunter looked down at me and raised his eyebrows mischievously.

"Come one, now, you owe me a ride on the twisty slide," he said.

There were a few ways one could interpret that, I thought. I laughed. "Ladies first!" I said, running to the slide. I couldn't help it. When I was with Hunter my inner child tumbled out and would not be controlled.

Hunter laughed and chased after me, catching me on the stairs and grabbing me around the waist. I turned, eye to eye with him now that I was two steps higher. I put my arms around him and kissed him. He held me tight and all my worries disappeared. There was only him and me and the warm, glowing feeling inside me.

I wiggled out of his arms and ran up to the top of the slide. I jumped and flew down the twisty shoot, squealing. Trevor followed, more slowly, as his large frame didn't quite fit on the little slide. I laughed watching him.

"Maybe I'll stick to the swings," he said, standing and stretching. Then he looked at me impishly and lunged at me, tickling me until I couldn't breathe.

"You didn't even give me a chance to say no!" I protested.

"Come on, let's go home," he whispered, kissing my neck.

"Uuuhhh," I moaned, grabbing onto him and pressing my body to his. His breath sucked in.

We walked back, our hands pinching, tickling, and caressing each other as we went. Hunter pressed me up against the front door, kissing me and tickling me as we swung the door open.

"Where did you two get off to?"

I looked up and saw Trevor sitting in the living room. I stopped giggling, surprised to see him there.

"What are you doing home?" Hunter asked.

"It's after midnight, I got tired. It's my house, too," he said. He said it matter-of-factly, but I felt the tension in the room rise. We really should have gone to my place.

"I know it is, Trevor, but I thought we had an agreement," Hunter said.

"We did. And I just got back. The night's over. Go ahead and do whatever you were doing. I'm going to bed." Now he sounded irked.

"Come on, Trevor," Hunter began.

"Look, I just don't think it's fair, alright? You already get to have her as your girlfriend whenever your family's around. I'm gonna have to pretend to be the doting friend for every holiday and any time your horde of sisters is in town. Just because I have no family, I get the short end of the stick," Trevor said, standing.

"Don't pull the orphan card," Hunter said, and I almost gasped. He never spoke like that. "You promised me tonight and this isn't cool."

"You know, stop being such a little kid. I let you have her for the night, stop complaining," Trevor said crossly.

Now I was mad. "You LET him have me?" I said, my voice raised. "I am not an object, Trevor Bond! And I'll make it easier for you since it's so hard. I'm not coming to Thanksgiving. I'm staying in town to work and go to David's wedding."

I regretted it immediately. Both of them looked at me with hurt in their eyes. We hadn't discussed the wedding, and I knew they were going to be upset I wasn't coming to Thanksgiving on the farm. I was disappointed, too, but David's wedding was two days before Thanksgiving, and I needed to be in town. There was a lot of work to do.

I was still livid, regardless of their wounded expressions. They knew I wouldn't tolerate them betting on me, passing me around, or objectifying me. And for Trevor to say something like that pushed me beyond the point of self-control. The bitch had been awakened and it wasn't going to be good for either of them.

"I'm sorry, Daphne," Trevor started, taking a step toward me. I raised my hands in front of me.

"No! Don't even think you're going to touch me! I'm going home and I'll be working the rest of the week. Don't call me. Don't text me. I don't want to see you!"

"Daphne," Hunter said, a catch in his throat. He looked like he was going to reach out to me, but then thought better of it.

I turned and slammed the door behind me, driving off with squealing tires. "Uuuaaahhh!" I screamed in my car as I drove. I gripped the wheel until my hands hurt.

I hardly left the office or the courthouse all week. Wisely, they did not call me. I pushed my personal life out of my head and concentrated on our clients. It was so much simpler when all I had to think about were other people's problems.

On Sunday I slept in. I was going to take one day away from the office, tie things up on Monday, and take Tuesday off for the wedding. I woke feeling trepidatious. I wasn't sure how I was going to feel at David's wedding. I didn't know if I could make it. I wished Reed were here.

I decided to try on my dress. I realized I'd lost a little weight in the last few weeks and wanted to be sure it still fit. I would have to remember to eat more when I worked. When I was with the boys, Trevor always made sure I ate. Since I hadn't been with him, I'd been forgetting.

I pulled on the slinky black dress and appraised myself in the mirror. Which shoes? Prim and proper patent leather kitten heels, or my black Louboutin stilettos? One said co-worker, one said fuck me. I was feeling more in the second camp. I slid the red-soled shoes onto my feet.

There was a knock on my door. I looked out the peephole, but all I could see was yellow. "Who is it?" I asked through the closed door.

"Two wretched and penitent boyfriends. Can we please talk?" Trevor's voice came from the other side of the door.

I opened the door and Trevor held out a fistful of yellow roses. Hunter stood behind him, looking at the floor.

I stepped back and motioned them to come in. "You could have called first," I said.

"You told us not to," Trevor said, the corner of his mouth turned up. "We brought you these. Yellow is friendship, right?" He handed me the flowers.

"Thank you. For the flowers and for respecting my wishes and giving me my space," I said. I went and put the flowers in the kitchen and came back. They both stood there like statues.

"We're real sorry, Daphne," Trevor began.

"Real sorry," Hunter piped up.

"It was wrong of us to treat you like that. We understand that. It's just been hard, with Reed away, and figuring things out. We're bound to make a few mistakes. But we never want to disrespect you. We think the world of you, Daphne."

They stood, looking at me with hope and longing on their faces. They were absolutely adorable.

"I'm sorry, too," I said. "I've been so wrapped up in work that I haven't been giving you both the time you deserve. It's hard for me having Reed away. You know he keeps my fiery side tamed. I don't mean to lash out at you. There's just so much to do, with Da-... me being the only lawyer in the office right now." I almost said David but thought better of it. No need to bring him up now.

"Oh, beautiful," Hunter said, taking that as his cue. He grabbed me in his arms and hugged me tight. He felt good. "Come on, Trevor, you need to get in on this."

Hunter set me down and Trevor wrapped his arms around me. I leaned into him. His strong arms came around me and I was home. The place where nothing bad could ever happen.

"You haven't been eating, have you?" Trevor asked. "You've lost weight."

"Mmm," I said, nuzzling him.

"Come on, get dressed and we'll take you out to lunch."

"Don't you like my dress?" I asked, smiling coyly.

"That's a dress?" Trevor asked. "I thought it was underwear."

"It happens to be a designer gown," I said.

"Who designed it," Hunter asked, "Victoria's Secret?"

"You two wouldn't know fashion if it bit you," I said laughing.

"What were you doing today that you were wearing that out in public?" Trevor asked.

"I was just trying it on for Tuesday," I said.

Trevor and Hunter shared a look.

"What?" I asked.

"That's what you're wearing to the wedding?" Hunter asked, his face twisting.

"Yes," I said.

"I know we've been grumpy about this wedding, but we decided we'd like to go with you," Trevor said, suddenly.

"But you're leaving for Paris tomorrow," I said.

"We can change that," Trevor said.

I became suspicious. "Exactly when did you make this decision?"

"Well, when I saw your black widow outfit. You look more like you're going to a funeral in your underwear, Daphne. I just think maybe it would be better if we were there," Trevor said, his voice getting louder.

Hunter put his hand on Trevor's elbow. "Shut up, Trevor," he whispered.

"Oh, no, Trevor, please, go on. Tell me what you *would* approve of me wearing. In fact, why don't you go out and pick out all my clothes for me, tell me when and where I can go, chaperone me at every social function, and spank me when I'm bad!" I yelled.

"Wouldn't say no to the spanking," he mumbled.

"Stop it!" Hunter said, glaring at Trevor.

"Get out!" I shouted. "Both of you! I'm disgusted right now. I have given my heart to you, to both of you. I've never given you a reason to mistrust me! Now you come into my home and tell me I look like, like, like a slut? I've always told you everything. And you are both still keeping secrets from me! How dare you!"

"Secrets?" Hunter said quietly.

"Yes! Trevor's big secret. Your whole damn life is a secret to me, Trevor! I love you! I want to know you, but you won't let me in. And you, Hunter, you're keeping his secret for him, which makes you just as bad. Get out!"

I stormed over to the door and flung it wide. Trevor walked out, but Hunter stopped next to me and hung his head.

"Get out," I hissed. "I know where your loyalties lie."

Hunter followed Trevor out the door and I slammed it shut. I kicked my shoes across the room and tore off my dress, throwing it on the floor. I crawled into my bed and cried.

24

The Wedding

I got up early that morning so I could sit through four hours of meticulous grooming. I wasn't showing up to this wedding looking like anything less than a supermodel. I would turn every head there or die trying. Including David's. Marriage wasn't the death of him, after all. And everyone got divorced. What chance did he have with someone he'd only known for a few months?

I knew David loved me. He might not realize how much yet, but I would do everything in my power to show him we were meant to be together. I'd been wrong. Reed had been wrong. He'd twisted everything to make it look like this insane relationship could work. And now I was paying the price.

My heart had shattered into a million pieces. But no matter. I would pick them up and lock them in a cement box where they could never be touched again. I would get my perfect match- handsome, driven, wealthy- and I would marry him and live happily ever after. That's how it worked in the real world. Not whatever fantasy I'd been living in for the last three months.

My hair was blown and brushed until it shined in long, blonde waves down my back. My make-up was done to perfection, blood red lips and nails to match my Louboutins. A corset that cinched my breasts up to my chin and put them on display for the world to admire. I looked in the mirror when I got back from the spa. Movie stars wished they looked like me. I grabbed my matching Louboutin clutch and headed to the party.

It was a quaint little affair in the backyard of Camile's parents' house. A smaller version of Camile greeted me as I came through the front door. Must be the little sister. I'd heard a bit about them. Supposedly the oldest sister was quite a beauty. I wasn't impressed. But I would have liked to take a bite out of her date. Now, there was a man.

I headed straight for the bar. Grandpa was mixing drinks and he tried to say something witty as he poured my old-fashioned. I stared him down over the top of my black sunglasses and he shut up. I walked around and sipped my drink.

"Miss Williams! How nice to see you!"

"Good afternoon, Judge Brown. I thought I heard you were presiding over this little ceremony. How's everything? How is Marjorie?" I asked.

Judge Brown was a friend of David's and I liked him well enough. Things usually went our way in his court. I wasn't sure how much of that had to do with my assets, but I had my suspicions. Couldn't hurt to remind him how much he liked them now. I ran the edge of my glass lightly against my cleavage.

"Oh, she's just fine. Got a new car last week and she's been speeding around town. Have to keep her out of traffic court..." he slowed his speech as he watched me. "Yes, sure is a hot day today, isn't it?"

"Mmm, I'm feeling quite warm," I said. "It's been too long since we've been in your chambers, Judge. Hope we'll get on your docket soon."

"Yes, ahem, yes. I should probably go take my place now. It's been just fine seeing you, Miss Williams."

I smiled to myself as he walked away. Good thing for the robe or everyone would probably be able to see what I just did to him. Guess

I've still got it. But he was an easy fish to catch. I needed more of a challenge. I looked around.

"Hi there, Ben, Sebastian," I said, sauntering over to two of our co-workers from the old firm. They were a couple, but Ben swung both ways. More of a challenge for sure. "How've you boys been?"

"Hello, Daphne," Ben said, reaching out his hand. I placed my fingers in it lightly, and he kissed them.

"Why, Ben, you old so-and-so. I sure have missed having you around. You know you were always my favorite researcher? I wonder if we might steal you away sometime. I could *use you*."

Ben smiled at me and blushed.

"Hi Daphne," Sebastian said, not reaching out his hand at all and eyeing me.

"Lovely wedding, isn't it?" I said.

"Oh yes. Did you see David's tux?" Sebastian said. "It's incredible. I have to know who his tailor is, I mean, uh!"

"Oh, I saw him. He looks very nice." I fanned myself with the program.

"Nice?! He's like an Adonis!" Sebastian went on. "Bet you're feeling the loss right now, I mean, I always thought you two were going to end up together after he offered you partnership and all."

"Oh, no, it was never like that with David."

"No sweetie? You're wearing black at his wedding."

Damn, Sebastian played dirty.

"What, this old thing? Well, I only wear it when I don't care how I look," I said, quoting my daddy's favorite movie.

"Very cute. Jimmy Stewart, right? Now there was a cutie..."

I gave up as Sebastian and Ben started in on the Jimmy Stewart or Cary Grant argument they always had. Sebastian had clearly read my intentions, or else he was just a catty old queen. Either way, he'd shut me down before I could toy with Ben.

I moved on. I looked back at the bar and decided another drink would suit me just fine, now that grandpa had left and some cute, young thing was standing back there. I sauntered over and asked for another Old Fashioned, leaning on the bar, squeezing my breasts between my arms. He dropped the soda can, his eyes as wide as saucers, and it sprayed loudly before he could stop it.

"Why Daphne Williams, how ever are you, honey?"

I turned and there was Laney Shimms. She used to work the front desk at our old firm. David had invited *her*? She was the only woman in the entire building, probably in my entire professional career, who was nice to me. I used to like her. Today I hated her; hated everyone. Wanted to make everyone as miserable as I was.

"Well, hi there, Laney, how are you doing? What a surprise to see you here! Never thought David liked you that much."

She stuttered a little, but she was too polite to outright object. "Oh, we still keep in touch. He's like a son to me, you know."

"I can see that, seeing as how your own son is a drunken loser. Pretending David's yours make you feel more accomplished somehow?" I was starting to feel that first drink.

"Well, I don't mean, yes, um, no. Is everything ok, dear?"

"Bless your heart, you're just so sweet to worry about me. I'm wonderful. I mean, look at me."

"I am, dear."

"And how about you, Laney? Fallen off the Weight Watcher's wagon again?"

"Oh. Yes. It was nice to see you, Daphne." She tottered away, the blubbery old fool.

I threw back my second drink and set my glass on the bar. They were beginning to seat people for the ceremony. I toyed with the idea of toying with the bartender. He barely looked legal, though. Even I wouldn't be able to get myself out of a statutory rape charge. Besides, I wouldn't give Trevor the pleasure of being right.

I was not a slut. I was a bitch. The biggest bitch in Charleston. I took a seat along the aisle, hoping to draw David's attention to my long legs, or even Camile's. Let her feel doubt every time David was with me.

I sat through the ceremony for appearance sake. Didn't want David to see me go before all the crap about loving each other forever. It was bullshit. No one loved you forever. No one really loved anyone. It was all a myth.

After the ceremony I wandered and drank some more, pissing off a few more people. Guess I was never going back to the old firm. Not that I needed them. *Monroe and Williams* was beyond successful, and we would continue to be if I had anything to do with it.

I walked by a couple sitting at a table chatting intimately. I stopped by the man's elbow and bent down, whispering in his ear loud enough for his companion to hear, "You were wonderful, lover." His date turned purple as I walked away.

Finally, the 'happy couple' was back and I could get out of there. As soon as I could I congratulated David, avoiding Camile, and took off. I had no desire to stay for dinner and dancing under the stars.

I sped home as fast as I could. As soon as I got inside, I stripped my dress off and threw it in the fireplace. I turned the gas on and watched it burn while I cried myself to sleep.

25

Implosion

By Friday morning I was over all of it. I'd not heard from Trevor or Hunter, and that was just fine with me. I was back in the office by sunrise. The place was completely deserted, being the day after Thanksgiving, and all. But that suited me just fine. It seemed right for me to be completely alone today.

A little after ten a.m. my phone rang. It was an unknown number. I was bored, having worked so much over the last few months that I'd actually wrapped most everything up nicely. So, I answered the call, hoping it would be something interesting. I wasn't disappointed.

"Hello, Daphne Williams."

"Hello. Is this Daphne Williams of *Monroe and Williams*?" a male voice asked.

"Yes, it is. With whom do I have the pleasure of speaking?"

"My name is Smith. I need to get in touch with David Monroe. It's urgent."

Smith. Clearly that wasn't true. I could hear the deception in his voice. "Mr. Smith, I'm sorry, Mr. Monroe won't be available until after the holidays. But perhaps I can help you?"

"Look, if there is any way to get a message to him do it. He'll want to hear what I have to say," Mr. Smith said mysteriously.

"Of course, I can get him a message, but it may take a few days. Are you able to give me the details?"

"Just tell him Belcaron. We have the Notori papers and we want to speak with him. It has to be David Monroe. Anyone else and we'll destroy the papers. And no law enforcement."

Holy Hell! Belcaron! David had been trying to get to them for years. And of course, it was falling in our laps when he was gone on his stupid honeymoon. "Yes, Mr. Smith. I will alert him right away. I know he will want to speak with you. Mr. Monroe has given me full disclosure on Belcaron. If you would allow me to be liaison while Mr. Monroe is out of town, I am sure we can get things started."

"Yeah, ok, maybe."

"I will send him the message and be in touch soon. Contact me by phone at this number only, nothing in writing, including text or email. Please give me your number."

As soon as I was off the phone with Mr. Smith, I started a message to David. He was far out in the desert, cell phone off, email sporadic. I wasn't sure when he would get the message. He had to go into town at some point, right?

Although if *I* was out there with him, he'd never even make it out of the bed. I allowed myself to fantasize for a few minutes. But the fantasy left me unsatisfied and... bored? That was strange.

I focused on the message. I had to put this in a way David would understand but could never compromise us in the future if the email ever got out. I pulled out the code book we used and wrote him a jaunty little email with a hidden message only he would understand. We were both painstakingly cautious about putting anything in writing. It was yet another way we were professionally compatible.

I'd just sent the email when my phone rang again. I looked down at the screen on my desk. Reed. My heart leapt into my throat.

I was suddenly frantic. We hadn't spoken in weeks, before everything had imploded. I wavered between lying and telling him everything was fine, or telling him the whole truth and nothing but the truth, or just telling him I never wanted to see him again.

But I desperately wanted to see him again. I had pushed thoughts of him out of my head, telling myself it was over, it hadn't worked, I was moving on. But seeing his name on my screen sent a tornado through me that broke down every wall I'd put up.

I answered the phone. "Reed!" My voice sounded small and squeaky.

"Hi Daphne," he said, sending a torrent through me. The sound of him saying my name caused every emotion I'd forced down to swell to the surface and I couldn't fight the current anymore.

"Reed!" I sobbed. "It's so good to hear your voice."

"Darling, what's wrong? You haven't been working too hard, have you?"

"I've been working, and I've been fucking it all up. Everything," I said in a small voice. I hated myself for telling him. He was trapped, thousands of miles away, and wouldn't be able to do anything about any of this for weeks. But I was being eaten from the inside out and I knew Reed could make it all better.

"Oh, Daphne, I wish I could have called sooner. I know what this week has probably done to you. Spill it, Williams. What happened?"

"Have you talked to the boys yet?" I asked, scared now.

"No, I called you first. I needed to hear your sweet voice. I've got enough men to talk to around here," he laughed.

"Oh, lord, Reed. I've been awful. It's been awful. It's just not going to work."

Reed was silent. After a moment I went on. "Hunter and Trevor have been fighting. And I've been fighting with both of them. Well, mostly Trevor. He's been impossible. He won't let me in, Reed." My voice cracked. "I just can't do it anymore. It's too hard." I started to cry.

"Tell me more," Reed said quietly.

"I was a terror at David's wedding. Oh, Reed, I was so mean to Laney Shimms!"

Reed chuckled a little. "Not Laney Shimms!" he said.

"Stop it, you brute! This isn't funny!" But his laughter calmed me. It should make me angry, I thought, but it didn't. "Reed, you should have seen the dress I wore. Black, lace, and not much of it."

Reed took a deep breath. "Now you're trying to kill me. Please don't tell me any more about that," he said, his voice thick with desire.

"I didn't go to Thanksgiving. I stayed to work."

"Oh, Williams," he sighed. "I can't even leave you alone for a few weeks and you implode. Where are the guys now?

"I don't know, and I don't care!" I yelled into the phone. "You should have heard what Trevor said to me!"

I told Reed the whole story. Everything. Including my plans to get David to fall madly in love with me after his honeymoon. When I talked about my behavior, I felt ridiculous. Reed listened patiently.

"Have you got it all out of your system, now?" he asked quietly.

"Mmm-hmm."

"Good. Now listen up, Williams. Suck it up! We all have our issues and part of being an adult is being able to deal with your own shit."

"Reed!" He never cursed at me.

"Miss Williams, you've heard worse. Don't go getting all dainty on me now. Trevor is being a real asshole, granted. He has his reasons, but it's no excuse. I'll punch him in his big mouth when I get home for you. But Daphne, we love you. We all love you. And even if you go out and burn every bridge, piss off everyone you ever knew, chase after David until you look like a fool, we'll still love you. And all you'll have done is hurt us and yourself. Has any of this made you any happier?" he asked.

"No."

"Then stop being a spoiled little brat and step up to the plate. When I come home in three weeks, I want to see the strong, confident, goddess I fell in love with. If you're not that woman then I don't want to see you."

"If that's the way you feel, then maybe it's better if we don't see each other," I said petulantly. How dare he call me a brat! It infuriated me. "And tell your friends that I don't want to see hide nor hair of them, either! You can all go to Hell!"

I hung up on him and crossed my arms over my chest, anger surging through me. I hated that they were all keeping this thing from me, whatever it was. I hated being called spoiled more than almost anything. I hated this whole, damn mess!

Suddenly the sight of my office made me sick to my stomach. I needed to get out of there. I went home and found a half-bottle of bourbon in my liquor cabinet. By midnight it was all but gone.

26

Summer

I drank my way through the weekend. It didn't help. By Monday I felt like a dried-up husk. Everyone would be back in session today. I had a few smaller cases to work before Christmas. Oh, god, Christmas. The thought made me physically ill.

It would be my first Christmas alone in a very long time. I usually had someone to share it with. I decided I would go home and pretend I was a child again. My parents would coddle me, and I could forget about everything.

But David was coming back just before the holiday and he'd want to get going on Belcaron. Or maybe he wouldn't. He seemed to have lost some of his blood lust lately. Camile was making him soft. No matter. I hadn't lost any of mine.

As the days passed, I became more and more morose. I drank myself to sleep every night. It was becoming a problem. Then one night there was a knock on my door. I'd just gotten home and poured myself a nightcap. I wasn't happy with the interruption. I looked out the peephole and saw a little blonde head.

"Summer?" I said, opening the door. "What in heaven are you doing here?"

"Daphne!" she cried and threw her arms around me. "I missed you so much!"

"Get in here you crazy little thing," I said, stumbling back, spilling my drink on my arm. She grabbed her suitcase and marched in.

"Oh, Daphne, you have to come back, you just have to!"

"What in the world are you talking about? And does your momma know you're here?"

Summer hung her head. "No, ma'am."

"How in the world did you get here all on your own?"

"I used all my money to buy a plane ticket, and then I got an Uber from the airport. Please don't call momma! She'll tan my hide!"

"Honey, you can't just run off and not tell your momma. She'll be worried sick."

"I told her I was staying the night at Sally's house. She's covering for me. Momma won't worry."

"Still... How'd you even get on a plane alone?"

"I'm smart. I figured out how to get around all that stuff. But that don't make no never mind. You need to come back with me now!"

"Honey, Hunter and I aren't on the best of terms right now..."

"I know!" Summer yelled. "That's why I'm here! It's killing him, Daphne! He's miserable. I hate it! I just hate it!" She started to cry.

We were sitting on the sofa and I pulled her into my arms. "I know, honey, I hate it, too. But it's complicated."

"Don't you love him anymore?"

Yes! Yes, I did! I loved him so much. But it didn't change anything. He hadn't even tried. "Of course I love him," I whispered.

"Then call him! Tell him! He thinks you hate him."

"I'm sure he doesn't think that." Did he?

"He does. He said it's all his fault and he's ruined the best thing that ever happened to him, but he can't betray his best friend, whatever that means. Trevor can go suck an egg as far as I'm concerned."

I laughed. "Well, regardless, I need to let someone know you're here."

"Then call Hunter, please! My folks will kill me! Hunter's at his house here, now. He can come get me."

Oh dear. I wasn't sure how I felt about that idea.

"Please, Daphne!" Summer cried, tears running down her face. She looked so pitiful.

"Ok, fine. But you call him. And I'll send you over in a car. He doesn't need to come here."

Summer's face lit up. "Ok! I don't have a phone, though. Can I use yours?"

Great. "Fine. Here you go."

"Thank you," she said, taking the phone and dialing. "Hi, it's Summer," she said after a moment. She was silent for a moment while Hunter said something, and then she said quickly, "Because I'm at Daphne's house. Come get me!" and she hung up.

"Why you little devil!" I said. But secretly I was pretty impressed. She was a quick thinker and a brave little thing.

"I'm not leaving until you talk to Hunter. I'll refuse. I'll hold onto the curtains so you can't drag me out," she said, crossing her arms across her chest and looking at me defiantly.

"Or I could just call your momma," I threatened.

"I don't care anymore. Let her whoop me. If it gets you two dummies to talk to each other it'll be worth it."

"It really means that much to you?"

"Yes."

"Fine. We'll talk. But Summer, we can't just... It's not something that... It won't be fixed that easily, that's all."

She just sat there looking smug. I sure did like this girl.

"Can I braid your hair, Daphne?" she asked after a minute.

"Right now?"

"Yeah. There's something I want to try. You look tired. Let me fix you up. For Hunter."

"Ok." Great, I could look tired and have a silly braid in my hair when he got here. Wouldn't that just win him over. I went and brought her back the supplies she asked for and she got to work.

"There," she said, finishing. "Much better. You have such lovely hair for braiding. It's so long."

There was a knock on the door. My stomach clenched. I stood and opened the door. Hunter stood there, a worried look on his face. He was wearing the hat I'd gotten him. He quickly took it off and held it in his hands in front of him.

"Evening, ma'am," he said.

"Hi Hunter," I whispered. "Come on in." I stood aside so he could enter and shut the door behind him. I stood there, facing the door for a moment, trying to get a hold on my swirling emotions. He looked so good.

I heard Summer greet him and I took a deep breath and turned around.

"You are in serious trouble, young lady!" Hunter scolded her. She just jumped into his arms and hugged him. His face softened and he smiled a little. Oh, she was a little devil, alright. Had him wrapped around her little finger.

Hunter set her down and turned to me. "Can we talk, Daphne? I have something I'd like to say to you."

Summer stood behind him, beaming.

"Sure," I said.

"Summer, sit on this sofa and don't move a muscle or I swear I'll call momma right now and you won't leave your room til you're thirty-five. I'd like to talk to Daphne alone."

"Yes, sir!" Summer said, planting herself on the sofa.

"Bedroom?" he asked me.

I led the way, and he closed the door behind us. I sat down on the bed and he stood by the door, looking at me. I skootched back and leaned against the headboard. "Well, come on, sit down, then," I said.

Hunter sat down on the bed next to me. Then he blushed. He actually blushed. My heart softened. "It's not like you haven't been in a bed with me before, honey," I whispered. He turned a deeper shade of pink.

"Daphne, I want you to know I didn't know Trevor was keeping things from you. He never discussed it with me. I didn't think you knew anything about it. I never thought about it at all, actually. Guess that was dumb of me. I knew you two were fighting over something. I just thought you'd worked it out," he said quietly.

"Not quite," I said.

"I know. That's why I'm here. I've been thinking, *a lot*, and it's not right. I don't want to break Trevor's trust, but you're my friend, too. And it doesn't work if we don't tell each other everything. So, I also need to tell you how I feel."

"You always tell me how you feel," I said.

"No, not always. I tried to keep it from you, how I felt when you would talk about David. I know I'm not good at hiding my feelings, but Daphne, I wanted to die inside whenever you said his name. Reed told us everything about how you feel about David. I thought I could just ignore it, but I can't. And it made me angry. I know it's been a barrier between us. And it made me realize something. You and me, we don't work."

A lump rose up in my throat. Tears stung my eyes. This was it, then. Did it even matter that I didn't feel that way about David anymore? That I'd never *really* felt that way? Was it too late?

"And you and Trevor don't work, either. And not you and Reed. You and me, we have something good and pure. But I can never give you what David could. I know that. It's why I hated thinking about you spending any time with him. But you have to, don't you? So, it just doesn't work. And me and Trevor, we can't do this, either. And you and Trevor, you're both smart and sophisticated, but without me and Reed you both have a hard time finding that connection in your hearts. And when it's just you and Reed, it's too dark for both of you. I know your heart, Daphne. And I know his. The two of you would destroy each other without us."

The tears rolled down my cheeks, but Hunter went on.

"What I'm saying is, it only works if it's all of us. It's the craziest thing I think I've ever said, but it's true. I don't want you without them. You and me, we would love each other. We would get married, have a few babies, live on the farm. But eventually, you'd want more. You'd need more, and it's part of what I love about you. You are an amazing person, Daphne. You need the world, the city, the thrill of victory. And you help people. I know you don't want to believe it, but your heart is true. All you need is someone to show you."

Hunter finally looked at me and our eyes locked. His soft brown irises looked right into my soul. I felt the truth in everything he'd said, and my soul cried out for it. I couldn't speak. I didn't know what to say, for once. Hunter grabbed a tissue off the nightstand and dabbed my cheeks.

"So, I'm here to tell you something and I hope it won't ruin everything. Trevor knows who his parents are."

Shock settled over me. He'd always said he was an orphan, grown up in the system, hopping from foster family to foster family, never making a real connection with any of them. "Why would he lie about that?" I asked.

"He didn't really lie. He didn't know, until he turned twenty-one. Everything he told you about his childhood was true. When he found out, both his parents were already dead. His father had left him a trust that he could access after his twenty-first birthday. But there was a catch. He can't touch it until he gets married."

Hunter looked at me, trying to convey something to me, but I didn't understand. He went on.

"See, his momma was American. She met his father when she went on vacation in Dubai. She got pregnant, but his father was already married. So, she came back to the States to have the baby, but she died from some complications during the birth. She had no family, so Trevor went into the system. It's a real shame what we do to children," he said sadly.

"But what about his father?" I asked.

"Well, his father apparently never forgot his mother. He loved her, I guess. But he was never going to claim an illegitimate child. See, his father was some kind of king over there. Owned a lot of oil and an airline. The airline is what he left to Trevor."

Well that explained a lot.

"He set up the trust just before he died, to be executed on Trevor's twenty-first birthday. That's the first time Trevor found out about any of this. Guess his dad kept tabs on him all his life. Anyway, when Trevor found out about it, he went wild at first. He was a millionaire overnight. But then he found out about the marriage clause. He'd got himself in a heap of debt by then. He's been working his way out ever since. He and Reed, they were good friends already, then. Trevor almost got married once before, so he could get the money, but Reed stopped him. I met them a little while after that."

"I don't understand," I said. "Why would Trevor keep this all from me?"

"Because he loves you. He loves you more than anything. And he wants you to love him. *Him*. Not his money, or his airline, or his fancy car."

"What fancy car? His jalopy looks like it's going to fall apart at any minute."

Hunter laughed. "That's not his car. See, the trust gives him an allowance, and part of it is paid out in cars and free travel on the airline he's inheriting. That's why I always get first class tickets back home whenever I want. Trevor just drove the loaner car when he was around you. You'd like his real car, I think."

"Oh my gosh! It's the black Ferrari, isn't it? I wondered why y'all never seemed to fix that one. Holy cow, Trevor's a prince!"

"Yeah, but don't say it to him. He hates it. He detests it, actually. Wishes it would all go away."

I pulled my knees up to my chest and rested my forehead on them, hiding my face from Hunter. They all thought I was a money-grubbing, power-hungry, status-seeking bitch. And maybe I was. Maybe Trevor was right to keep this from me. A few months ago, I would have done everything I could to marry a prince. But that's not who I was anymore.

"That's why he's not fighting what's going on right now," Hunter said.

"What's going on right now?" I asked, looking up at him.

"His dad's family is challenging the trust. They want to take it for themselves. He's not fighting it. He wants to be free of it before he talks to you again. He was going to tell you, after the money was gone."

"Oh." I started to cry. Then I started to sob. Suddenly the bedroom door burst open and Summer came running in.

"You big meanie! You made her cry!" she shouted, and jumped on the bed, wrapping her arms around me.

"Summer, I told you to stay out there and mind your own business," Hunter said in a gruff voice.

"I was, but I could hear Daphne crying all the way out there and you're just such a dummy, Hunter!"

I started to laugh, and my crying stopped. Hunter laughed, too.

"What's so funny, y'all? Why're you laughing at me?" Summer said, bewildered.

"I'm not laughing at you, honey," I said. "And Hunter didn't make me cry. I did. I've made some bad choices and now I have to live with the consequences. Hunter was trying to make it better."

"Oh my gosh! You're pregnant, aren't you! Hunter, you have to marry her!"

Hunter and I burst out laughing even louder this time. Summer got mad.

"Stop laughing! I know what consequences means. And you better step up and be a man, or I won't let you be my brother anymore!" Summer wrapped her arms protectively around me and glared at Hunter.

"Summer, I'm not pregnant," I soothed her, hugging her tight. "But I appreciate your defending my honor."

Summer looked disappointed. I thought Hunter did, too. If only it were something so simple as a baby.

"Give us another minute, Summer," I said, wiping tears from my face. She smiled, like she knew everything was ok. I hoped she was right.

"I've got to see that trust," I said.

"No way! That's the last thing Trevor wants. Don't go messing around in this, you hear?" Hunter warned me, wagging his finger at me.

I smiled wickedly at him. "You know, when you order me not to do something, it makes me want to do it even more?"

"In that case, DO NOT kiss me right now," he said, resting his chin on my knees and looking into my eyes.

My heart swelled with love for him. I gently put my lips to his and when they met a heat pulsed through me, down to my toes and out through my fingers.

We both heard a little snicker at the door. We opened our eyes and stared at each other, smiling. Hunter reached a long arm over and grabbed a pillow, launching it at the little face peeking through a crack in the door.

"Ow!" Summer said as it hit her square in the nose.

"Serves you right, you little spy! Get in here!" Hunter yelled. Summer bounced onto the bed. "Now, what are we going to do with you? How should we punish her, Daphne?"

"Well, let's see, what are the charges? Spying," I said.

"Going AWOL," Hunter said.

"Threatening and coercing a member of the bar," I added. "Hmm, since I'm the closest thing to a judge here, I sentence you, Summer Falco, to two, five second terms of tickling, to be served consecutively, starting now!"

Hunter and I both attacked her, and she screamed bloody murder. I hoped no one would call the police.

"Alright, you've served your sentence. Did you learn your lesson, young lady?" I asked.

"Does this mean you two are back together?" she asked hopefully.

"Yes," we both said at the same time. We all broke out in laughter.

"Then I've learned that I am always gonna have to make sure my dumb big brother does what he's supposed to do. Jeez, Hunter, it's gonna be like a full-time job watching after you. Hey!" she screamed as he tickled her again.

"Do you think Ginny would let Summer stay with me for a few days?" I asked. "It is winter break."

Summer's face lit up. "Oh yes, please Hunter! You can ask Momma! She always listens to you!"

"Do you really think we ought to reward her for this behavior?" Hunter asked me.

"I sure do," I whispered. "I sure do."

27

Homecoming

R eed was coming back today. None of us had spoken to him since we'd patched things up. Or mostly patched them, anyway. Trevor still wouldn't speak to me. We were going to pick Reed up at the docks today. Summer and I waited for Hunter to pick us up. My heart sank when I opened the door.

"He didn't come?" I asked, letting Hunter in.

"No. He's left town. Went to the farm. Said he'd see Reed there for Christmas. I'm sorry, Daphne."

"It's ok, Daphne. We can see him when we all go home," Summer said. "He can't be mad forever cuz Hunter told his dumb old secret. Who cares if he's a prince, anyway? He's not even a real prince. Doesn't have a horse or crown or anything."

I didn't care about his money. I knew it. But Trevor didn't, and I had no idea how to show him.

"Alright, ladies, your chariot awaits. Don't wanna be late to get Reed," Hunter said, shooing us out the door.

"I don't think there's any chance of you being late anywhere, the way you drive," I said.

"Oh, you should go out muddin' with Hunter sometime. It's insane!" Summer said, glee in her voice.

"I'm sorry, y'all, but muddin' is not something I will ever do," I said, smiling at their expressions.

"Maybe you're not a real Kentucky girl, after all," Hunter teased me.

"Says the vegetarian," I teased back.

Summer giggled.

We waited with all the other families for the sailors to come off the ship. I watched with an eager heart and hungry eyes for Reed to appear. Sailors lined the decks as the huge floating city docked. My eyes searched, but I couldn't spot him.

"Where is he, Hunter?" I asked, bouncing up and down.

"Calm down, he'll be here," he said.

"I just can't wait!" I squeaked.

"You sure are good friends with him," Summer said. She didn't know how right she was.

"He's my best friend," I said, then quickly added, "after you and Hunter, of course." Hunter chuckled.

The gates opened and people began to deboard. The crowd went wild around us. People were waving signs and screaming. There were balloons everywhere. I even saw people carrying a giant sheet cake with 'Welcome Home' scrawled in frosting on top.

Then I saw him. He was coming down the gangplank in his flight suit. Oh, god, he looked good. Hunter jumped up and down, waving and hollering and somehow Reed spotted us. He started running. Suddenly my head felt dizzy and my knees were weak. I couldn't catch my breath.

"Hunter," I said, and I felt my legs give out. Everything went black.

When I opened my eyes, Reed was standing in front of me, Hunter holding me up under my arms from behind. My breath rushed in and I wrapped my arms around Reed's neck, pressing my lips to his, holding him so tight I thought I'd never let go.

I practically attacked him, devouring his mouth, his cheeks, his neck. Reed cleared his throat and whispered in my ear. "Daphne, I'm happy to see you, too." He chuckled. "But maybe we save something for later?"

I stopped kissing him and looked into his eyes. He looked to the left, and my eyes followed his. Summer stood there, jaw dropped, staring at us. I felt the heat rise to my face. I'd forgotten everything when I looked into Reed's crystal blue eyes. Everything but him.

With a Herculean effort I pulled out of Reed's arms. I looked at Summer apologetically.

"What is going on here?" she demanded.

"It's alright, Summer," Hunter said. "We're all just very good friends."

"I've never kissed my friends like that!" she said, not believing a word of it.

"And you better not, for at least ten more years!" Hunter laughed. Summer looked at him like he was crazy.

"You don't mind?" she asked.

"Mind what?" Hunter said.

"That!" Summer said, waving a hand at me.

"That Daphne loves Reed just as much as I do? Nope," he said, and smiled.

"What's Momma gonna say?" Summer said, almost to herself.

"Let's not tell Momma for now, ok?" Hunter said. "And I won't tell her you actually ran away without telling anyone." He winked at her. Summer seemed satisfied for the moment.

"Can we go home now? I'm so ready to see my own bed," Reed said, and we all made our way to Hunter's truck. "Where's Trevor?" he asked.

"He's already at the farm," Hunter said, giving Reed a look. Reed seemed to understand. He always seemed to understand.

Summer climbed into the little backseat of Hunter's truck. I thought about sitting back there with her, to avoid any further awkwardness, but stuffing my long body in that tiny space did not appeal to me. And I wanted to be next to Reed so very badly. So, I took my place in the middle. After all, the cat was already out of the bag.

I held both their hands while we drove to their place. If Summer noticed, she didn't say anything. I was euphoric sitting there between them. Everything I'd worried about over the last three months seemed to evaporate into the ether. Reed was back and it felt so right again.

We got back to their house and the boys unloaded Reed's bags. His duffle was almost bigger than him and I wondered how he even lifted it. But he hefted it over his shoulder like it weighed less than nothing.

We had a quiet dinner together after Reed showered and got settled back in. Summer was tired out from our three-day slumber party. I'd made sure she had a good time at my place in way of thanks for interfering in the very best way. By nine p.m. she was lying on the sofa, her eyes closing. Hunter carried her into his room and tucked her into his bed.

He came back and took his spot on the sofa next to me. I felt him move my hair to the side as I kissed Reed. I couldn't wait. As soon as Summer was out of the room, I'd attacked him again. Now we were making out like teenagers, his incredible hands roving over my body.

Hunter's lips came down on the back of my neck, his mouth closing over the spot he'd just exposed. My breath rushed in and I thought I might faint again. I moaned against Reed's mouth.

"Uuuhhh, you'll be the death of me, Daphne," he whispered, and sat back against the arm of the sofa.

"But what a death it would be," I flirted. Then I moaned as Hunter's mouth continued on my neck.

Reed laughed. "No doubt about that. But, y'all, I'm a little out of the loop. Care to catch me up? I see we're all friendly here again," he said, waggling a finger between me and Hunter.

Hunter reluctantly stopped kissing me. He'd been banned from the house since Summer was staying with me, and it had been over four weeks since we'd been together. Needless to say, we were all on the edge of insanity. I didn't think I'd ever been celibate so long, not since I lost my virginity fifteen years ago.

"Well," I began, "you were right, as usual. I was being a... brat." I choked on the word a little. "Summer showed up on my doorstep three days ago, having run away from home and refusing to leave until Hunter and I got back together. There was nothing we could do. She'd set her mind to it."

Reed laughed.

"Hunter told me about Trevor," I said, looking into Reed's eyes. "I understand why y'all kept it from me, I do. It hurts, still, but y'all have shown me what I was and what I can be. And I want to be what you see me as, Reed. I want to be the woman you think I am, and Hunter, and Trevor, I hope. I hope Trevor can see me as more than a status-obsessed gold-digger someday."

"He doesn't think that, beautiful, really," Hunter said quietly behind me, his head resting by mine.

Reed just looked into my eyes and I thought he might cry. His eyes were intense, and I could feel his love for me rolling off of him in waves. "Does Trevor know?" Reed asked.

"Yeah, he knows," Hunter said. "He's pretty ticked off at me. But he refuses to talk to Daphne until it's all over."

"I guess I should go give him that punch in the mouth after all. He's still acting like an ass."

"No, don't Reed," I said, and he laughed.

"Ok, anything for you," he smiled.

"Anything?" I asked, raising my eyebrow.

"You know it," Reed said.

"Good. Then you're going to help me get my hands on that trust."

Reed looked at me in shock. Hunter groaned behind me.

"What?" Reed said, almost angry.

"I don't mean like that! Honestly, when will y'all really, truly trust me? How many times do I have to prove myself to you?"

Reed looked chagrined. "Sorry," he said. "What do you mean?"

"I want to help Trevor take care of his Trust. These things can drag on for decades in court, even if he rolls over and lets them screw him. And I'm not willing to wait that long," I said.

"Decades?" Hunter said weakly behind me. "Suddenly your plan is sounding better."

"There's a plan?" Reed asked.

"Yes. I know how to take care of this once and for all, but I need inside help. I need you two to do a little spying. Maybe a retrieval mission. Nothing you can't handle. Since Trevor won't talk to me until it's all over, let's make it be all over."

Reed looked speculative. "Fine. I'm all caught up now." His eyes moved down my body and his hand moved to my knee, his fingers grazing me and moving slowly up my thigh. He slid the hem of my skirt up until he could see the top of my stocking. "God, I've missed you," he whispered.

I took his face in my hands and kissed him, my breath rushing out as his hand gripped my thigh and ran up my skirt to squeeze my ass.

"Bedroom," I breathed.

Reed moaned, and in one swift motion he was up on his feet and I was thrown over his shoulder just like his duffle. I squealed, but threw my hand over my mouth, not wanting to wake Summer.

Reed carried me into his room and gently laid me across the bed. I stretched out and looked at him and Hunter, standing over me, side by side, their eyes devouring my body. I started to hyperventilate.

Hunter turned and locked the door quietly. Reed stripped off his t-shirt and my breathing came even quicker. Then Hunter was lying beside me, whispering in my ear.

"Shhh, beautiful, it's alright." He turned my face to his with gentle fingers and his soft lips gently coaxed mine. I reached my hand up to his chest and my breathing slowed as I felt his steady heartbeat there.

Hunter kissed me long and slow, his large hand cupping my face. I ran my hand up his chest to caress his soft beard. Oh, god!

Reed's hands slid up my legs, from my ankles to my thighs, and I felt them disappear under my skirt. I felt his mouth on me, licking and sucking my inner thigh just above my garters. His hands were grabbing my ass and his mouth moved over my panties. I felt his hot breath as he kissed me and closed his mouth over the top of my silk underwear. He reached his hands up and pulled my panties down my legs. His hands came back up between my thighs, pushing my legs open, spreading me before him.

Hunter slid his hands under my top and pulled it up and over my head. He sat up and took his shirt off, too. He leaned over me, gazing into my eyes for a moment, before lowering his lips to mine again. His hand came around my back and unfastened my bra. Gently he slid it off my arms. One large hand cupped my breast, massaging it and teasing my nipple.

"Aaahhh!" I moaned into Hunter's mouth as Reed's tongue pushed between my lips. Hunter moved to my breast and soon two tongues were sliding over my most sensitive areas. Reed's mouth was hot and hard on me, his tongue pressing and urging my clit to orgasm. Hunter's mouth moved slow and sensually, tongue and teeth moving in perfect tune, sending waves of pleasure down my body.

I wanted more. I wanted them both inside me. I wanted to take them in me and make them feel physically everything I felt for them.

All the love, the lust, the need I had. I wanted them to know. But before I could say anything, my orgasm hit me like a truck.

My body was slammed with wave after wave of intense pleasure. My muscles contracted to the point of near pain. Lights danced behind my eyelids. I grabbed onto Reed's hair and bucked my hips into him. He lapped at me and held my thighs apart, shoving his tongue into me.

My other hand ran down Hunter's back, my nails digging into his hard flesh. I screamed and Hunter's mouth came over mine, muffling my cries. I panted heavily through my nose as I came down, Hunter's mouth still working on mine.

I opened my eyes and fell into Hunter's soft gaze. He smiled at me and I smiled back. He was so sweet, so very handsome. And I loved him. "Make love to me, Hunter," I whispered.

I propped myself up into a semi-sitting position on the plush pillows. Reed's eyes met mine and I motioned for him to come. He slid up next to me, but I grabbed his thigh, pulling him over me so he was straddling my shoulders.

"Oh, my days," he whispered when he saw what I wanted. "You are an incredible woman, Daphne."

Hearing my name on his lips drove me insane. I wanted to make him scream it. I grabbed his huge cock with one hand and his ass with the other. I ran my tongue around the tip, looking up into his eyes. His blue eyes burned like sapphires. I took the head in my mouth and sucked, circling my tongue faster. Reed shuddered and grabbed the top of the headboard, a low moan erupting from his chest.

Then I felt Hunter between my legs. I couldn't see him. I could only feel him, and it felt amazing. He teased me with the head of his cock, slipping it in, then out, then a little deeper. I started to pant. Then he slid in, the whole length of him, pushing deep inside me.

"Uuuhhh!" I cried out, my hand clamping down on Reed and my eyes rolling back in my head. Having my sweet Country inside me again was almost too much. He filled me and probed me and drove me wild.

I grabbed Reed's ass and pulled him into me, deep throating him until I had him all. "Daphne!" he moaned, and I felt a flood break loose between my legs. I was going to cum again, and soon.

I slid Reed's cock out of my mouth and looked up at him. "Fuck me," I mouthed.

"Dear lord," he whispered.

I took him back in my mouth and pulled him into me, moving him back and forth until he took over. I felt him swelling. He wouldn't last long this way. And that was what I wanted. I wanted to swallow him. To take everything he'd built up waiting to be with me. I sucked him and licked him and took him deep in my throat, meeting his thrusts with eager lips.

Hunter was moving slower, teasing me still, building me into a writhing, throbbing abyss of pleasure. He could slow build me like no one else. I could feel the orgasm coming for minutes, prolonging the pleasure. He slid his long length all the way out, and all the way back in again, letting me feel every inch of him. Every stroke caressed me inside until I was ready to explode.

I could feel Reed getting close. I could feel myself getting close. Oh, god, I was going to cum! My pussy started to throb, long and intense, the muscles contracting around Hunter. I screamed around Reed's cock and he swelled, watching my face as I came. And then he was cumming in me, throbbing in my mouth, and my orgasm peaked. I couldn't think, cum dripped down my chin and I stroked Reed with my hand, running my tongue over him and crying out.

Reed collapsed next to me, panting and sweating, his chest glistening. And now I had a view of Hunter and I watched him pump into me. "Oh, Hunter!" I cried, my orgasm continuing to spasm around him. He moaned low and long.

"Lay down, honey," I whispered to him. "I want to finish you."

Hunter collapsed onto the bed and I crawled onto him, lowering my mouth to his lap. He was slick with my juices and I stroked him before taking him in my mouth. "Oh, Daphne," he moaned, tangling a hand in my hair.

Reed had been watching Hunter fuck me and now he was ready again. I saw him stand and walk behind me and I started to drip again. I felt his hands run over my ass and up my back and I raised my hips up to him, spreading my knees apart. Reed ran his cock up and down the length of me, rubbing my clit, sliding in, then rubbing my clit again. Little squeaks escaped me as I sucked Hunter and tried not to scream.

Then Reed sunk into me. He wasn't gentle about it, he drove into me, his thick cock stretching me to the edge of reason. I did cry out, the feeling so intense I couldn't breathe. He rammed into me again and again, his cock hitting that special spot until I was dripping wet and mad with desire.

I felt Hunter swell in my mouth and the taste of his pre-cum drove me over the edge. My orgasm exploded again, sending my head spinning. I wanted Hunter's cum, and I sucked him hard, my hand stroking him, my tongue working, and he burst in my mouth. I lapped at him and milked him until he was done.

Reed slammed into me one more time and I felt him burst, hot and hard as I swallowed Hunter. It was so much more than I'd ever experienced. My orgasm continued to throb around Reed, making him moan.

My legs gave out and I slid down onto my stomach, Reed sliding with me and landing on top of me. My head fell onto Hunter's hip and my eyes closed, my head spinning. Reed was slick against my back, our bodies covered with sweat. Hunter stroked my hair and my breathing slowed.

I don't know how long we lay there, but I never wanted to leave. Reed kissed my shoulder and whispered in my ear, "I love you, Daphne."

I rolled over underneath him and off of Hunter's lap. I wrapped my arms around his neck and stared into his eyes. "I love you, too," I whispered. He kissed me softly.

"Hey, what about me," Hunter teased.

"I love you, too, man," Reed said, sending Hunter into a laughing fit.

I crawled into the middle of the bed and nestled the whole length of my body against Hunter's side, my chin resting on his chest. I looked up into his beautiful face. I reached up and stroked his face. He blushed.

"I love you, Hunter, so much," I said.

Reed laid down next to me, running his finger absently up and down my hip. It was blissful.

"Whose toothbrush should I use tonight?" I asked, and Hunter laughed again.

"What's so funny?" Reed asked.

"I'll tell you sometime," I said. "But right now, I just want to sleep. I never want this to end."

Hunter and Reed both kissed my cheeks at the same time, squishing my face between them.

"Mmmm, you boys sure know how to treat a girl."

My eyes were closed, and I couldn't stay awake any longer. I felt soft lips touch mine, gentle and tender. I kissed Hunter and my heart glowed. He moved away and another set of lips replaced his, firmer, more insistent, but just as full of love. I kissed Reed's lovely mouth and drifted into slumber.

28

Breakfast

Bang! Bang! Bang!

I was jolted out of sleep. Someone was pounding on a door. My eyes opened slowly, my lids heavy with sleep.

Bang! Bang! Bang!

"Daphne!" Summer's voice came through the door. I bolted upright.

On either side of me my men lay, comatose in sleep. They stirred, but not much. I climbed down to the foot of the bed and off, stepping over to the door. I whispered through the closed door, "Just a minute, Summer, I'll be right out."

I looked around. I was still wearing my garter belt, but I needed to put on a bit more than that. I found my bra and top and skirt and threw them on. I unlocked the door and slid out, opening it as little as possible. Summer tried to peek inside, but I blocked her.

"Where's the fire, girl?" I whispered, hustling her down the hall.

"I'm sorry, Daphne, I didn't know what to do," Summer said, looking like she might cry.

"About what, honey?" I asked, suddenly worried. I could see the sun was just coming up. What was she doing up so early?

"I'm bleeding," she whispered.

"Oh!" I said, understanding. "Is this your first time?"

"Yes ma'am."

"Oh, honey-child. I've got some things in my purse, come on now." I wrapped an arm around her shoulder, and we walked into the living room to get my purse. I pulled out a pad and walked her back into the bathroom.

"You know how all this works?" I asked her, helping her clean herself up.

"Yeah, my sisters told me. Of course, it had to happen at my brother's house!"

"I know, honey. It's never convenient. It's a curse and a blessing, I guess. How are you feeling? Are you in any pain?"

"A little. Not much."

"Well you just let me know if you want something for that, ok?"

"Thank you, Daphne!" she said and threw her arms around me. I held her, feeling a little overwhelmed. She was becoming a woman and I was here to see it.

"Come on, you want some cereal?" I asked.

"Sure," she said, all smiles again. The Falcos were the happiest family I'd ever met. It took an awful lot to drag them down.

We went to the kitchen and I made coffee while Summer poured cereal. Of course, all Hunter had in the cabinet was Cap'n Crunch. Normally I wouldn't touch the stuff, but it felt wrong not to join Summer in a celebratory breakfast. So, I sat down at the table with her and we ate sugar-coated corn blobs. I could feel myself getting fatter.

But it wasn't really important to me, I realized. I lifted my coffee mug. "Congratulations, Summer!" She lifted her orange juice cup and we clinked glasses.

"Guess I'm a woman now, or something. I don't feel any different."

"It doesn't really work like that. But you're not a kid anymore. It's pretty great being a woman, though. You have a lot to look forward to."

"I want to be just like you, Daphne." She beamed at me.

"Aw, sweetie, thank you. That makes me feel pretty good. But you are your own amazing person, and I think you're going to do even better than me."

Summer blushed and she looked just like Hunter.

"Are Hunter and Reed both in there with you?" she asked, taking a bite of cereal.

I felt like blushing now. I wasn't sure how much to tell her. It felt silly to try to hide it from her, she was a very intelligent person. But I wasn't her mother, or even her family. What was it my place to say?

Huh. Since when did I ever stay in my place? There hadn't been a 'place' made that could contain Daphne Williams. I decided to be honest with her.

"Yes, they're both in there."

She giggled and a smile spread across her face. "Do they like to be together, you know, like that?"

Oh, dear, this wasn't the conversation I expected to have today. "It's really not proper to ask, honey. We didn't mean for you to see us like this. I'm real sorry about that. I'm usually the first one up."

Summer smiled again. "I knew I wanted to be like you."

I didn't know what she meant by that, but I felt like I should change the subject before I got myself in trouble. But Summer beat me to it.

"There's a boy I like," she said conspiratorially. "His name is John. He's a year ahead of me. Next year I wanna talk to him. Will you help me? I'm so nervous around him!"

"Sure, I will. There's really not that much to it." My own little protege, I thought.

"Thanks, Daphne."

"So, tell me all about John," I said, sipping my coffee.

Summer could talk a blue streak, just like her brother. I leaned back and listened, enjoying my coffee. The sun was high when

Hunter walked into the kitchen. He smiled when he saw our little scene.

"Morning, beautiful," he said, kissing the top of my head. "You, too, squirt." He ruffled Summer's hair. "Y'all save me some cereal?"

Hunter bustled around getting cereal and pouring coffee. I watched him move around the kitchen, not able to take my eyes off him. I'd missed him so much.

He sat down in between us and sipped his coffee. "Mmm, mmm! Daphne, you make the best coffee I've ever had. I should marry you right now just for that."

I was stunned. I was dazed. I was dumbstruck. I froze, staring at Hunter. But he just went on eating his cereal and poking Summer in the ribs when she tried to steal a sip of his coffee.

"Tell her, Daphne," Hunter said to me.

"What?" I'd missed what they said.

"Tell her she shouldn't drink coffee. It'll stunt her growth."

"I didn't drink coffee, Summer, so if you want to achieve supermodel height, you shouldn't either."

Hunter smiled at me. "See," he said.

"But, on the other hand, you may need coffee if you have to deal with this all of Christmas break," I said, motioning toward Hunter.

Hunter poked me in the ribs, and I jumped. Reed strode into the kitchen. He went about silently making his breakfast, turning to me once and winking at me when the others weren't looking. It sent a shiver through me.

"I need to get home and pack, boys," I said. "What time is our flight tomorrow?"

"Nine a.m.," said Hunter.

"You don't suppose Trevor cancelled my ticket, do you?" I asked, suddenly worried.

"No, beautiful, he wouldn't do that," Hunter soothed me.

"Alright, then. We have until nine a.m. to make our plan."

29

Going Home

I sat with Summer on the plane, leaving Reed and Hunter to sit in the row behind us, much to their disappointment and Summer's delight. I bought a Seventeen magazine quiz edition for her and we did all the quizzes. Not surprisingly, I got an even mixed result on the 'Who's Your Soulmate' quiz.

When we took off, I felt confident, calm, and optimistic. As we landed, I began to feel unsure. What we were doing was illegal, though not dangerous for the boys. I hadn't told them, but I could lose my license to practice if things went badly.

We deplaned and the boys got their rental car. I was going to stay with my parents, away from Trevor, not wanting to poke the bear. Summer sat in the front with Hunter, and Reed held my hand in the back. I pressed myself as close to him as I could. Being away from them now was going to be more difficult than ever.

"You doing ok?" Reed whispered to me.

"I think so. I'm worried, that's all."

"Your hands are sweating. You don't need to do this. Just come to the farm, talk to Trevor. Once he sees you, he won't be able to stay away," Reed said, kissing my hand.

"You're sweet. But it wouldn't change anything. He'll never let me in while this is hanging over his head."

"Then don't worry, Daphne. If anyone can do this, you can. You're a phenomenal lawyer, and Hunter and I will make sure everything goes well on our end."

I knew they would. If I were only relying on Hunter, I'd never go through with this. He was a terrible liar. He wore his emotions on his sleeve. But Reed would be there, and nothing would ruffle him. I laid my head on his shoulder and closed my eyes, just feeling him.

We pulled into my folks' driveway and parked the car. We were all going to have lunch and I suddenly remembered to be nervous about that, too. I didn't want to lie to my parents, but there was no way I was telling them I was dating three men. Well, two currently, anyway.

We'd decided that as long as we were in the state of Kentucky, or with my or Hunter's family, Hunter would be my official boyfriend. It was just easier that way. Even three counties over people talked, and I didn't want to do that to my parents. Reed seemed fine with whatever arrangement suited me.

Before we got out, I turned to Reed, kissing him softly. "I love you," I whispered.

"I love you, too, Daphne," he whispered back, a little smile on his face.

We piled out and Hunter grabbed my bags, carrying them in like the dutiful boyfriend he really was. He just wasn't the *only* one. Momma and Daddy were running out the door, all smiles and hugs.

"Deedee! You come here girl!" Momma said, running up and grabbing me.

"Hi Momma," I said, squeezing her back.

"Oh, it's just so good to have you here for Christmas! And all your friends. Come here and give Momma a hug, now!" she said, attacking Hunter first, then Reed, finally stopping in front of Summer. "And who is this gorgeous young lady?"

"Summer, ma'am," Summer said.

"Well, come give me a hug, then Summer! You know, you look so much like Daphne did. What are you, about thirteen?"

Summer's face lit up. "Yes ma'am."

"And how have you boys been?" Daddy said, shaking hands. "It's good to see y'all again. Nice to see Daphne with someone that brings her home once in a while." Daddy gave me a raised eyebrow and I laughed. He'd hated Chad.

"Daddy!" I said in mock embarrassment. I ran into his arms and he hugged me tight.

"Come on now, y'all. Get inside before you freeze your toes off," Momma said, hustling everyone inside. I went in and took a deep breath. Home. Daddy had the fire going and it was cozy and warm.

We spent the afternoon eating and talking and I was more comfortable than I had ever been sitting at my parents' table with a boyfriend. They seemed to love Hunter, especially Daddy. His infectious happiness kept everyone laughing.

I took Summer out to meet Theo. She was stunned speechless for a few minutes, something I didn't think was possible. I hadn't told her that I had an affinity for braiding when I was her age, too, and Theo was a Friesian. Jet black with the longest, most beautiful mane and tail you'd ever seen. With my long, blonde hair, and his flowing black mane, we'd won every show we'd entered. Theo seemed to love Summer, too.

Too soon it was time for them to leave. My heart sank and my anxiety returned. Summer jumped in the back of the SUV, leaving me alone with my men.

"I don't know if I can do this," I said to them, my voice shaky.

"Aw, beautiful, you don't have to, you know," Hunter said, taking me in his arms. "We can figure out a different way to help Trevor."

"It's not that. I meant spend days apart from you. I just got you back." I laid my head against his chest and listened to his heart. I tried to memorize its rhythm to use later if I needed it.

Reed grasped my shoulders from behind and buried his face in my neck. "You don't know how hard this is for me, Daphne," he whispered. "Maybe I should stay here with you." He said it in a joking way, but I knew he truly wished he could. So did I.

I turned in Hunter's arms until I faced Reed, wrapping my arms around him. I kissed him long and hard. I felt his breath come faster. "Oh, honey," I breathed.

"We'd better go, Hunter," Reed said dolefully.

"Love you, beautiful," Hunter said, kissing my cheek from behind.

"I love you, too."

I waved to them as they drove down the driveway. My heart felt like it was being pulled from my chest and going with them. It was going to be a long holiday.

Dinner with only me and my parents was much quieter. But it was just as nice. I realized how much I missed this. I hadn't come home for a holiday since I couldn't remember when. Work always seemed to get in the way.

After dinner, my father brought out the bourbon, his best bottle, and he set three glasses on the table. My father was conservative in many ways, but he'd taught me to drink before I'd gone away to college. His theory being I'd get in a lot less trouble that way. But college had been easy. I'd never needed to drink then. It was my thirties that were proving to be a problem.

Momma and Daddy looked at me and we all took a drink. "Alright, what's going on with you two," I asked, smiling at them.

"We're just so happy to have you here, baby," Momma said. "Hunter and Reed sure are good boys. And that sister of Hunter's! What a beauty! He's gonna have to keep an eye on her."

"Summer is already pretty good at taking care of herself," I said, laughing.

"She's a lot like you that way," Daddy said. "So," he said, taking another sip, "tell us what's really going on with the four of you."

My mouth dropped open and I hastily closed it. "What ever do you mean, Daddy?"

"I mean, why isn't Trevor here? Isn't he part of the package?"

I wasn't sure what he was saying. How much of the 'package' did he know about? I decided to go with as much of the truth as possible.

"He's mad at us right now. Mostly me, I guess. He won't talk to me right now. But it's alright. We'll be friends again. I'm just giving him his space."

"You know, if they wanted to stay here, we would be happy to have them. Just keep it in mind."

Daddy was offering to let men stay in our house with me? What in the world was going on? I think he read the surprise on my face.

"You're an adult now, and we want you to come home to see us. We understand if you want to bring someone with you. We just hope that one of them, at least, will make an honest woman out of you and give us a grandchild."

"Daddy!" I said, shocked. I looked at my mother, but she had the same determined, no-nonsense look on her face that my father had.

"Deedee, you've changed since you met them. It's been a good change. We've heard from you more in the last few months than in the last ten years. We just want to support you, however you need to be happy."

I didn't know what to say. I was dumbfounded. I just stared at them. Then Daddy laughed.

"Deedee, I always said there was no man good enough for my little girl. But maybe you've found a way to prove me wrong. Yes, sir, if anyone could figure out how to get around the polygamy laws, it would be you." He and Momma laughed hard. I still couldn't speak.

Finally, I found my voice. "How... How did you know?" I said in a small voice.

"Oh, it's not that hard to see. Spend five minutes in a room with y'all and you can't help but know," Momma said.

"Now, my vote is for Hunter, but you marry one of them, please, so I can enjoy my retirement. I don't think I could stand you bringing home another Chad," Daddy said, and Momma shivered and made a disgusted noise.

I started to laugh. "Well, I just don't know what to say to y'all." I felt tears in my eyes. I wiped them away.

Momma reached over and hugged me. "Oh, Deedee. You are a very special woman. You've always needed more. If the Lord is offering it to you, I say take it."

But maybe it was the Devil after all.

30

Christmas Eve

I snuck out of my parents' house at two a.m. to go parking with two men in the back of an SUV. If only it were as naughty as it sounded. Unfortunately, it was much naughtier.

Hunter met me at my front door, and we walked down the dark, deserted street. Reed had parked a bit down the road, away from any houses. I climbed in the back and Hunter sat in front, closing the door.

"Shouldn't one of you have stayed back in case Trevor wakes up?" I whispered.

"He's not going to wake up," Reed said in a mock whisper. Then he used his normal speaking voice, "And I think it's alright if we talk out loud, Williams. You really get into this spy stuff, don't you?"

"Even if he did wake up, I don't think he's gonna be looking for his laptop. And if he does, I'll just tell him I couldn't sleep and decided to go over some work stuff," Hunter said.

Guess they'd thought of everything. I opened the laptop they'd left in the back and started searching. Hunter had a list of passwords he'd either already known or gotten from Trevor without much trouble.

I stuck my flash drive in the side and started copying files. Luckily Trevor used his personal computer for work and everything else. It was all on here. Correspondence, trust agreements, letters from law firms. And names. The names of the people trying to break the trust.

This was where the gray area became black and white. I was going to use my leverage and the full force of *Monroe and Williams* to find out anything and everything about these people that I could use against them. Thankfully between Belcaron and Camile, David was still completely distracted. I wasn't sure how I was going to keep this from him. It was going to be dirty, and I hoped I wouldn't come out too soiled.

I started to breathe hard, feeling my anxiety rise as I looked at everything. It was a very well-written trust. Breaking it would indeed take years. Unless Trevor got married first and claimed it. But that wasn't going to happen. I couldn't get a breath in.

"Hey, hey there," Reed said from the front. "Calm down. What are you finding on there?" He reached a hand back and rubbed my knee.

"Everything." I said. "It's everything I'm going to need. Y'all did a good job." I panted again.

"So why are you having a fit back there?"

"I just hate doing this. I hate going behind Trevor's stubborn back," I said.

The two of them laughed from the front seat. But then Reed squeezed my knee. "This is really ok, right? You're not doing anything you could get in trouble for?"

Darn him, it's like he was always in my head. Usually it calmed me, the way he knew me. But tonight, it had the opposite effect. "No, it's fine."

"Reed, are you sure we should go along with this?" Hunter whispered.

"Not really," Reed said.

I closed the computer. "Well, too late. Here's your computer. Your part is done. And you know what'll happen to you if you try to tell me not to do something."

Reed and Hunter looked at each other and both got out of the car at the same time. They opened the two back doors and slid in, sitting on either side of me.

And then they were both biting my neck, sinking their teeth in, on either side. "Uuuhhh!" I cried.

"Whatever you do, Daphne, don't make love to us," Reed whispered in my ear. Then his hand slid up my leg, under my coat. "What is going on under here?" he said as his hand explored.

"A little Christmas Eve present I thought you'd like," I said teasingly. I unbuttoned my long coat. Underneath I was wearing red satin lingerie with white fur trim. And knee-high black boots. It was silly, but I couldn't help it when I saw it in the store.

I opened my coat and their eyes went wide. I took the coat off and was suddenly chilled. It was cold in the car. My nipples stood erect through the sheer fabric.

"Oh, darling, you're cold!" Hunter said, running a hand over my breast. He tore off his shirt and leaned into me, kissing me, his hot skin pressed up against mine. His hand slipped under the silky fabric, his fingers finding my nipple.

"Uuuhhh, Hunter!" I moaned.

Reed's hands were exploring the silken fabric, too. He had them up the little skirt of the lingerie top and was working my panties down. His fingers slid down my thighs, leaving a trail of fire behind them. His mouth moved back to my neck and his hand slid up in between my thighs. One finger slipped inside me and I moaned against Hunter's lips.

They were so eager, so aroused, their hands and mouths everywhere at once. All I could do was feel them roving over my body, stimulating every part of me until my entire body was pulsing. Then hunter pulled me onto his lap, facing him.

"I need you, beautiful. Oh, Daphne," he whispered, and I could feel him, hard and ready, pressing against my slit.

I lowered myself onto him, slowly taking him all the way in. I was dripping wet and he slid into me up to the hilt, taking my breath away. Hunter pulled my body to his, crushing me to him, and began pumping into me.

He was so deep inside me I could barely take it. I was going to cum on him and it was going to be soon. I laid my head against his shoulder as he held me to him, and I opened my eyes. Reed's crystal blue irises watched me and burned with desire. When his eyes met mine, my orgasm erupted and a wail ripped from my chest. My whole body was rocked, but my eyes never left Reed's.

Hunter could feel me cumming on him and he swelled inside me. He moaned my name and I felt him shoot into me. I pressed down onto him, taking him deep inside, my arms wrapped tightly around him.

"I love you, Hunter," I whispered as he came down. "I love you so much."

"I love you, too, Daphne," he said, kissing my lips.

I slid off Hunter's lap and turned to Reed, who was sitting with his back against the door. The look on his face took my breath away. I laid back against Hunter and he cradled me against his hot chest. I spread my legs wide for Reed and slid a finger down, into myself and back out. He watched, then climbed on top of me.

I could feel the weight of him pressing me into Hunter. His massive chest crushed me, but I only wanted to hold him tighter. My arms came around his back and my nails dug in as he entered me.

Reed filled me until I couldn't breathe. I moaned, all the air being forced out of my lungs, then rushing back in again as he pulled out and I felt the exquisite caress inside my body.

"Oh, my love," I whispered in his ear. "My darling Reed. I've needed you inside me so badly! Uuuhhh!"

"Daphne," he moaned. I could feel myself dripping on him, Hunter's cum, my cum, making a puddle under me. Knowing Reed would cum in me soon made my pussy convulse.

"Oh, god, Reed, I want to feel you cum in me. I need you!"

He slammed into me and I screamed, cumming on his hard cock. He pushed in deeper and I came so hard my head spun. And Reed kept thrusting, harder and deeper. Then I felt him pulse and he was cumming in me. I could feel it and I moaned with him.

Reed kissed me hard, his tongue finding mine. His massive arm held my body to him, and we lay there, panting.

Reed laid his head on my shoulder, his lips brushing my neck. I could feel his breath coming in and out of his chest, slow and steady. I laid my head back and felt Hunter's heartbeat. It was the most wonderful place to be, smashed between my two lovers, having sated them and been sated by them. But it wasn't complete. I missed Trevor.

"Mmm, Santa sure filled my stocking," I laughed.

Hunter's laugh was so loud it startled me. Reed just chuckled against me.

"Come on boys, you need to go. Trevor could wake up early. It is Christmas morning, after all. I wish I could be there with you," I said sadly. Christmas morning on the farm sounded like the most magical thing I could think of.

"Then come," said Hunter. "Stop worrying about giving Trevor his space."

"That is a very bad idea. He'd have to watch me be your girlfriend again and I don't think he's in a good place for that right now. Not after David's wedding. He doesn't understand yet. But he will," I said quietly.

Then I laughed.

"What's so funny?" Hunter asked.

"I didn't tell you yet, but my parents have us all figured out."

"What?" they both said simultaneously.

"Yep. Daddy even said you could all stay the night in his house. I about fainted."

"You mean we could've been doing this in a bed?" Reed said, shifting and almost falling off the bench seat.

"Yes, but he'd probably be standing outside the door with the shotgun afterwards. He said one of you better make me an honest woman, so he doesn't have to worry about Chad coming back," I laughed.

"Sounds pretty good to me," Hunter said into my hair.

"God, I hope none of us have to worry about that yank coming back," Reed said, putting his clothes on.

I turned my face up to Hunter and he looked into my eyes, a longing there that pulled at my heart. "Daddy's vote was for you, sugar," I whispered to him. A mile-wide smile spread across his face and he kissed the top of my head.

I sat up and Reed held my coat up so I could slip back into it. I grabbed my panties and stuffed them in my pocket. I really didn't want them to go. But I had a lot of work to do, and we all had to be up for Christmas morning in a few hours.

Hunter and Reed walked me back to my house, my hands in each of theirs. I kissed them both goodnight and slipped inside. The glowing feeling lasted in my heart until I felt the flash drive, heavy in my pocket. I ran up to my room and began my research.

31

Christmas

It was after eight when I finally padded downstairs. I'd stayed up until the sky began to lighten doing research. I'd found out a lot. I thought I had what I needed to end the lawsuit. I just didn't know if I was willing to pull the trigger yet.

I yawned as I came down the staircase, stretching my arms.

"Good morning sleepy head," Momma said. She was sitting in the living room sipping coffee. "Santa came, baby!"

"What?" I asked, rubbing sleep from my eyes. I looked and there were indeed new presents under the tree. And the old stocking from my childhood that Momma put up every year had been filled to overflowing. "Wow. I thought I'd get coal this year."

"Oh hush, you've been very good."

"I don't know about that, Momma."

"Well, I bet all those people you help would say so. You know, I hear about you and David all the time, even up here. How you fight for people who've been wronged, and you get them the medical help and time off work and things they need. I'd say you've been very good."

"I get paid pretty well for it, Momma. It's not a selfless act."

"You keep trying to tell yourself that, but we know you could be at a bigger firm, making more money. You could be fighting for the other side, but you're not. Ever wonder why you do that?" Momma asked.

I never had. I thought I wanted to be with David, to learn from him, and because we really did work well together. But when I thought about it, that was because I did care. I cared that our clients got a fair shake. I'd never realized it before. "I guess you're right, Momma."

"You know I am. Momma always knows best."

"I need coffee," I said, shuffling into the kitchen.

"Morning sunshine!" Daddy said from the kitchen table where he sat reading his paper. He sounded just like Hunter. No wonder Daddy liked him.

"Morning Daddy. Merry Christmas." I poured myself coffee and took a long drink. It was divine.

"Merry Christmas, kiddo. Sure is nice to have you here. It's been too long."

"I know. I promise I'll come back more often."

"You ready to open presents? Momma's been sitting out there for two hours waiting for you. She's pretty excited."

We joined Momma by the tree, and I passed out gifts to everyone like I used to do. Daddy got scarves for me and Momma, which we promptly traded. He never could remember the styles we liked. Then Momma went behind the tree and pulled out a big box. She had a wicked grin on her face as she handed it to me.

"We special ordered this for you, Deedee. We really hope you can use it," Momma said. Both my parents smiled at me. Nervously, I opened the box.

"Towels?" I asked.

"Well, take 'em out!" Momma said.

I lifted a towel out of the box. 'Hers' was monogrammed on the front. I lifted out the next towel, 'His' was embroidered in the same navy blue. There were two more towels in the box. I pulled the next one out in disbelief. 'His'. And 'His' again when I pulled the final towel out of the box. My parents burst out laughing and I wanted to die of embarrassment.

"Are you two for real right now?" I asked. "I think you're going senile and I'm going to have to put y'all in a home soon," I said, stuffing the towels back in the box.

"Don't you like them, Deedee?" Momma said and they both collapsed in a fit of giggles on the sofa.

"Very funny."

We spent the rest of the day catching up. I told them everything. How all this craziness came to be. About my poor behavior. About the trust. They were intrigued by Trevor's story. And they stood by my decision to 'interfere', as they put it. I'd never been so close to them.

The next morning my folks dropped me off at the airport and I promised to come home soon. Daddy gave me a stern warning to be careful, and I said I would. I hoped I wasn't lying to him. I flew back to Charleston alone and the city felt a little emptier.

I went straight to the office and got to work. No one else was in, even though it was a Monday. I decided not to make my assistant come in til tomorrow. By that evening I'd set everything in motion. Now I just had to wait. They would respond one way or the other, and everything would hinge on that.

I picked up my phone and my hand shook as I called Reed. I needed to hear his voice.

"Hi," he said in a monotone. I could hear lots of voices in the background.

"Hi," I said, my voice shaking. He didn't sound very happy to hear from me.

"Hold on a minute," he said in the same uninterested tone. I started to breathe hard. "Ok, I can talk now. How are you, *baby*?"

That was a pretty good joke for him, but I couldn't laugh. I was starting to hyperventilate. "Reed," I breathed.

"Hey, now, what's going on? Everything ok?"

"I don't know. I did it. I could be in big trouble. I'm freaking out a little."

"Good grief, Williams, what did you do?"

When he used my last name like that it always calmed me. Brought me out of my head and back down to earth. "Maybe a little bit of blackmail?" I squeaked.

"Oh, for crying out loud. You know, you're making it real hard for me not to punch Trevor. Ok, tell me."

I explained everything I'd done, and Reed listened. He was a little shocked, which was hard to do. I would have been smug if I wasn't so terrified.

"I'm going to come back as soon as I can, ok? I'll get the first flight out. Oh Daphne," he sighed, exasperated.

"I know," said. "I know."

There were a few moments of silence. Then I broke it. "Don't tell Hunter, please. He'll just worry. And maybe think less of me. And I don't want him to."

"Daphne, Hunter will never think less of you. If anything, he'll be even more awed by you. You've stuck your neck out for a friend without being asked, without even knowing if there will be a reward in the end. Honey, you are magnificent."

I didn't know what to say. So many thoughts ran through my head. Why was I doing this? For Trevor, or for me? There was no 'us' anymore to do it for. But I still held onto the hope that there would be. So, was I completely selfish, or selfless? I gave up. I needed Reed here to sort out my head.

"Thank you. Please come back to me," I said. And I realized I'd never said that to a man before. I always made them beg me for every second of my time. It was like I billed them for hours, and the payment was emotional, not monetary. But now I could admit to myself and to another person that I needed them. It was a revelation.

"I will," Reed said.

"I need you, Reed!" I said, wanting to scream it from the rooftops.

"I know." He said it quietly. And he did know. He knew everything in my crazy head, and he loved me for all of it.

"I have to go," I said. "I need to make a phone call."

"Yeah, you do."

Frustrating, impossible, wonderful man. I hung up and called Trevor.

32

New Year's Eve

"Trevor, I have something I have to tell you. And since you won't answer my calls, I'm leaving a message. I hope you will at least listen to it.

I need you. I NEED you, Trevor. I love you. I know you don't want to hear it and you can't understand right now, but I never loved David. Have Reed explain it to you.

None of it works without you. Not me, not Reed, not Hunter. We need you. Have Hunter explain it to you.

Trevor, I need the world. And you are the only one who can give it to me; give me faith in humanity. I need your mind, your intellect, and, ok, your body. I'll admit it. But without you, I can't be me. I'm not whole. You pull me out of myself, bringing out the best me, making me better. I can't explain this over the phone. Please, just talk to me."

I ended the call. I was drained. Mentally, emotionally, physically. I'd done everything I could today. All the balls were in other courts. I went home and crawled into bed.

I woke to soft kisses on my shoulder and a warm body sliding into my bed. Reed! I rolled over and he took me in his arms. I snuggled into him, running my fingers over every exquisite ridge of his abdomen. Just having him here lifted a weight off of me.

Reed kissed me softly on my lips, pulling me in tighter. I flung my arms around him, pressing my breasts to his hard chest. His hand slid down my body, grabbing my thigh and gently pulling my leg over him. And then he was inside me.

Slowly, quietly, Reed pushed into me. A soft moan escaped me and was muffled by his kiss. Oh, god, Reed! I loved him so much. My need to be physically close to him was overwhelming, and he seemed to need it, too. We'd been apart for so many months, and then never alone. I clung to him, taking him into me.

Reed made love to me, gentle and slow, but with a burning desire that flamed through me. The heat between us grew until we were both covered in sweat, still clinging to each other, still moving as one until we burst at the same time. Reed's hand seized my thigh and he thrust deep inside me. My leg locked around his back, holding him, my fingers clawing his back.

It was a silent climax, only the sound of our breath coming in and out in heavy gasps. We didn't move. We didn't let up on the hold we had on each other. We were still until our breath slowed, and I opened my eyes.

Reed's beautiful blue eyes gazed at me. I smiled and kissed him again. We both collapsed onto our backs, intertwining our fingers and savoring the afterglow. I could have stayed there forever. But I had to get to the office.

"Wanna be my assistant today?" I asked, turning my head to his gorgeous face.

"Mmm, that could be fun. Will you wear those black shoes with the red bottoms and a very short skirt, and tell me I made the coffee wrong and need to be disciplined?"

"You are so naughty," I said, playfully smacking him. "But sure, I mean that's how I treat Henry all the time."

Reed rolled over and grabbed me, kissing me hard. "Vixen," he said.

"Really, I was going to make poor Henry come in today, but I'm sure he'd much rather have the day off. And the less he knows about this, the better."

"Yes, boss," he said, kissing me again.

Reed looked adorable in his suit and tie. I'd never seen him wear one. He was the sexiest assistant I'd ever had, no offense to Henry. He was good, too, executing everything with military precision almost before I asked. It was nice having an assistant that could read your mind.

That evening David popped his head into my office. "Hey, Daphne, did you take on a new client?" he asked, looking at his phone. He glanced up. "Oh, hello," he said, seeing Reed.

"David, you remember Reed Butler from Nathaniel's party? He's helping me out today. I gave Henry the day off."

"Yes, of course, nice to see you again." David extended a hand to Reed, then turned to me. "Are you working on a trust case? Bond?"

Oh shit. "Yes, it's for a friend. I'll take care of everything; you don't need to worry about it."

"Alright. They sent a response to my email by mistake, I'll forward it to you. Since when do you take on trusts? Anyway, whatever brilliant maneuvering you did, they're dropping the challenge. Sorry, I read it before I knew it was yours. You really are a savant, Daph. I'm taking off, see you tomorrow. Nice to see you again Mr. Butler."

David disappeared, closing the door behind him and I collapsed into my chair. Reed fell into the chair in front of me and blew out a long breath. We looked at each other and smiled. I opened my email and read. Reed sat, watching my face.

"Oh my god! They're agreeing to everything!" I squeaked.

Reed smiled. He just watched me as I typed and scribbled and began setting everything up for the transfer. I was beyond frenetic. But Reed was calm, a look of reverence on his face.

The wheels of justice moved like molasses during the holiday week. No one was in their offices and there was only so much I could do. By New Year's Eve I was feeling pretty confident everything was ironed out, but I was as nervous as a pregnant nun. They could still back out.

Reed was going to take me out for New Year's Eve. He was being very mysterious about it. We were sitting in my living room in front of the fire. I was already dressed, but Reed was taking his time, still in the suit he'd worn to the office today. I'd decided to give Henry a real holiday week. I was enjoying my new assistant too much.

"Daphne, I've been wondering if you'd wear that black dress you told me about sometime. The one with 'lace and not much of it'?"

"How do you remember that?"

"It's been staring in my fantasies since you told me about it."

"I'm sorry, honey, but you're looking at it."

Reed gave me a questioning look.

"I burned it. In the fireplace." I motioned to the flames.

Reed laughed. "Well, you weren't exaggerating. There's not much of it."

"Are you going to get dressed or what? If you're going in a business suit, then I am way overdressed."

"No, I'm not dressing. I'm not taking you out."

"What? You'd better be joking, Reed Butler. It's New Year's Eve!"

"I'm not joking. I'm not taking you out." There was a knock at the door. "But that's probably your date now."

I looked at him, confused, and starting to get frustrated. "What in heaven's name are you talking about?"

"Well, go on, answer your door." I stood and he spanked me hard on the bottom.

"Oh, you're gonna get it!" I said, glaring at him and swatting his hand away. He just chuckled at me.

I looked through the peephole and my knees went weak. I flung the door open.

Trevor stood in front of me in a tuxedo, a huge bouquet of daffodils in his hand, and that adorable curl falling across his forehead. I sucked in a breath and clamped my hand over my mouth.

"Hi, Daphne," he said softly, a little smile on his face.

"Trevor," I breathed.

"I brought these for you." He handed me the bouquet. Pink and white daffodils. I had no idea where he got them this time of year.

I took the flowers and motioned for him to come in. "Thank you."

"I hope you like them." He stopped in front of me. "The roses didn't work out so well for me the last few times. The single daffodil went over a lot better, as I recall. I thought maybe if I brought every single one in the city…"

Tears were threatening my eyes. Then Trevor smiled at me, flashing his adorable dimples. My breath caught.

"Well, I've got to get going," Reed said, standing. "Good to see you, Trevor." He patted Trevor's shoulder. "Daphne." He kissed my cheek.

"Thanks, Ace," Trevor said, and Reed walked out the door, closing it behind him.

"What are you doing here?" I asked.

"Why is it you never sound happy to see me?" he smiled.

"You never answered me. You never called, never texted. I thought…" I didn't know what he wanted. I couldn't let myself hope.

"I'm sorry about that, truly. My head just wasn't on straight. Will you sit with me, Daphne?"

"Yes, just let me put these in some water." I ran into the kitchen and grabbed a vase, setting it on the counter and gripping the edge of the sink. Tears poured down silently and I caught my breath. I dabbed at them with a towel and put the flowers in the vase.

"You sure look beautiful," Trevor said as I came back and sat beside him.

"Thank you."

"Can you forgive me?" Trevor took my hand and looked into my eyes.

"There's nothing to forgive!" I squeezed his hand.

"Oh, my girl, I don't think I deserve you. I've been a fool. I know you know everything now, and by some miracle you understand. Reed and Hunter explained it to me. And now I understand, too."

"Oh, Trevor," I whispered, draping myself over him. He pulled me in close.

"You smell incredible," he said, nuzzling my neck.

Fire shot down my body. I moaned.

"Let me take you out?" Trevor asked.

I pulled back, looking into his eyes. His lovely, dark and light eyes, the flames of the fire reflected in them.

"If you really want to," I breathed.

"I do. So, stop making it near impossible for me." He leaned in and kissed me softly. I closed my eyes, feeling his lips meet mine. The soft skin just touching, then pressing lightly, sending sparks down to my toes. Trevor pulled back.

"Come on, angel eyes. I'd like to take you on a real date for once."

I was elated and disappointed at the same time. I wanted him to take me in his arms and never let go. But here he was, ultimate sophistication in his tux, asking to take me out on the town on New Year's Eve. It fulfilled a lot of fantasies for me.

Trevor stood and held his hand out to me. I placed my hand in his and he pulled me up, crushing me into his arms and kissing me for real this time. My body went slack in his embrace and I thought I might faint. But his strong arms held me to him and the fire on my lips kept me conscious.

I was in Trevor Bond's arms again and everything was going to be ok.

Trevor released me and held my hand, leading me out the door. We walked out the front of my building and there was the car. The shiny, black Ferrari I'd admired every time I'd been in the shop. Trevor opened the door for me, and I stepped in. It was as luscious inside as it was out. I allowed myself to stroke the soft leather seat once before Trevor slid in beside me.

"I hope you never let Hunter drive this," I said, smiling at him.

Trevor laughed. "Heck no! You think I'm crazy? I'd let you drive it, though. If you'd like."

He knew I would.

"You want to drive it now?" he said, a sly smile on his face.

"Yes!"

We switched seats and I ran my hands over the wheel and the stick shift. Trevor watched me, grinning.

"Hey now, don't make me jealous of my car. I'll have to go get the loaner and take this one away from you."

"Oh, please don't. I promise this stick has got nothing on yours."

Trevor's jaw dropped and he took a second to recover. "Well, alright then," he stuttered.

I started the car and released the brake. I grabbed the stick and took off down the street, getting it up to fourth gear before the stop sign at the end of the block.

"Holy Moses woman!" Trevor screamed. "Let me drive, I changed my mind!"

"Not a chance," I said, speeding off again. The car was a dream to drive. My daddy had an affinity for sports cars, and he'd taught me how to drive in his Porsche Spyder. I'd nearly destroyed the transmission, but Daddy kept me at it until I was almost a pro. We both liked to go fast.

"I've never seen anyone handle a car like you, except for Reed. You have a lot of hidden talents, don't you?" he winked.

"A few," I winked back.

Trevor directed me to the French Quarter and we dropped the car with a valet. He almost drooled when I handed him the keys. More for the car than for me, I thought. It might have bothered me once, but Trevor took me in his arms, and nothing mattered. He hugged me and walked me into *La Serre*.

"How long have you been planning this date?" I asked, surprised. "It takes weeks to get reservations here, maybe years on New Year's Eve!"

"It's not a problem. I can get reservations pretty much anywhere in the city," he shrugged. "Bonjour. J'ai une réservation pour deux sous le nom de Bond," he said to the maître de.

I nearly fell over. "You speak French?"

"I learned a little overseas."

We were ushered to a little candlelit table, off to the side of the dining area, quiet and private.

"I've never been here," I said, my eyes dancing over the gorgeous room. The walls were a deep Kelly green, and golden filigrees adorned everything. The ceiling was made entirely of glass, and the full moon was visible high above. In one corner a pianist played softly on an enormous grand piano, something slow and melodious.

"I hope you like it," Trevor said, gazing into my eyes. He took my hand and kissed my fingers lightly.

A pulse shot through me down to my pelvis. "It's incredible."

"Bonsoir Monsieur, Madame. Est-ce que vous voulez quelque chose à boire pour commencer?" our server said.

Trevor tore his eyes away from mine. "Boinsoir. Bollinger Les Vieilles Vignes Francaises, s'il vous plaît."

"Très bien."

Our waiter shuffled away, and I stared at Trevor. "Seems like you have some hidden talents of your own. How long were you overseas, anyway?"

"Long enough. Daphne, I don't want to keep anything from you anymore. I was married before. Her name was Gigi. It's why I speak French."

"Married? But..."

"I know, the trust. It didn't last. And it wasn't recognized here, in America. We split and I had the marriage annulled before making it official here. It wasn't hard, seeing as how I walked in on her screwing her best friend on our wedding night."

The waiter was back and pouring out glasses of champagne. "Est-ce que vous avez choisi?"

"Oui. Daphne, would you like to see the menu, or do you trust me?"

"I trust you. Anything is fine," I said, completely uninterested in food now.

"Qu'est-ce que vous voulez commander?" the waiter asked.

Trevor ordered something I couldn't begin to understand. I heard *végétarienne*, so I felt safe that I wouldn't be eating snails or calf's brains, at least.

"I'm so sorry," I said, after the waiter left.

"Don't be. It would have been a disaster. I got off pretty easy as it was. I was young, dumb, and horny. I thought I loved her. Thought I might die when she did me like that. Thank God Reed was there to help me through it. If I'd got my hands on that money, I'd probably be dead now. Drug overdose, or speedboat accident, or something. And Daphne, I realized something when I met you. I know what it is to love someone now. And all I want is for you to love me. And if you need all of this," he waved his hand toward the room, "then my love, I'll give it to you. I'll give you everything I have."

Tears threatened again. I reached my hand under the table and found his knee. I caressed him and took a deep breath. "Sweet, wonderful man. All I want is you. I love you more than anything, don't you know that?"

"But you said you needed the world..."

"*This* is not what I meant. You are my world, Trevor. You and Reed and Hunter. But *you* are the one that makes the rest of the world palatable to me. It's in me to love humanity, somewhere, deep down. It surfaces now and again, when we get a particularly heart-wrenching case that I know is unwinnable, but I take it anyway. You are the one who showed me that part of myself. And you are the only one who can cultivate it."

Trevor's eyes teared now, and I pressed my lips together so I wouldn't cry. No sense ruining my face in a beautiful place like this.

"Oh, Daphne, you don't know how much that means to me."

"And I'm sorry, Trevor. So sorry. For David, for all my fool-headedness. And now that you've told me about Gigi, I'm even more sorry."

"It's alright. I *am* a grown man. I should be able to tolerate you being around male co-workers. Just give me some more time before you talk about David, ok?"

"Of course."

The food came and it was divine. I found myself ravenous. The champagne was like nothing I'd ever tasted. I ate until I was fit to burst.

"Are you sure you don't want some more?" Trevor teased me after dessert. I almost never ate cheese, but I'd finished off the entire plate. It was too good, and I was too happy to care.

"Don't go making me self-conscious, now. You'll never get my dress off later."

Trevor's face fell. "Now that would be a darn shame. Daphne, you're a goddess. I worship at your feet. There has never been a more perfect, beautiful woman. How am I doing?"

"It's a start," I laughed.

Trevor stood and held out his hand. "Dancing in the *Starlight Room*?"

Would the surprises never end? "I'd love to."

Trevor drove this time, taking me to a New Year's Eve party at the most beautiful ballroom in the city. The balconies looked out over the water outside a wall of windows. At midnight there would be fireworks over the bay.

"May I have this dance?" Trevor asked, holding his hand out and bowing to me.

I curtsied and took his hand. He whisked me out onto the floor and spun me around. He was incredibly light on his feet. He held me tightly in his arms as he moved me around the room.

"You can dance, too? Did they make you go to prince school or something as part of that trust? I didn't see that clause in there."

"What?" Trevor asked, his eyes going wide.

Oh god! Why had I just said that? Why did I always say the wrong thing to him?

"Trevor, there's something I should tell you." I told him everything we'd done, and placed the blame solely on myself, saying I coerced the boys into helping me. He looked unconvinced.

"Daphne, how can you ever expect me to trust you when you do something like this?" Trevor led me off the dance floor and over to a table in the corner where it was quieter.

"I know. I wanted to help you, desperately. And I think I have. If you want me to undo all of it, I will. But if you sign the agreement, it will all be over, and you won't have to spend years in court. Really, I was doing it for you."

Trevor looked at me, exasperated. "You are fool-headed, you know that?"

And then he kissed me. He took me in his arms and held me to him like he'd never held me before. His lips crushed mine, his tongue pushed into my mouth, devouring me. I couldn't breathe. I couldn't think.

"Daphne, I wasn't lying when I said I would give it all to you. If this is what you need to be with me, it's yours. You don't have to go behind my back. Marry me, Daphne. Marry me now and I'll claim the trust. I love you!"

My head spun and I thought I would faint. It was what I had always dreamed of. My prince charming was begging me to marry him. And, lord, he was charming. The little curl fell over his forehead and I reached up to smooth it back. He smiled and I ran my hand over his dimple.

"No."

Trevor's face fell. "What?"

"No. I won't marry you."

"Jesus, Daphne, you give a man some real mixed signals, you know that?"

"You still don't understand. I'm not after your money, Trevor. I didn't fix the trust so it would go to you. I just fixed it so those greedy miscreants wouldn't get it."

Trevor stared at me and then he laughed.

"What's so funny?"

"I just didn't think I'd be so happy that you turned me down, that's all."

"Ouch."

"Oh, come on now, angel eyes. You know I want to marry you, don't you?"

"You do?" I started to hyperventilate.

"Yes, I do. More than anything. And now I know you want me, too."

"Oh Trevor!" I threw my arms around his neck and squeezed with all my might. His hands came around my waist and he pulled me into him.

"Kiss me Daphne?" he said, a question that was really a command.

I pressed my lips to his and he kissed me tenderly, but with an ardor and devotion that burned into my soul.

"It's almost midnight," he whispered. "Dance with me so I can hold you in my arms my love."

He spun me out onto the floor again and I reveled in being in his arms. I laid my head against his shoulder.

"You don't have any other secrets you'd like to divulge to me while I'm in this very good mood, do you? Might be a good time to do it." He chuckled in my ear, his chest rumbling against me.

"Oh lord, I hope not," I sighed.

"Daphne, who is getting the money, if it's not me, and it's not them?"

"The Children's Fund. They're a legal organization that represents children who have no guardians or whose guardians are not able to help them. They also build and run teen homes for kids who are aging out of the system. I've done some pro-bono for them and they are top-notch. But I can change it if you don't like that."

Trevor squeezed me tight.

"Trevor, I can't breathe!" I squeaked.

"Oh! I'm sorry. You're extraordinary, Daphne," he said quietly.

"I know."

Trevor laughed, his chest rumbling against me again. It was the best feeling in the world. Suddenly a huge 'BOOM' shook the room. I jumped in Trevor's arms.

"It's just the fireworks," he laughed. "Almost midnight."

People began counting down around us. Trevor stood, his hands holding my arms, his eyes staring into mine.

"Seven, six, five, four, three, two, one!" the screams erupted around us.

Trevor lowered his mouth to mine and kissed me. I slid my hands up his chest and around his neck, tangling my fingers in his hair. He kissed me forever. Around us people sang 'Auld Lang Syne'. The song was over when we finally broke apart.

We walked out to the balcony and watched the fireworks. Trevor stood behind me, his arms around my waist, his hard body pressed to my back. I grabbed his hand and raised it to my lips, kissing each of his fingers while the fireworks exploded around us.

"Would you like another dance?" Trevor asked when the show was over.

"Take me home," I said, looking into his eyes.

33

At Last

Trevor drove back to my condo. I kicked my shoes off the minute my feet were inside.

"I don't know why you insist on wearing those," Trevor said.

"So you'll look at my legs," I giggled.

"Trust me, I'm looking anyway," he smiled.

"Mmm, this makes me think of the first time I had you over here. Care for a re-enactment?"

"Something like that," he laughed. Then he scooped me up in his arms and carried me to the bed, laying me down gently.

"Make love to me, Daphne. Oh, god, I love you so much!" Trevor was on top of me, burying his face in my neck, his lips and tongue working me into a frenzy.

"I love you, Trevor!" I moaned.

Trevor's hands slid down my body and grabbed the hem of my dress, pushing the fabric up to my waist. His fingers trailed over my garter belt, then one hand came around and grabbed my ass, squeezing me, making me cry out.

He pulled me up to sitting and slid the dress over my head, then laid me back down, his body pressing onto me. I kissed his lips and ran my hands through his hair, over his back, and around his bulging biceps. I tugged at his bow tie, and unbuttoned his shirt, revealing his sculpted chest. My breath caught.

Trevor knelt over me, straddling my thighs, and took off his shirt. I watched with hungry eyes. He reached down and removed my bra, his eyes devouring my breasts. His mouth came down on me, his hand taking a breast and kneading it, working it with his tongue.

"Uuuhhh!" I cried, and he moaned on me, sending tingles through my sensitive flesh.

"Oh Daphne, you're amazing. Your body is incredible!" He reached down and unhooked my garter belt, pulling it down and off in one swift motion, along with both stockings and my panties. "I need to feel all of you."

Trevor slid his hands up my body as he kissed me, running his tongue over my bottom lip. I quivered. I bit his shoulder and grabbed his hard, round ass, pulling him to me. His cock pressed into my hip and I throbbed with desire.

"I need you, Trevor. I need you inside me!" I whispered.

Trevor groaned and stood, removing the rest of his clothing. His eyes ravaged me, and mine devoured him, settling on the wings and hammers tattoo on his arm. God it was sexy.

Trevor laid back down, taking me in his arms, his knee coming up between my thighs and spreading me open to him. I felt myself drip at the thought of him inside me. And then he was there. He looked in my eyes and I raised my hips to him, pushing the head of his cock inside me.

Trevor moaned and pushed the length of his shaft into me. My whole body trembled. I cried out, low and guttural from my chest. Shocks pulsed through my chest and I gripped Trevor's back. He slid out and thrust into me again, sending another shockwave through me.

We were frenzied, manic, weeks of lust, desire, and longing pouring out and into each other. Our bodies became one; wanting, needing, feeling as one. I knew we would cum together. I could feel him swell and throb and my own rapturous build coming to a peak.

I pulled his mouth to mine, our lips and tongues meeting, before we both screamed out, our bodies pressing together, trying to get closer as we throbbed around each other. My heart pounded near out of my chest, and my body pulsated in Trevor's arms.

He held me to him, his body rigid, but his arms cradling me. Tears ran down my cheeks as I came down from my orgasm. I kissed his sweet face, his lips, his neck. He kissed me back, holding me in those wonderful arms.

"I love you, Daphne Olivia," Trevor whispered.

"I love you, Trevor."

We lay there, holding each other, just looking. Just feeling. It was the best way to start the new year I could imagine.

34

Airplanes

I stretched out in the late morning light. My eyes flew open. Had I dreamed it all? It just couldn't be true. But it was.

Trevor lay sleeping beside me, his back rising and falling rhythmically as he lay on his stomach. His tousled curls fell in disarray on his head and I reached out and toyed with one, pulling it and watching it bounce back. My heart throbbed.

I watched him for a long time. My eyes moved over every inch of him. He was beautiful, and he was mine.

My phone buzzed on the nightstand. I picked it up and it was a text from Reed.

-Can we come over?-

My heart swelled.

-Yes, my darlings, please come over-

I sighed. I felt Trevor's lips on my shoulder. He kissed my skin softly, running his hand over my belly and pulling me into him.

"Good morning, angel eyes," he whispered.

"Hi."

"How'd you sleep?" Trevor asked.

"Like the dead. The very happy, very satisfied dead. It's almost eleven!"

"Mmm, perfect New Year's Day. Guess we missed the parade."

"The parade? Really? Parades are just about the most boring things I can think of," I said.

"Oh, thank god. I'd be happy to never have to sit through another parade. But Hunter loves them."

"Of course he does," I giggled. "Guess one of us will have to take him sometimes. They're on their way over."

"They're probably chomping at the bit to see if you accepted my proposal or not."

"You told them you were going to propose? What did they think of that?" Thoughts ran rampant through my head. How would they feel if I'd said yes? I could only legally marry one man. It didn't seem fair.

"My darling, we all just want you to be happy. Whatever you chose would make us all happy."

I snuggled into Trevor's chest and his arms came around me. I was happy, truly happy. "Let's get dressed. We have a lot to do today."

"It's New Year's Day. Don't tell me you have work to do. I was thinking we wouldn't get dressed all day..." Trevor kissed me and I shivered, shocks running through me.

"Mmm, come on. I need to show you something, all of you. Before you sign the trust agreement. I want to file it tomorrow. Remove the axe from above my head."

"Axe?"

"I may have slightly skirted the law in setting this whole thing up. But don't worry. The settlement terms were more than satisfactory. I don't think anyone will be complaining. I'll just feel better when it's over."

"You broke the law? Daphne." Trevor looked at me, fear in his eyes. "I'm so sorry. I wish I wasn't such a blockhead. Give it to me now. I'll sign it."

"No. Go get dressed like I told you, now. Before the boys get here. I don't know how long my willpower can stand against the three of you."

Trevor smiled. "Well, at least we have sheer numbers to our advantage, because you hold all the other cards, angel eyes."

Trevor kissed me and went to take a shower. When he was done, I slipped in. I came out of the bathroom wrapped in my silk robe to see three gorgeous men sitting on my bed, all eyes on me. I ran over and jumped in Hunter's lap, throwing my arms around his neck. He smiled a huge smile.

"I missed you!" I said kissing him. He held me tight.

"Missed you, too, beautiful."

I hugged him again, then leaned over and kissed Reed. "I'm still mad at you for dumping me last night. That was very sneaky," I laughed.

"Sorry," he smiled. "Means to an end. So?"

"So what?" I asked.

"What was your answer? Trevor won't tell us."

"I said no."

Trevor laughed. "She wasn't gentle about it, either. Flat out 'NO!' right to my face. Didn't even act like she was thinking it over."

"So, where does that leave everything?" Hunter asked, his voice quavering.

"It leaves us here, all together, finally. Trevor is going to sign the agreement, and none of us will have to worry about being millionaires anymore," I laughed. "Well, I might. I don't plan on retiring anytime soon, so you'll all just have to deal with it. Now, shoo, out of my room. I'm getting dressed."

"Can't we stay and watch?" Trevor smiled at me.

"No! Out, you naughty boys! I have something y'all need to see and you're making it really hard for me."

They filed out and I put on my cutest shorts and a silk top tied at the waist. "All right, I'm driving, come along now," I said emerging from my room.

"Here, eat this," Trevor said, handing me a glass with a straw. I took it and sipped. Mmm, strawberry-mango and orange.

"Thank you, lover," I said, and we all headed to the car.

I drove to the airfield and pulled up to the huge hangar.

"Are we flying somewhere?" Hunter asked.

"No, not unless Reed wants to fly us somewhere. Come on inside," I said, getting out of the car. I led them inside and looked around. I hadn't actually seen it yet with my own eyes, and it was even better than I thought it would be.

"Wow!" Reed said. "These are beautiful. Whose are they?"

"Trevor's," I said. "If he wants them."

"What?" Trevor asked, searching my face.

"I didn't give away all the assets in the agreement. The cash is going to the Children's Fund, and the airline is going to the people challenging the trust. Though I don't think they deserve it. I find a little carrot with the stick gets things done much more quickly. But these are the private planes. The ones your father used when he was here, and for his friends. I held them back. The hangar, too. I thought maybe..."

Trevor grabbed me in his arms and kissed my neck. "You're amazing," he whispered in my ear.

"And, I won't bore you with all the legal stuff, but you don't have to get married to claim it. It's yours as soon as you sign."

I thought I saw disappointment on his face, but only for a minute. Then he was smiling from ear to ear. He scooped me up again and held me in his warm, strong arms. He sighed against me, crushing my whole body. He held me there, against his chest, his breathing hard and uneven. When he pulled back his eyes were damp.

"Does that mean you like it?" I asked.

"I love it. I love you." Trevor kissed me.

"Well, shoot, does this mean we get to work on planes now, boss?" Hunter said, smiling a huge smile.

"Lord, I think it does," Trevor whispered, looking into my eyes. "And now I have everything."

Reed cleared his throat. "You looking for a pilot?" he asked. "I might know someone."

"Woo!" Hunter yelled. "Come here, you two!" He wrapped his long arms around me from behind and kissed my neck.

"Come over here, Captain Butler," I said. Reed was running a hand down one of the shiny planes.

"Captain has a very nice ring to it," he said, kissing me softly on the lips.

"Ok, then. Whenever you're ready we can go to my office and make it official. I'll be able to file everything tomorrow."

The boys looked at each other.

"When can we fly them?" Trevor asked.

"It'll take a few days at least to get all the paperwork done. If I can speed things through. Maybe a week?" I answered.

They shared another look and now I felt left out. "Why?"

"No reason," Reed said, taking my hand and kissing it. "Can we look inside?"

They spent the next hour under the hoods and in the cockpits of the half-dozen little planes. One could fit a few dozen passengers, but the rest were fairly small. They were pretty, though, sleek and shiny.

I sat in the hangar office, watching them through the glass, my heart glowing. They were having so much fun. Reed made his way in to me. Hunter and Trevor were still looking at engines.

"So," he said, taking me in his arms and looking into my eyes, "can you take some time off soon? So we can all go somewhere together, just the four of us? No work."

"I think I can swing that. David owes me some time off, and our load is pretty light for now. Vacation sounds wonderful."

"Good then. As soon as we can fly that Piper M350. Lord, I can't wait to get her in the air." His eyes sparkled.

"Where will we go?" I asked.

"Do you think you'd let me decide? Make all the arrangements?"

"Since when do you ask for my permission, Captain Butler?"

"Since I found out how sneaky you can be when you want to find something out. And I really don't want to make you mad right now," he laughed.

I poked him in the ribs, and he jumped back. I grabbed him and kissed him. He held me tight.

For the next nine days I had a different man in my bed every night. I never knew who was going to be waiting for me when I got home. They had worked that out amongst themselves. And every night was a revelation. The three raw pieces of my heart grew back together into one glowing, full organ.

Trevor had signed the agreement and I'd filed it the next day. Yesterday he'd gotten the keys to the hangar. Today was my last day of work for two weeks. I had no idea where we were going, and I'd told David I would be out of touch. He was very surprised.

I left early, a few hours after lunch, having wrapped everything up and put a bow on it. I was excited to see who would meet me at home today. I barely even knew I was driving before I was home and walking in my door.

I walked in and froze, letting the door slam shut behind me. Trevor, Reed, and Hunter stood in my living room looking as handsome as could be.

Hunter was wearing the fedora I'd gotten him, along with a leather jacket and khaki pants. I wanted to tear open that button down shirt when I saw him.

Reed was wearing his dress blues, his broad chest straining the jacket, his square jaw accentuated by the white, black, and gold cap.

My heart pounded in my chest when I looked at him. He smiled his small smile at me.

And Trevor, oh, lord, Trevor, he had his millionaire playboy look on today. Fitted dress shirt, unbuttoned just enough to give me a peek at the toned pecs beneath. Sport coat, dress pants, and Ferragamo shoes. I started to breath hard.

"Don't you all look..." I couldn't finish, I just stood there and undressed them with my eyes.

"Look boys, we've got her speechless," Trevor said, smirking. "Didn't think that was possible."

Reed stepped forward. "Ma'am, we're here to whisk you away. We'll wait while you pack. We're going to a quiet spot on the Georgia coast for one week. You probably won't need very many clothes."

I smiled at him devilishly. "Not many, or not *any*?"

Hunter blushed and looked at the floor, Trevor laughed, and the corner of Reed's mouth turned up, his crystal eyes sparkling.

"I'll be right back then," I said, going into my room and locking the door. My breath was coming fast, and I was excited beyond reason. A week, isolated and alone with all of them! It might kill me by the end, but it would be worth it.

I showered and lotioned and perfumed my body. I pulled out a very naughty black satin lingerie set and put it on under a skin-tight crimson sheath that left little to the imagination. Tonight, we wouldn't need to imagine anything. I slipped on the Louboutins for Reed.

When I came out, they all jumped up and stared. I walked across the room and their eyes followed me silently. I carried my suitcase over to the door, but not one of them moved.

"Well? Is one of you going to take my bag down? Or maybe y'all want to stay here while I go?" I teased them.

They jumped. Hunter got to my bag first and scooped it up, holding his arm out. "After you, ma'am."

I swayed my hips as I walked, leading them to my car, feeling their eyes on me.

"Aren't we going to take the truck?" Hunter asked.

"No, sugar, I'm driving," I said.

"Only to the hangar," Reed said.

They loaded their luggage into my trunk, and I drove us all to the hangar. Trevor jumped out and opened it up and I parked my car inside. I stepped out and the boys began loading the luggage into the sleek little plane Reed loved so much.

"Care to be my co-pilot, ma'am?" Reed asked, holding his hand out to me.

"I'd love to!" I said, taking his hand and pressing myself to him.

"Love the shoes," he whispered.

Reed led me to the plane and helped me inside. There were rose petals sprinkled everywhere, their deep scent filling the air.

"Oh!" I said, holding my hand to my mouth.

Inside the little plane was nicer than my Mercedes. Reed sat me down and fiddled with things, handing me a headset.

"You're going to want your sunglasses. And don't touch anything," he said, rather authoritatively. It made me want to touch something. But the panel was pretty intimidating. I'd never been in a cockpit before.

Reed climbed in the other side and Hunter and Trevor took their places in the back. I looked over my shoulder at them and grinned. They looked good enough to eat.

"So, can I touch this, Captain Butler?" I asked, sliding my hand up his thigh.

Reed's eyes met mine. "Vixen," he whispered. "Put on your headset."

"Yes, Captain!" I said, saluting him.

"Wrong hand," he smirked.

The engine roared to life and I jumped a little. Up here in the front I could see everything. I started to get nervous as we sailed out of the hangar. Reed was on the radio talking in pilot code. It was incredibly sexy, and I had to squeeze my hands between my knees to stop myself from putting one in his lap. I put my sunglasses on.

We went slowly at first, but then started to pick up speed. And before I knew it, we were in the air. My stomach dropped as we left the ground and I felt dizzy. I closed my eyes, scared of what I was seeing. It felt like I was floating in the air, nothing holding me up. It was very different from sitting in the back with the tiny window. I felt Reed touch my leg.

"Open your eyes, silly girl. You're missing it." His fingers played over my knee, then ran up my thigh before he put his hand back on the yoke.

I opened my eyes and squeaked. Reed laughed.

"Don't you trust me, Daphne?" he asked, his voice sweet and seductive. When he said my name, a pulse ran through me.

"Yes, Reed," I said into my headset.

"You wanna try her out?" he asked, an excited smile on his face.

"I don't know," I said, my hands shaking.

"It's ok, I won't let anything happen. Just put your hands on the yoke like this." He guided my hands, caressing my fingers as he pressed them onto the handles.

My adrenaline spiked when he let go. I froze, my hands gripping the thing.

"You're flying," Reed said. "Now, take her a little to the right, slowly."

I turned the yoke and the plane began to turn. I squeaked. Reed laughed. I had a wicked idea. I pushed the yoke in, not too hard, but it had more of an effect than I was expecting. My stomach was in my throat and Reed grabbed his yoke, evening us out. Hunter and Trevor yelled something from the back.

"You are insane, sometimes, Williams!" he hollered, but his eyes were smiling.

I laughed. "Got you!"

"If I let you fly some more will you promise not to kill us?"

"Not with my flying," I said, running my hand up his leg again.

"Dear lord," Reed mumbled.

"How long are we in the air for?" I asked.

"About an hour."

"And, do you have to be up here the whole time?"

Reed looked at me speculatively. "It's a really good idea, yes."

"Hmm, but maybe I could distract you *a little*?" I asked coyly.

"I thought you didn't want to kill us while we were in the plane," he said, but there was fire in his voice.

"I'll be back soon," I said, and took the headset off.

I couldn't wait any longer. I was going to explode. Reed's uniform, hearing him on the radio, it was too much. But I thought I might give him a little show first. I climbed between the front seats and into the back, where Hunter and Trevor sat next to each other, facing the front.

I laid across both their laps and their eyes opened wide. Reed turned and looked back at us and I smiled wickedly at him, placing one spiked foot up on the window of the plane and running my hands down my body. I grabbed the hem of my dress and slid it up, revealing the black satin garters and thong. Hunter and Trevor both sucked in a breath.

"Touch me," I said to Hunter. My ass was in his lap and I could feel him growing against my hip. Trevor was poking into my shoulder.

Hunter ran his hand from my ankle, slowly up my leg, gliding over my black silk stockings. His fingers dug gently into my thigh and I moaned, pulses shooting through my pussy. Slowly his fingers made their way under my thong and he dipped one into my wet spot, sliding it up and playing with my clit.

"Ooohhh!" I moaned. I looked up at Trevor and he looked as devilish as I felt. "You, too, go on now."

Trevor's hands came down on my breasts and he worked them out of the dress and began playing with my nipples. I screamed with pleasure and looked at Reed, who was watching me intensely.

Hunter sunk two long fingers in me and my body spasmed, my back arching. "Aaahhh!" I screamed while he fingered me. "Stop, Hunter," I breathed. "I want to cum on you."

Hunter looked like he might faint. I stood, as best I could inside the plane, and tore my dress off, revealing the black satin corset cradling my breasts. I knelt down and unzipped Hunter's pants and pulled him out. I put my mouth on him and gave him a few good pulls, feeling him swell. I loved sucking his cock the most. His look of complete and utter worship made me ache.

"Sit on the floor, right here," I told him. I straddled his hips, giving Reed the best view of my backside. I wanted him to watch Hunter's long cock sliding in and out of me. The thought almost made me cum as I slid him into me, slowly, taking every inch one at a time.

I rode up and down his hard cock a few times, feeling my ecstasy build. Then I reached over and pulled Trevor out of his pants, stroking him. I leaned my head down into his lap and took him in my mouth. He moaned, watching me.

I sucked Trevor hard, taking him deep, moving my tongue on the underside of him. He was so hard, ready to burst almost. Guess my show was working. I felt my orgasm coming and I rode Hunter faster and grabbed onto Trevor's cock, running my hand up and down while my tongue worked his head. I felt him swell and my orgasm exploded.

I slammed down on Hunter, taking his full length, making him cry out as I throbbed on him. He grabbed my hips and thrust into me, making me cum again. The man was incredible.

Trevor burst in my mouth and I greedily swallowed him, squeezing out every drop with my hand, my tongue running around and around his head.

Hunter pulled me onto him, thrusting up so hard he lifted me off the ground. I felt him shoot into me and I screamed. My pussy still throbbed from my orgasm.

I kissed Trevor's thigh and laid against Hunter's chest, kissing his neck. I slid off of him and crawled to the front, squeezing between the two seats, putting my head in Reed's lap. I looked up at him, my pupils dilated with arousal.

"Jesus, Daphne," he said, sucking in his breath.

I opened his pants and released him. He sprang up, hard and sticky with pre-cum. He was incredibly aroused. I took him in my mouth and moved my tongue until he cried out and his head flew back.

Then his hand was on me. Oh god, his hands were like magic. He kept one hand on the yoke, but the other slid down my back and he plunged his fingers into me, stroking and caressing me inside. I moaned on his cock and his chest rumbled. Then his fingers slid down to my clit and I pulled my mouth off him, the pleasure so intense I couldn't breathe.

He circled my clit and I sucked him back into my mouth, gripping him with my hand and working him furiously. I wanted him so badly, wanted to taste him, wanted to cum on his god-damned magic fingers.

"Uuuunnnngggghhhh!" I screamed out as my orgasm hit me. I went down on Reed again as my juices poured onto his hand. I felt him swell and throb and then he shot into my mouth. He plunged his fingers into me again and I almost choked but managed to swallow everything without spilling a drop.

I put him back away and turned around to grab my dress. Hunter and Trevor were staring at me, their eyes like saucers. I smiled smugly to myself as I slid back into my dress. I found a napkin and cleaned myself up a bit. I was a tad messy. Then I went back up front and sat down next to Reed, putting my headset back on.

No one said anything. Reed just stared out the front of the plane, a look on his face that was part shock, part awe, and part euphoria.

Finally, Reed spoke. "I think I'm going to have to teach one of those knuckleheads back there to fly if we're going to be doing this often. I didn't think I'd ever find something I wanted to do more than fly."

"Are we going to be doing this often?" I asked, smiling at him.

"Well, if the four of us go into the charter business, then it seems likely."

"Charter business?" I asked.

"Yes. Trevor has already started a business plan. He's been putting in hours doing research. He thinks we can run a successful charter and touring business with just the planes in that hangar. Of course, we will have to hire another pilot, as well. I'm sure Trevor is dying to tell you all about it."

Interesting. I liked the idea. "But I don't know anything about planes. I'll stick to being legal counsel for y'all, if that's ok."

"Honey, nothing you do is *ok*. You are extraordinary in every way. We're almost there. Don't touch anything," he warned me again in his military voice. It made me kind of hot when he did that.

"Stop telling me not to do things, you know what it does to me," I teased him.

"Yes, Williams, I know," he smiled.

35

The Cabin

The landing was even worse than taking off. I couldn't keep my eyes open no matter how hard Reed laughed. Seeing the ground hurtling toward me was terrifying. I didn't think I'd ever make a very good pilot.

There was a car waiting for us at the airfield, and a little hangar just for Jillian, as Reed had named the plane. I jumped behind the wheel before they could say anything.

"Which way?" I asked when they had all gotten in.

"Here you go," Trevor said, putting the address into my phone and putting it in the holder on the dash.

"Thanks lover," I said, gazing at him.

The cabin wasn't too far from the airfield. We were there in twenty minutes. And a cabin it was. Small, rustic, tucked away next to a nature preserve. No neighbors. Perfect. The boys unloaded the luggage and I stretched before trying to navigate the dirt and stone path in my Louboutins. I hadn't really thought that one through.

Reed unlocked the door and opened it for me. I stepped into a fairytale. The floors and walls were warm glowing wood. A huge stone fireplace dominated an entire wall. It had three arched openings, and a warm fire glowed inside.

On the other side of the room, and as far as I could tell it was the only room, was a curved staircase made of logs and twisting, vining branches that extended up the length of the staircase and across the balcony which served as the second floor hall. A tiny kitchen with a rustic wooden table was tucked into one corner.

I gasped. Candles glowed on tables, and there were flowers everywhere. Gauzy curtains blew in the sea breeze. The wood paneling made it dark and cozy inside, even during the day. In front of the fireplace was an enormous furry white rug, surrounded by plush sofas and chairs.

I kicked my shoes off and walked onto the rug. It felt like a cloud. I turned and saw the boys carrying our bags upstairs. They were so efficient sometimes. Well trained by the Navy, much to my delight. I followed them up the stairs.

"This doesn't look like it has eight bedrooms," I teased.

"Nope. Only two," Reed said.

"Two?" I asked, apprehensively.

Trevor came back through a door and took me in his arms, looking down into my eyes. "I hope you'll be comfortable with that. I know you *always want more*, but *I* think it's twice as many as we need." And the way he said it made me shiver.

"Let's see!" I said, kissing him on the cheek and running in one of the two doors up here. I stopped and frowned. Inside the little room were two twin beds. At least there was an en suite. I turned around and Hunter was standing behind me.

"Look at that little pouty lip," he said, grabbing me around the waist. He picked me up in his arms until my eyes were level with his. "That just about drives me crazy," he whispered and lowered his mouth to mine.

I forgot about the bedroom. I forgot about the cabin. I ran my hands over Hunter's shoulders and melted into his embrace. My lips parted and I slid my tongue over his bottom lip. He tightened his arms around me, and I wrapped my legs around his waist.

"Ahem." Reed cleared his throat.

"Find a room you two," Trevor laughed.

I unwound myself from Hunter and he stuck out his bottom lip, pouting at me. I kissed it and grabbed his hand, dragging him into the other room.

Now this was more like it! The biggest bed I'd ever seen sat in the center of the tiny room. There was one little window and the gauzy curtains blew in the breeze. Two nightstands and a painted wooden chest at the foot of the bed were the only other furniture. And there was an en suite with a jacuzzi tub.

I pulled Hunter's hand until he was in front of the bed. I pushed him down and climbed up on top of him. I unbuttoned the top buttons of that sexy shirt and kissed his chest and up his neck.

"Oh, beautiful," he sighed.

"I was just kidding," Trevor said. I looked at him and stuck out my tongue. He smiled. "Don't tease me, angel eyes."

"You can tease me," Hunter said, pulling me back to him.

"Hunter," Reed said from the doorway.

Hunter sighed. He looked into my eyes. "I love you, Daphne." He sat up with me in his lap and scooped me up, standing and carrying me out of the room.

"Eee!" I squeaked. "Hunter Falco, what in the world are you doing?"

Hunter just smiled at me indulgently and carried me down the stairs. I clung to his neck and prayed we wouldn't both go tumbling down. Reed and Trevor followed behind.

Hunter set me down gently on the sofa and the three men stood in a row facing me. I ran my eyes over each of them and smiled. My heart was so full of love for them.

"Daphne," Reed said, and a shiver ran down my spine when he said my name, "we have something we'd like to ask you."

"Alright," I said, curious.

All at once they knelt before me. My heart raced in my chest. Reed reached out and took my hand in his.

"Daphne, I love you. I can't say I loved you from the moment I saw you, we both know how that went, but from the moment I saw your soul, I loved you. You are, without a doubt, the most extraordinary woman I have ever met. Without you I feel empty. Our souls are meant to be together." Reed pulled something out of his pocket and held it up to me. It was twisted and silver, set with a beautiful pale green stone. "Say you will be mine forever."

Reed looked into my eyes, searching my face. Tears stung my eyes.

"Yes, Reed," I whispered. "I love you so very much."

Reed slipped the ring on my left ring finger and kissed my hand. His eyes sparkled. He took my hand and placed it in Hunter's. I started to breathe hard. I couldn't believe this was happening.

"Daphne, you are the most beautiful woman, inside and out. I've wanted to marry you since the first time I saw you sitting in my momma's house. You fit there, much as you think you don't. All I want to do for the rest of my life is make you happy. Say you'll be mine." Hunter pulled a ring out of his pocket. It had the same twisted silver band but was set with a diamond.

"Yes, Hunter, my darling. I love you," I said.

Hunter's smile beamed at me. He slid the ring onto my finger, and it locked in place with Reed's ring. "I love you," he said, then placed my hand in Trevor's.

Trevor looked up into my eyes and didn't speak. I was lost in the brown and blue, my breath coming in shallow gasps. My head spun and I fainted. When I came to, Trevor was leaning over me, a smile on his face.

"Why is it you always give me the hardest time?" he said, lifting me back to sitting and taking my hand in his. "Are you alright?"

"Yes, I'm ok," I whispered.

"Good." Trevor placed my hand between both of his and looked down at our hands. Then he raised his eyes to mine and smiled, his dimples taking my breath away again.

"Daphne Olivia," he dropped his eyes again, clearing his throat. When he raised them, his eyes were dark and intense.

"I never thought I would find you. I was determined to be a life-long bachelor. The day you walked into my shop my *mind* started to change. You were smart, and funny, and a living goddess. After the first morning I woke up with you, my *heart* started to change. It wasn't the amazing night we spent together, and it *was* the most amazing night of my life. No, it was when I looked in your eyes that morning. You took a place in my heart that day. But now I know you, all of you, and you have become more precious to me than anything else I could ever have in my life. Please, Daphne, take my ring, and tell me that I will be yours, and you will be mine?"

Trevor pulled a ring out of his pocket. It had the same thin, wavy band as the other two rings, but a deep blue stone was set in its center. He looked into my eyes and I inhaled sharply.

"Oh, Trevor, yes! It's what I want more than anything!" Tears came to my eyes as he slipped the ring onto my finger and twisted it to lock with the others. I looked at my hand and moved it in the light. The colors of the stones shifted and changed. It was magnificent.

I threw my arms around Trevor's neck, sliding to my knees on the floor, and kissed him deeply, pressing myself to him. His strong arms came around me and I melted into him. I pulled back and looked into his eyes, smiling. His arms slid down my sides and he released me, turning me toward Hunter.

I looked into Hunter's gorgeous brown eyes and my heart glowed. He looked at me softly, and his sweet smile made the tears fall down my face. I ran a hand over his fuzzy cheek, pulling his face down to mine, our lips meeting gently, slowly. Then Hunter's arm was around my waist and he pulled me to him so forcefully my breath rushed out. His kiss became pure fire and I moaned into his mouth. Country had been holding out on me all this time.

Hunter pulled back and blushed, still looking in my eyes. I giggled, almost shy myself after that kiss. Hunter sighed and glanced at Reed. My eyes followed his and locked with the crystal blues of my very best friend.

I moved over in front of him and wrapped my hands around his neck. "This was all your idea, wasn't it?" I asked. He nodded. "Oh, Reed," I sighed, and our bodies moved together as one. The moment our lips met a beam of bright sun illuminated the room, blinding me even with my eyes closed. The sun was setting and suddenly everything was orange. We opened our eyes and we both laughed quietly.

"You really do bring the light into my life, Daphne," he whispered.

His blue eyes glowed in the sunset and a fire lit in me. I crushed myself to him, pushing him down onto the soft carpet. I kissed him and he pulled me harder to him, his hands on my back, sliding down, one grabbing my bottom.

"Oh, Reed," I moaned. "You look so darn good in your uniform! I just can't take it anymore!"

"Feel free to take it off if it's bothering you that much," he laughed.

"I'm bothered alright," I purred at him. His smile disappeared and he bit into my neck, grabbing me around the waist and rolling me over to my back. He hovered over me, looking into my eyes, and then he sat up, straddling me, holding me down.

"Well boys, now that we've got her, what *should* we do with her?" Reed said, grinning wickedly.

Hunter and Trevor came and sat on either side of me. Trevor placed a pillow under my head. Their eyes were hungry.

"Oh, god!" I moaned, closing my eyes.

"Eyes open, Williams," Reed commanded in his military voice. My eyes flew open and my pussy throbbed. He was the only man I'd ever known whose orders made my *loins* burn instead of my temper.

Trevor's hands came down on the top of my dress and he pulled my breasts out in one quick motion. His mouth came down and began working my nipple. Hunter took the other in his mouth and I cried out. It was incredible.

Reed began to unbutton his dress coat. He slid it off his arms and pulled his shirt off, revealing his sculpted body. My eyes roved over him as he reached down and began to take off his belt. Slowly he unbuckled it and unzipped his fly, looking in my eyes. My pussy throbbed again, and I thought I might orgasm before he even touched me. Agonizing pleasure shot down my body from Trevor's and Hunter's mouths.

Reed pulled his cock out, stroking it. I watched every move, desire coursing through me like whitewater. I whimpered and Reed smiled libidinously.

Reed stood, removing the rest of his clothing. Hunter and Trevor started on mine. Together they made short work of my dress. Reed reached down and pulled my thong off. And then all their mouths were on me.

Reed dove between my legs, his hands spreading me wide, his fingers pressing into my flesh. He stroked and massaged up my thighs, sliding two thick fingers into me and pressing hard.

"Uuuhhh!" I screamed, and Reed's tongue coursed up my dripping crevice, circling my clit. "Reeeeed!" I cried.

Hunter's hand was in my hair and he was kissing up my neck, biting and sucking and driving me insane. His mouth came down on mine and he kissed me deeply, languorously, his tongue sliding in and exploring my mouth.

Trevor unzipped my corset and his mouth moved down my abdomen and back up to my breasts. Flashes of pure ecstasy flew down my body as Trevor's tongue moved on me. His hands slid down and unhooked my garters. He slipped my stockings down my legs.

Reed's tongue pressed harder, his fingers slamming into me. My body began to spasm, my back arched, and I came with a feral cry. Reed lapped at me, his hands moving over my thighs, holding me open for him. His tongue moved over my pulsing clit until I cried out in excruciating pleasure, every muscle in my body trembling.

Trevor and Hunter moved away, down to my feet. They knelt there, removing their jackets, then their shirts, both gazing down at me. Reed sat back, wiping his mouth, his eyes dark and burning with a raging fire. The beast was out.

Trevor grabbed hold of one ankle, Hunter the other. They spread me wider before Reed, kissing my ankles, my calves, their mouths moving up my legs.

Reed knelt before me stroking his enormous cock. He was huge, aroused to the point that I could see the blood pumping in his veins. Trevor and Hunter held me, watching my face as Reed sunk himself into me.

Hard and fast and deep he plunged into me, hitting the aching throb inside me. I moaned, my hips bucking up to him, but he pinned me down with a hard thrust. Reed pumped in and out of me, while Trevor and Hunter held me open for him. I was completely at their mercy and it was more erotic than anything I had ever experienced. I let go. I couldn't control any of it. All I could do was feel it.

And feeling it was magnificent. Reed's thick cock filled me until I thought I would split in two. His hard thrusting made me throb inside and I felt my orgasm coming again.

"Oh, god, I'm going to cum!" I half moaned, half growled. Reed's body came down on mine and he pressed me to the floor.

"Cum on me, Daphne," he whispered in my ear. "Let me feel you cum on me." He slammed into me and I burst on him. Hot, wet rivulets ran down me as my pussy clamped down on Reed. Trevor and Hunter released my legs and I wrapped them around Reed's body, spasming wildly as he slammed into me again and again.

The aching, throbbing slowed, and I remembered to breathe. My eyes were rolled back in my head and I shook it, trying to see straight. I panted and collapsed, and Reed slowed his strokes, caressing me inside, bringing me down so he could bring me back up again. Oh, god, he wanted me to cum again.

Hunter and Trevor stood at my feet and began unbuckling their pants, watching Reed fuck me below them. I watched as they both emerged, long and hard, so ready.

Reed stopped and pulled out of me. He sat me up and moved behind me, sliding the corset off my back and tossing it aside. He began to rub my shoulders. Hunter and Trevor sat on the sofa in front of me, stroking themselves. The sight made me pulse anew, and I knew what I wanted.

I leaned forward, staring into Hunter's eyes and grabbed hold of him. I brought my mouth down on him and he moaned. He loved this so much and it made me so hot to see it. I ran my tongue around the head, licking, then sucking with my lips, stroking him with my hand.

"Daphne!" Hunter yelled. At the same time Reed slammed into me from behind. He filled me, pressed into me, and his body came down over my back, hot and slick with sweat. I moaned, running my mouth up and down the underside of Hunter's long dick.

Reed fucked me deep, getting to that special spot and bringing me close to my peak again. He grabbed my tits in his hands and rolled my nipples, sending shockwaves through me. I could feel him swelling even more and I knew he would cum soon.

And then he did. He shot into me, his hands moving down to my hips and pulling me to him. He thrust into me so hard I cried out. I could feel him throbbing and the spurts of his ejaculate inside. I was so close to cumming I couldn't stand it. But he pulled out.

And Trevor took over. I watched him rise from the sofa and disappear behind me. I was a dripping, throbbing mess, and I needed release. I took Hunter deep in my throat and rubbed my tongue on his base and he howled. I worked him up and down, getting more and more turned on with each stroke.

I waited an eternity, so close to orgasm, for Trevor to enter me. His hands moved over me first, sliding up my backside, over my back and down my sides. He grabbed my hips and held me still while I furiously sucked Hunter's cock.

Slowly Trevor pushed the tip of his cock into me, then slid it back out. I was so close it was absolute glorious torture. I felt the tip enter me again, a little further this time, then slide back out. A guttural cry broke from my throat. Trevor slid in again and this time he kept going.

Achingly slow he slid into me, every inch of him causing me to throb more. I started to pant through my nose, and I sucked Hunter harder, my frustration building.

"Uuuhhh, Daphne Olivia, goddess! You feel like no woman ever!" Trevor cried, and his fingers dug into my hips as he pulled me into him, thrusting his full length into me.

I pulled off of Hunter and cried out. "Oh, Trevor, god, please!" I begged. "I can't take it. I need to cum on you!"

Trever moved slowly out and back in again, circling his hips until he hit me in the exact spot, and I cried out again. Now he held my hips to him and pumped, pumped, pumped right into that spot until I was trembling all over and my knees threatened to give out.

"Uuunnnggghhh!!!" I cried as his cock hit me and I finally released. I ground up against Trevor and he slammed into me hard, pushing and pumping deep in me as I came around him. I could feel every inch of him inside me, my muscles tightening and releasing on him, my cum and Reed's, dripping down my legs.

I moved my lips back to Hunter, raising my eyes to his as I took him in my mouth. His eyes were almost black with arousal and he watched my face as I came down from my climax. I watched him as I brought him to his.

Up and down that long cock, around with my tongue, deep in my throat. I craved it, I hungered to be filled from both sides. Trevor took me deep again and I deep throated Hunter. His eyes went wild and his cock swelled.

"Daphne!" Hunter cried, his hand tangling in my hair as he came in my mouth. He bucked up and I pressed my mouth onto him even deeper. He whimpered and moaned and throbbed in me. I sucked him until he collapsed back onto the sofa.

Trevor pulled out of me and laid me down on the soft rug. He looked into my eyes as he lowered himself onto me. I reached my hand up to tangle in his black curls. He smiled at me and the dimples made my breath rush in.

Trevor kissed me softly as he slid into me. Gently he made love to me, rocking my body with his. He ran his hands up my sides and tangled them in my hair, kissing me deeper. I wrapped my legs around his and moved my hips with him, feeling him, savoring him.

I felt him tense, knew it was coming. I held him to me, wanting to feel his body in mine, to feel him release into me.

"I love you, Trevor," I whispered in his ear.

He shuddered and his strong arms came around me, pulling me into his chest, wrapping me in their love. He held me tightly and came in me, his chest rumbling and heaving, his lips devouring mine.

"I love you, Daphne Olivia," he whispered as his spasming slowed. "So much."

36

Happily Ever After

"It's absolutely stunning!" I said, holding my hand out in front of me. I shifted my fingers in the light and the colors in the stones shifted. "I've never seen peridot, diamonds, or sapphires shift like this."

"That's because those aren't peridot, diamonds, or sapphires," Reed said.

We were all lying in the enormous bed after making love this morning, and all of last night. Hunter had me in his lap, cradled against his chest. Trevor and Reed were on either side of me.

"They're not your birthstones?" I asked.

"They look like it, but they're actually all your birthstone," Trevor said, taking my hand and kissing it.

"Alexandrite? But it's impossible to find!" I said, very surprised. "And in these colors! How did you ever get these?"

"We have a Russian friend who happens to be a jeweler. We owe him big now," Reed said. "We'll probably be giving him and his friends free plane rides for life."

"Oh, tell me about the business plan!" I said, getting very excited.

Trevor went over everything in detail and the more he talked the more excited we all became. Trevor's eyes sparkled like I'd never seen them. Reed had a look of longing when he talked about the planes. And Hunter, well Hunter was just as happy as he always was, which made me unbelievably happy, too.

The days in the cabin flew by. The boys took turns sleeping in 'my room' with me. It was wonderful to have them one by one, but also to have them all. It was even nicer that they had their own man-cave to retreat to. And their own bathroom. I didn't know if the seat would ever be down in my home again.

And sixteen Months Later...

"Ok, one more push! That's it, now stop," the doctor said. "Here she comes. It's a girl!"

The doctor held up my daughter, Virginia. She was so small, and so beautiful, with a head of blonde hair. She screamed.

"Alright, who would like to cut the cord?"

Hunter stepped up and grabbed the scissors. He cut right through the cord with a smile on his face. The nurses whisked Virginia away and Hunter followed her. I felt a little left out.

"Are you doing ok?" Trevor asked softly, putting a cool compress on my head.

"How do you think I'm doing?" I snapped at him. But he just smiled.

"Ok, Ms. Williams, get ready. I'm going to need you to push again. Ok, now."

I was getting tired of this doctor. I was just tired. I'd been in labor over twenty hours now. And I had to do this three times. I didn't think I could do it.

"I can't," I panted.

"Come on, Williams, you can do this," Reed whispered in my other ear.

"Nnnggghhh!" I screamed, pushing down hard.

"Good, good! Ok, stop now. Here he comes!"

A wail filled the air and the doctor held up another tiny, blonde baby. It had to be Kody.

"Gentlemen?" the doctor said, holding the scissors out.

Reed stepped away from me and took the scissors, cutting through the cord with a stoic expression. He disappeared, following the nurse. I started to cry. I definitely couldn't do this again.

"It's alright, angel eyes," Trevor whispered in my ear, his cheek next to mine. "I'm here. We'll do it together."

"I can't Trevor. I can't do it. I'm so tired." Tears ran down my cheeks.

Trevor slid his arm under me and held me tight. He kissed my bare shoulder where the hospital gown had fallen down. I took a deep breath and reached down deep in myself. In Trevor's arms I was safe. Nothing bad could happen. I could do this.

"You're almost there. You're so strong, I'm in awe of you Daphne," Trevor said against my shoulder.

"When you're ready Ms. Williams, just one more time. Wait for a contraction, alright?"

"Trevor," I cried quietly, gripping his arm and feeling the pressure of the contraction coming.

"I've got you, honey," he whispered, holding me.

"Eeennnaaahhh!" I screamed, pushing with the last of my strength.

"Good! Here he comes! Here he is!" the doctor said, holding up a beautiful baby with black curly hair and olive skin.

I began to cry. "He's beautiful," I choked out.

"Here you go, Dad," the doctor said, holding the scissors out to Trevor.

Trevor took the scissors and looked like he might faint. He cut the cord, his face going white. The doctor laughed.

"Just try to stay on your feet, son. You'll feel better in a minute."

Trevor was back at my side, stroking my hair. Hunter and Reed came back, each with a little bundle in their arms.

Trevor kissed my forehead. "Good job, Momma," he said.

"Where is Sterling?" I asked, worried. "Shouldn't you go with him?"

"He's fine, the nurses are fixing him up to meet you," Trevor said, looking into my eyes.

"Alright, Ms. Williams, I just need you to deliver the last placenta, now. Give me a little push," the doctor said.

"I think I'll stay up here with you," Trevor said, his face turning white again as I pushed the placenta out and the doctor went to work with a needle and thread. "I'm so proud of you, honey."

I looked into his brown and blue eyes and I felt completely at peace. Trevor stroked my hair and I turned my head to see my babies.

Hunter sat down on the bed next to me and held a perfect little face up to mine. She opened her eyes and two dark gray irises met mine. She was the most beautiful thing I'd ever seen.

"Hi Virginia," I whispered. "Aren't you the prettiest little thing? You and me, we're gonna have to be a team. I'm so glad you're here to help me with all these boys."

Hunter laughed his gregarious laugh, startling the nurses. They all giggled, though, susceptible to the infectious laughter.

Reed stood behind Hunter cooing at the little bundle in his arms. He was completely unaware of anything around him.

"Reed," Hunter elbowed him. "Let Momma see her baby."

Reed looked up and suddenly seemed to see us. He lowered Kody down to me and two little crystal blue eyes looked back at me. Just like my Reed.

"Hello, gorgeous boy. You look just like your daddy," I said. Reed smiled and pulled Kody back into his arms, cooing at him again.

"And here is your last little gentleman," the nurse said, handing Trevor a little blue blanket with a mop of black hair sticking out the top.

Trevor stood from my side and took the baby into his arms. "Hi there, little man," he whispered. "Look at you! You look just like your momma, don't you?"

"What are you talking about, Trevor Bond, he looks just like you," I sighed.

"Uh-uh," Trevor cooed. "You've got your momma's eyes."

Trevor sat down on the bed and brought Sterling down to me. Two bright blue eyes stared back at me.

"Just like you, angel eyes," Trevor whispered, kissing me.

"Alright, now, Momma," the nurse said, elbowing her way in. Time to breastfeed. Let's see who wants to go first."

"I do," Trevor mouthed at me. I giggled and made a feeble attempt to smack him. My arm fell limply by my side. I was exhausted.

"Ladies first," the nurse said, placing Virginia in my arms.

I pulled a breast out and awkwardly held my baby. This did not come naturally to me. The nurse grabbed my breast and the baby's head and gently latched her onto me.

"Just like this, sweetie. Just pop her on there. Oh, look at her go! She's a natural. You won't have any problems with her," the nurse said.

"She's got her daddy's appetite!" Trevor said, punching Hunter on the shoulder.

Hunter howled with laughter. "Good girl," he said.

"Everything looks wonderful, Ms. Williams," the doctor said, moving to my side. "It certainly has been a joy to witness this pregnancy and birth. I've never seen anything like it. Triplets via heteropaternal superfecundation. I don't know that I've ever even read about a case. And carrying them to term and delivering them, well, I've just never seen anything like it. Congratulations, folks."

"Our Daphne is extraordinary in everything she does, doc. Thanks," Trevor said, shaking the doctor's hand.

"Hetero super what?" Hunter asked.

"It means three eggs and three sperm, son," the doctor answered him. "We'll still do the buccal swab, but I'm almost positive these children came from three different fathers. Just incredible," the doctor mumbled. "Can't wait to write the paper."

The doctor and nurses left, leaving us all alone for a few minutes. Virginia sucked at my breast and I watched her perfect little mouth move. It was a miracle, that's what it was. I looked at all my boys and thought what a miracle it all was. Hunter leaned down and kissed the top of my head, watching Virginia eat.

Oh lord, we were going to need a much bigger house. Maybe even eight bedrooms.

THE END

Don't miss out!

Visit the website below and you can sign up to receive emails whenever J.C. Fairbanks publishes a new book. There's no charge and no obligation.

https://books2read.com/r/B-A-HAWH-TXDAB

Also by J.C. Fairbanks

Love and Desire
Two Days In Florida
A Kiss in Carolina
Love and Desire in Paradise

Standalone
Daphne, Woman of Law

Watch for more at https://www.facebook.com/jcfairbanksromance.

About the Author

I love to write about love. True love, passion, and romance are the best things about life. I fall in love with all of my characters in every story, and I hope you will, too. In my real life I am living my happily ever after every day with the love of my life and our four little ones. But let me tell you the story of how I started writing. One night I had a dream. It was incredible and I couldn't stop thinking about it for weeks. This dream was not your usual dream. It was so real that it felt like it had actually happened. In it I met Julia, Camile, Anika, Leo, David, and the whole family. I now knew these people and I was dying to find out what happened to them after I was yanked from my slumber by the alarm clock. It was nearly impossible to get out of bed that morning and even harder to stop thinking about them. My first novel, Two Days In Florida, was born. But I still had to know more. The stories just keep getting steamier and more romantic. I can't wait to see what happens next!

Read more at https://www.facebook.com/jcfairbanksromance.